OFFSIDES

Lori B. Scott

10-27-23

End Game Press books may be purchased in bulk at special discounts for sales promotion, corporate gifts, ministry, fund-raising, or educational purposes. Special editions can also be created to specifications. For details, contact Special Sales Dept., End Game Press, P.O. Box 206, Nesbit, MS 38651 or info@endgamepress.com.

Visit our website at www.endgamepress.com.

Library of Congress Control Number: 2022952384
Hardback ISBN: 978-1-63797-107-9
Paperback ISBN: 978-1-63797-106-2
eBook ISBN: 978-1-63797-098-0

Published in association with Cyle Young of the Cyle Young Literary Elite, LLC.

Cover by Dan Pitts
Interior by Typewriter Creative Co.

Scripture quotations marked (ESV) are from The ESV® Bible (The Holy Bible, English Standard Version®), copyright © 2001 by Crossway, a publishing ministry of Good News Publishers. Used by permission. All rights reserved.

Printed in India
10 9 8 7 6 5 4 3 2 1

OFFSIDES

LORI Z. SCOTT

END GAME
Press

Trigger warning: This story addresses human trafficking.

CONTENTS

CHAPTER ONE

OFFSIDES

My heart throbbed in my ears, and my breath came in heavy gasps.

The Cedar Creek High School striker dribbled the ball just out of my reach, her footwork fast. Still, I pounded after her, my face heating with exertion. My role as a center midfielder required stamina, and I drew deep on my reserves of strength to chase the girl.

Our center back, Erika, jumped into the gap between us, forcing number twenty-two to shield the ball. They battled it out with Erika employing her bulk as a weapon.

"Two minutes left!" Coach Hering boomed from the

sidelines, her voice cutting through screams of teammates and fans alike. "Stay on her, Dani!"

When I heard my name, I flicked a glance to Coach. In that millisecond, I registered her pointing at twenty-two with one hand and motioning at me with the other.

My adrenaline rocketed beyond high gear. Muscles tense, I tracked my opponent, ready to spring. Motion surrounded me. Players raced to the attack. Our goalie barked out orders to the remaining defenders. The ref, a blur of yellow jersey with black pinstripes, kept pace.

Every second counted.

If Erika could force twenty-two to move laterally, there'd be an opportunity to steal the ball. Anticipating that, I darted sideways. As our opponent booted the ball toward her wing player, I intercepted the pass.

With short, choppy touches, I gained control of the ball. In my peripheral vision, bodies changed directions, targeting me. Grunting, I kicked the ball upfield to our striker, Reb. She took off, weaving her way around lunging defenders. I charged after her, gulping air.

The screaming from the sidelines rose to a fever pitch. "Shoot it!" My friend Sol's shrill voice blared over the menagerie of noise.

A defender tripped Rebecca, but she recovered, pivoted, and reversed direction. Spotting an opening, I broke away from my defender and streaked up the middle, waving my hand. With a burst of speed, I pulled ahead.

Reb shot the ball my way. The field spread open before me. My leg made a solid connection, sending the ball arching toward the goal.

The ball zipped past the goalie into the net, and my heart soared. Score!

Screaming, I raced back toward my teammates for high fives. My brother, Nick, used to say nothing beat that feeling—driving hard, battling through sweat and fatigue and obstacles, and then scoring.

Before I took two steps, the whistle blew. The ref pointed at a spot on the field where the assistant referee held a flag out straight. "Offsides," he said, signaling for the ball. "No goal."

Offsides. Again? All euphoria drained out of me as the ref positioned the ball on the spot of the foul. I hated that rule. Why should it be a penalty when an offensive player received a pass beyond the last defender? Was it my fault their players were too slow?

"Dani!" Coach Hering folded her arms across her chest. Her face held a distinct scowl. "Fall back."

Sucking in air, I tromped to midfield, waiting for the opponents to initiate their indirect free kick.

Reb planted herself nearby. "Pass it back to me next time. I'll make the shot."

Next time. As if this time didn't matter. Here's a secret—it *always* mattered.

I nodded, avoiding eye contact. Her words made my stomach drop farther into the ground. Why did I always charge ahead without looking?

Our wingman, Wren, trotted up to me and patted my shoulder. "Don't worry, Dani. You just got too excited."

Too excited? How about I swooped into scoring position like a peregrine falcon while their lame defense reacted like Jell-O on a hot day? You ask me, they ought to strike offsides from the rules.

Still, we had to play by the book. And I knew better.

"My bad," I said, willing myself to accept Wren's comment and move on.

Twenty seconds after the ball went into play, the game ended with a disappointing 2–3 loss.

A bitter taste tainted my mouth and I stumbled to a stop. We could have forced overtime if I had held back just a little. If I'd checked myself. Too bad patience was not my superpower.

Dragging my feet, I joined my teammates by the sidelines. Coach Hering frowned, talking into the microphone on her cellphone. That was her way of taking notes about the game, dictating strategies we'd need to discuss and practice later.

"Tough game, girls. Hustle up." Apparently, she was too intent on plotting the next move to elaborate more. She gave us a dismissive wave toward the bus.

"Coach got that right. Tough game." Sol flicked a piece of grass off my jersey. "But you played well."

I grunted, acknowledging the compliment.

Coach hadn't played Sol at all. She made a better sports magazine model with her spotless jersey and dark hair swept into a crisp ponytail. Even her shin guards looked straight out of the package.

Meanwhile, my jersey was splattered with mud stains and sweat and clung to my skin. My breathing had a hitch too, like a fish out of water. "Thanks."

I wish I had Erika's stubborn toughness or radiated confidence like Reb, but expressing myself was another superpower I lacked. Instead, having summed up all I had to say with a simple word of gratitude, I opened my water bottle and gulped three swigs.

No one expects you to talk when you're drinking.

"I thought for sure we were going to score there at the end," Sol said, "but that number twenty-two, she was so destructive. I would have called a foul on her just for the way she glared at everyone." She scowled as if mirroring the girl's look, then broke into contagious laughter.

I chuckled, content to let the waves of Sol's perky personality sweep over me.

My best friend and I knew our roles well. She talked. I listened. She made dramatic entrances, and I quietly closed the doors after her. She called people out, and I calmed their ruffled feathers. The balance worked, which made hanging out with Sol easy. I didn't have to worry about filling awkward pauses, and she had a rapt audience for her stream of verbal material.

Seemingly distracted by Rebecca dumping water on her own head, Sol gave my shoulder a quick squeeze and moved on. I smiled as she worked her way around, high-fiving, commiserating, and joking.

Sol never complained about her lack of playing time. She always claimed to have joined the team for my sake. If I pushed her on it, she'd say, "Dani, we've been friends since kindergarten. I'm not letting your soccer addiction get in the way of that. Plus"—and here she'd channel an '80s vibe— "guys dig chicks who are in good shape."

Regardless of her motivation, Sol fit seamlessly with the team. Maybe her expectations for herself were so low, sitting on the bench didn't bother her. Or maybe she just liked being surrounded by a group of rowdy people that included me. I envied her for that outgoing bent. But whatever the reason, I couldn't imagine a team complete without Sol.

After changing from my cleats into slides, I grabbed a box of granola bars out of my bag and joined the girls packing up their gear. Without a word, I dangled a snack in front of each one, tossing it to them if they nodded acceptance. I knew how hungry I got after a game, so I always packed extra to share.

Reb held out her hand for one, but a frown creased her face. "Have you seen my towel?"

Squeezing my eyes shut, I retraced her steps in my mind. Final time-out. Rushed drink. Grab the towel off her bag. Face mop. Sloppy toss. The rag fell between duffels and landed …

I fished behind the ball bag and scooped her missing team-colored turquoise rag from the ground. "There you go," I said, passing it to her.

"Thanks." Pressing her lips together, she dotted her forehead with the cloth. "You need to shut down those offsides penalties. They're hurting us."

"Amen, sister," Erika said, handing me her bag. I held it while she changed her shoes. "I mean, one more step and you've got the score."

Face heating, I bobbed my head. Was everyone staring at me? Had I let them down?

Reb shrugged into her sweatshirt. "Even if you hadn't raced ahead, I doubt that defender could have stopped you. And I was open too. I might've scored."

Swallowing hard, I tucked a few empty snack wrappers into the front pouch of my bag. "Yeah. I know."

"When I played on the U10 team, our coach drilled offsides out of us. Except for those corner kicks." Erika stretched her arms overhead, probably working out some muscle kinks before reclaiming her bag. "For those, she always told us to get directly to the ball whether there's someone between you and the goal or not. Do you know why?"

I did. But my tongue chose that moment to freeze.

Sol came to my rescue. "The refs won't call offsides unless our legs get tangled. And speaking of tangles—" Sol put her hands on her hips. "Y'all look like a cyclone hit you. Anyone want me to braid their gross, sweaty hair on the way home?"

A sea of hands shot into the air.

Sol smirked. "Who's first?"

"Me!" Our goalie, Sandy, pushed forward. Her short ponytail looked like a firework explosion gone wrong. "My hair is so wigged out. I'll never get a brush through it."

"You got it." Sol pointed at the other five hands that were raised. "Hmm. It looks like I'm going to be popular."

I winced, knowing what was coming next. Growing up with Sol as a best friend meant I sat through every musical she could get her hands on ... *and* all their soundtracks.

"Please don't emphasize your point with a song from *Wicked,*" I murmured.

With a wolfish grin, she did exactly that.

"I'm gonna be pop-u-OO-lar." Laughing, she hooked arms with our keeper and headed toward the team bus. "This will be fun. Hey, why don't they let chickens play soccer?" Sol winked at me over her shoulder.

"Do I care?" Sandy groaned and shifted her duffle bag.

"You do," Sol said, not missing a beat. "You care because if chickens played, there would be too many fowls on the field."

"Boo ..." Sandy blew a raspberry.

I let the rest of my teammates surge pass me before falling in line behind them. When it came to the gossip afterwards, the chatter and debriefing time, listening from the shadows suited me just fine. Unlike me, the social spotlight belonged to Sol. Except on the soccer field. There, I was a glorious blaze of light.

At least when I wasn't offsides.

I had to find some way to get my game back on track and end my senior year strong. A little extra work, a little more effort ... I could do it.

"I'll save you a seat, Dani!" Sol called. She disappeared into the bus, surrounded by teammates.

Sweat beaded on my lip, and I swiped it away with the back of my hand. Maybe I could get my social life back on track too. A little extra work, a little more effort.

A little less like introverted me and a little more like extroverted Sol. She made making friends look easy. I'd rather sprint a thousand shuttle runs being chased by mountain lions than hang out at the mall—surrounded by people but still completely alone.

Maybe this year I could learn to come out of my shell. Blend in with the crowd.

Except the bus doors shut before I reached them, and I had to knock to get on.

So ... then again, maybe not.

CHAPTER TWO

ADVICE

After finishing Wren's hair, Sol called a halt to the braiding. "I've gotta stop or my fingers will cramp, and you don't want me *Les Misérables.* I won't be able to text or get on social media. And no one wants *that* tragedy on their conscience."

"Ha!" Erika called from her catty-corner seat. "No, I do not. You are an icon with words, Ms. Journalist. Who wants to mess with a writer? They'll put you in a story and kill you off."

Placing her hand on her heart, Sol gave a dramatic gasp. "I would never do that." She leaned forward and winked. "As far as you know."

"What I know," Wren said, "is that besides the sports

highlights, your advice blog is the only part of the school's website I read." She tapped my shoulder, and I swapped places with her, reclaiming my spot by Sol.

"I call a lie on the finger cramps." Reb patted her new braid and snapped a selfie. Two empty pouches of apple juice sat next to her. She'd apparently recharged without losing one smidgeon of audacity. "They look good enough to post a video in two seconds flat. And you only need one finger for that."

"In a pinch, you could use your nose." I modeled the move with my own phone, snapping a close-up of my nostrils. I passed the device over the seat so Reb could see it.

She barked a laugh and handed my masterpiece off to Erika. I allowed myself a grin.

"Fine. You want action? We'll make a video." Sol shifted her body, settling into the stiff vinyl cushion, and lifted her phone.

Erika and Reb opened their mouths wide and flashed *love you* fingers. Wren and Sandy hammed it up with goofy poses.

I stifled a giggle. I knew where this was going. No one minced words with Sol.

"Quit with the theatrics," Sol said. "I'm interviewing each of you one by one, asking trivial questions. Like, how many pleats are in a chef's hat?"

"What's a pleat?" Erika asked.

Sol's eyebrows dipped. "It's a fold. And there are a hundred of them. Do you know how much of the brain is made of fat?"

"Ten percent?" Wren asked.

"Wrong. Sixty." Sol's eyes gleamed. "I'll splice everyone's answers together, tag you, and post the video to my 14K followers for brutal scrutiny. Starting with—"

A chorus of *no's, I'm good, not me,* and laughter echoed. Sol had earned her space.

Switching off her screen, she elbowed me. "Now that it's only us, how are you feeling?" Sol lowered her voice. "I bet you're blaming yourself for our loss. Which is dumb, since we're a team, not individual players. No single person is responsible."

I sighed. "I could have scored."

"So could've a dozen other people a dozen other times." Sol leaned into me. "That's how the game works. And that's what makes it fun—the challenge. The struggle."

"Let's be clear here. It's the struggle followed by the *win* that makes it fun." I held up a finger showing how the scale tipped. "Besides, how do you even rank a close game on the mood scale? Very confusing. It's good, but it's mostly awful. Sort of like broccoli."

"You know I love broccoli." Sol drummed her fingers against her thigh and narrowed her eyes. "If you're really upset about it, what are you going to do? Every problem has a solution."

"Spoken like a true advice columnist." I kept my tone light because I appreciated Sol's upbeat attitude, and I didn't want her to think I resented her prodding. Far from it. I needed her to push me when I got discouraged like this. She forced me to look at situations with fresh eyes, something that kept me from turning my frustration inward. Still, coming up with a plan of action sat on my heart like a feral cat.

"Well?" Sol cleared her voice and sang. "How do you solve a problem like Dani the kicking-but-offsides machine?"

"Trust me, *not* with *The Sound of Music.*" I took a deep breath. "As in all things, there's a science to it. I need to be more aware on the field."

"Specifics?" Sol cocked her head. "I'm being serious here. I really don't know how ball or field awareness works. Which is probably one of the reasons I'm constantly warming the bench. Not that I mind, because then I don't get all sweaty like you do. But is it anything like being aware when a guy is checking you out?"

"Maybe." I considered Sol's point of view. She stood out like a swan among ducklings. What would she do if the entire boys' club team showed up on the sidelines? With a flip of her hair, she'd examine the crowd, note the body language, and know exactly where to toss a coy comment or plant a sly wink to lure the men closer. "Actually, yes."

Sol's lips twitched. "You know the routine. Break it down."

"I'd start by scanning the field before receiving the ball. That would help me predict how the play will unfold. That mental map would give me time to make a smart decision. To know where to stand, who might be open, or where the goalie might block." I folded my arms across my chest. I knew my stuff—on paper, at least.

"You've been playing for years." Sol shrugged. "How is this kind of thinking not natural already?"

I slouched. She had a point.

I should work on scanning and making snap decisions until it became automatic.

"I'll practice more. In a small, controlled space first, then a larger area," I said.

Mom might not like my kicking the ball around in her flower garden, but there was an empty lot down the road from our house. The front of the property line had three brick steps leading nowhere. Perfect for alone time with a soccer ball.

"You'll figure it out. Just keep working on it." Sol flashed a toothy smile. "And now that we've solved all your problems, let's take a look at mine."

She woke her phone and loaded her school email. "I want

your reaction to my responses to these letters for my *Heart and Soul* column before I publish it. This letter reads, 'Dear Heart, I went to Crates of Candy last week with my friend. Signs in the store clearly stated customers were not supposed to sample the candy. She filled a bag with jellybeans and then ate a handful of them out of the bag. When I pointed out that wasn't cool, she got really mad. She claimed she just wanted to see if she liked them or not, and since the candy came from a bag she planned to buy anyway, it wasn't stealing. And she said I should go—'" Sol paused. "I'm not going to read the next part because the school wouldn't allow that language in the blog. Let's just skip ahead and … 'She paid for the rest of the jellybeans, but it still bothered me. Was she stealing or not? Signed, Candy Confusion.'"

I whistled. I'd seen things like this happen before. People get touchy on both sides of the stealing or not-stealing issue. "I can only imagine the snark involved with this. What did you say?"

Sol straightened her shoulders. "I said, 'The candy was a bulk item that needed to be weighed to determine the cost. When your friend ate some, she decreased the weight of the product in her bag, which decreased the overall cost. Technically, that's stealing. If you want to ease your conscience, donate a quarter to the cash register next time you're in the store. If you want to save your friendship—' And that's where I got stuck. Any ideas?"

"How about 'eat a healthier diet?'" I arched a brow. "You can't go wrong with a bag full of broccoli, right? 'Cuz who wants to sample that?"

Sol's eyes widened. "That's perfect. It adds a touch of humor to a harsher truth, taking the sting off a potential relationship powder keg." Her fingers flew across her phone while she sang a tune from *Mary Poppins* under her breath. The topic of candy no doubt sparked her "Spoonful of Sugar" tribute. She ended with a flourish. "Good call."

A warm glow filled my veins. Sol's praise was butter on a stack of warm pancakes. I nudged her. "Got any more?"

"Do I?" She scrolled. "I've got one who wants to know what I think her boyfriend might like for their two-month anniversary."

"And you suggested what?" I squinted my eyes.

"I told her to buy him a key chain." Sol tapped her forehead. "You know—something that will make him think of her every time he drives his car."

"Not bad." I snorted. "But who buys two-month anniversary gifts? Tell her to wait for a year and then write you back for ideas if he's still around."

"Zinger." Sol typed into her phone. "I'm totally stealing that idea. Okay. And here's one who wants to know if she could date two different boys at the same time." Sol held up a hand. "I'm keeping my answer. I said of course she could. But it's not smart."

"Ha! No kidding." I frowned, trying to imagine bouncing between two love interests. "That's asking for trouble."

"But some people need you to spell it out for them, you know?" Sol pressed her lips together and shrugged. "Hello! Testosterone meets testosterone meets competition. Not pretty."

The bus slowed, and I glanced out the window. Our parking lot waited beyond the next stoplight, so I reached for my backpack. "Any other interesting letters?" Sol got a dozen a week. They were addressed to *Heart* if it was a matter of relationships and *Soul* if it was a matter of integrity or everyday issues.

"Nah." She shrugged. "Well, one, but I stuck it in a file where I keep all the creepy submissions. Some guy wrote wanting to know how I feel about dating older men."

"Are we talking a twenty-year-old?" I asked.

Sol shook her head. "More like thirty."

"Ew. That's like … ancient." I shivered as the bus rolled to a stop and the doors hissed open. "Sounds like some punk is trying to get a rise out of you. Do you know who submitted it?"

Sol tucked her phone away and stood. "Nope. The online forms are anonymous. Which makes everyone a suspect. I keep all the psycho emails in a separate folder. Clues for the police in case I ever go missing—ha-ha." She stepped into the aisle and turned back to catch my eye. "I don't let it worry me."

Unease settled in my stomach. "But what if you should worry?"

"Pfft." She flicked her fingers.

Frowning, I followed Sol off the bus. Didn't the news always warn girls to be on alert for predators?

Still, I lived in a small town and a safe neighborhood. Maybe I was being overly cautious. Wouldn't be the first time fear held me back.

My brother always pushed me to be bolder. To take chances.

One time, when he got grounded for sledding down the staircase on a cooking tray, I sneaked into his room to cheer him up. I expected to find him lying on his bed, miserable. Instead, he had on headphones and was lip syncing with a comb.

"Don't you feel guilty?" I'd asked.

"No." He'd crooked his arm around my neck. "Life is more interesting when you embrace your mistakes. Every single tumble is an adventure."

I could tell from the tightness in his eyes he didn't mean it.

That sometimes he regretted his impulsiveness.

The memory spurred me to pause outside my car and text him hello.

He sent back a raspberry emoji and a heart.

Despite his flaws, I owned some of his brazenness.

"Hey, Sol," I said as we climbed into my car. "Let's make a pact. This year, we are going to take a few chances. Try new things."

"Why?" She buckled herself in, a frown on her lips.

"I want to be more social." I shrugged. "More outgoing, like you." *And Nick.*

"You don't need to change."

"But I'm quiet."

"Exactly." Sol smiled. "Who said that was a bad thing? It's the old curly hair, straight hair conundrum."

I sighed. "Translate conundrum."

"Puzzle or problem." Sol shrugged. "People with curly hair always want straight hair and vice versa. But both kinds of hair have their advantages. Who's to say which is better?"

"Do we have a deal or not?" I asked.

"Fine. Deal." She lifted her chin. "Want to start with a new flavor of milkshake? Strawberry, maybe?"

"Ugh. That's pushing it." I started the car and revved the engine. "But I guess I've got to start somewhere."

Chapter Three

WORDS AND DEEDS

After dropping off Sol at her home, my unease over the creepy letter faded. I swung past Let's Shake on It to pick up a cup of chocolate ice cream for Mom.

Fifteen minutes later, I returned to a dark home. Even though I valued my solitude to recharge after a long day of crowded hallways, a loud lunchroom, and conversation, I still wished the house wasn't empty.

There was no helping it though. Mom missed my game

tonight because she was working a long shift. Dad was out of town for business and Nick was away at college facing his own demons. The emptiness of the house swallowed me.

I sent Nick another text—*Miss you.*

A few minutes later, he texted back. *Obviously. I'm adorable.* Followed thirty seconds later by a *JK. Miss you too.*

I sent a heart. After flicking on the lights in the entryway, I slid Mom's plastic-capped treat into the freezer and left a sticky note telling her where to find it in case I was asleep when she got home.

You made it through the day. Yay! There's a surprise for you in the freezer. Maybe I'll see you tomorrow. Love you!

I bet she would appreciate it if I cleaned the dishes before she got home too. My muscles ached to rest, but I rinsed the plates in the sink and tucked them into the dishwasher.

Was it weird that even though I enjoyed time alone, I still craved the company of loved ones? Dad could have talked me through my failure on the soccer field. Mom would have given en me a shoulder massage. Nick would have cracked jokes to cheer me up—after teasing me, of course. Instead, the silence, which normally gave my mind room to soar, closed in on me.

"Hey, Siri," I said. "Play instrumental music."

Soft violins and deep cellos warmed the barren space. The tension between my shoulders relaxed, and I hummed along—off key, like a yodeling goat with its tail caught in a vice. But with no one else around, who cared?

At nine thirty, I wiped my hands on a dish towel. It was too early for bed and too late for homework, so I grabbed a broom and dustpan instead. The floor needed cleaning. My shoes had tracked in dirt from the field.

But grime was less damage than a loss.

The game invaded my thoughts again.

Our team had more victories than defeats, but three-fourths of the season remained. Much as I loved soccer, I knew my journey with it would end after high school. I was good, but not college-recruited good. Although she was only a junior, Reb had already earned an athletic scholarship, but sophomore sensation Erika still had hopes of catching a recruiter's eye. Making it to the playoffs would help get her recognition.

My competitive drive sparked the longing to win, but the need to do everything possible to help my teammate find her dream fanned that desire to a flame.

Today's loss didn't help her cause. And no matter what Sol said, it was my fault.

With a white-knuckled grip, I swept the broom across the floor, replaying that last penalty over and over in my mind.

I worked hard to execute every play right. I thought I'd improved. But how could I compare to Reb's speed and precision? Erika's energy and spunk? Sandy's knowledge of the playing field? Even Wren got in on the scoring.

Watching the play unfold in my mind, my thoughts spiraled. Even so, I followed the trail. I was the one holding our team back from making playoffs. I wasn't fast enough. Strong enough. Smart enough. Good enough. Not on the soccer field. Not in the social arena. Would I ever be?

My phone buzzed, shaking me from my stupor. I pulled it out of my pocket and glanced at the message from Sol—a smiling snapshot of us she'd taken before the game. *Good night, Squirrel.*

Squirrel. Her nickname for me ever since I started darting across the playground chasing a soccer ball.

I had just enough reserves in my emotional bank to call her. "Don't tell me you're going to bed at ten."

"Yes, right after I publish my blog. And you should too. We both need our beauty rest." She paused. "Well, you need it more than I do."

I scoffed. "Are you calling me ugly?"

"No!" She laughed. "I meant it like, since you were on the field most of the game, you should be more tired than I am. Go to bed."

My body agreed with her, but my mind didn't. "I want to read the final version of *Heart and Soul.*"

"You can see it online in about ten minutes." Her voice held a hint of mischief. "Don't forget to like and comment on the post."

Sol and her multilayered words! "You're up to something," I said.

"Maybe." She drew the word out into long syllables. "I'll see you tomorrow."

After hanging up, I checked our school website for Sol's blog. The first two letters were ones we'd talked about after the game. But the last one? New.

Dear Soul, my friend is very talented, but hard on herself. How can I help her see how amazing she is?

My heart warmed. That sneak! Of course, since the letters were anonymous, Sol could submit one targeted at me.

I read the answer. *Remind her that mistakes are okay. That's how we learn and grow. And help her count her blessings, starting with having an awesome friend like you who cared enough to write me about ideas to cheer her up.*

Smiling, I texted one more message to Sol. *Thanks.*

And, once again, having summed up the totality of my thoughts with a simple word of gratitude, I waited for her answer.

It came a heartbeat later. *I don't know what you're talking about. Goodnight!*

The sneak!

I made a mental note to buy Sol some fancy notebooks and pens on my way to school tomorrow to say thanks. It would be a nice surprise.

I tossed my phone on the entry table, still restless from the game. Although Sol's encouragement helped, it would take more than words to work the anxiety out of my system. If I turned on the outside lights, I could practice my footwork in the driveway before heading to bed.

After slipping on an old pair of white Converse, I snagged my well-worn soccer ball—the one I'd named Betty in fourth grade—and headed out the side door. Mom would probably scold me for being out by myself this late, but I had just turned eighteen and figured I could handle myself in a quiet neighborhood.

In honor of my friend, I set up two cones and worked on Sole Rolls. The drill required me to control the ball with the underside of my feet while moving laterally. The dribbling move would help me skirt defenders and avoid getting tackled.

Keeping the ball close to my body, I rolled it forward, then stepped with the opposite leg in a one-two rhythm until I reached the other cone.

After twenty reps, I switched to another ball skill, then another. Muscle memory took over, and I lost myself in the motions. My breathing steadied, and a calm confidence flooded me.

I would be an asset to my team. I would help them succeed. I would not let them down. I would not go offsides. And we would go to playoffs.

Sweat trickled down my back and mosquitoes buzzed around my face before I decided to quit. Revived, I danced to the applause of an imaginary crowd.

That's when I noticed someone blending into the shadows, watching me.

My heart jumped to my throat. I snatched the ball and glared at the darkness, trying to intimidate the entity like I would a rival defender. Why had they stopped? How long had they stood there before I noticed? Better yet, why had they lingered in the darkness at this time of night?

The person stood for a span of maybe three seconds before the patter of footsteps revealed their continued journey down the road.

Shoring up my courage, I tracked the movements. My body shook with adrenaline. The shape paused and turned. The streetlight illuminated the wide-eyed face of a young girl, maybe fifth grade. One who, if I was not mistaken, lived a few houses down from me.

Releasing a hiss of air, I relaxed. I'd seen that girl sitting on her doorstep many times. Always alone. Easily overlooked. Invisible. *Kind of like me.*

I shook my head, scolding myself. It should take more than a sliver of a kid to spook me.

Still, what was she doing up this time of night? Did anyone miss her?

CHAPTER FOUR

COFFEE, TEA, AND GLEE

The next morning, an empty ice cream bowl sat in the sink with a sticky note. *Dani, thanks for the treat. You made my day. A few of our nursing staff is out with the flu, so I'll be pulling late shifts to cover the floor this week. I'm sorry! I love you SO MUCH. Can't wait for your father to get home! Mom.*

Soft snoring sounds came from behind the master bedroom door. I eased it open and slipped across the floor with quiet feet.

It was nice to see Mom without tension lining her face. Her ebony hair sprayed across her pillow, reminiscent of Sleeping Beauty. Her mouth opened slightly, the source of the heavy breathing. Everything about her, even her flushed, freckled cheeks and straight nose mirrored my own face, just with more wear-and-tear.

She still clutched her prayer journal in one hand. Not wanting it to get damaged, I worked it out of her grasp. A bookmark with a list of people peeked out, wedged in the spine, her barely legible cursive scrawled across it. Dad. Me. Nick.

She'd bought me a prayer journal too, a year ago. The notebook had a soccer ball cover, and she paired it with a grassy green felt-tip pen. "Prayer changes things," she'd said. "You should record your prayer requests. Revisit them later and write down how God answered them. You might be surprised at His love and faithfulness."

Me? Track prayers like a diet or the number of followers on social media? No thanks. Prayers hadn't changed Nick. Even my texts to him went mostly unanswered.

A brick pulled on my heart, and I closed the diary.

Mom's list was not my business. After setting the journal on the nightstand, I tucked the bedsheet over her shoulder and kissed her forehead. "I love you too, Mom," I whispered.

Since I still needed a gift for Sol, I drove to the corner store first. On the way, I couldn't help but scour my street, trying to catch a glimpse of the girl who had haunted my driveway last night. At her age, she might be waiting on a school bus about this time, or perhaps walking a family dog. But there was no sign of her.

Maybe I only imagined she belonged in the neighborhood and what I saw was a vagrant or even some absent-minded old lady going for a midnight stroll. If I had trouble sleeping, I might do the same. Shaking off my burning need to verify my suspicions, I put the girl out of my mind and accelerated to the market.

By the time I swung by to pick her up, Sol was waiting for me in her driveway. I'd wrapped her surprise in a bright floral gift bag.

She lifted the present before sliding into the front seat. "What's this?"

"For you." I checked my rearview mirror and backed out onto the road. "Please remember to like and comment."

She laughed. "Touché. And unexpected."

The bag crumpled as she rifled past the tissue, most of which ended up on the floorboard. From the corner of my eye, I saw her face light up.

"Love it," Sol said. "A notebook and a set of classic ballpoint pens, the kind you twist instead of pop to get the ink. Fancy."

Nothing beats making a friend smile.

"They're a good size to fit into your purse or backpack," I said. "No more jotting things down on store receipts or napkins. Now you can write your ideas down whenever inspiration strikes you."

She waved her phone in my face. "You know, there is this clever invention that allows you to click a button and talk into a microphone and record your ideas."

"But I bet you like the tactile and gritty and"—I searched for the right word—"the old-fashioned way."

"Call it antiquated. But you're right." She whisked the pen through the air like a wand. "It's perfect. Thank you."

"No, thank you for the encouragement." I slowed to make a turn. We had enough time to grab a drink on the way to school, and the drive-thru line for Coffee, Tea, and Glee was short. "Let's get drinks. My treat. For your blog. Your advice was exactly what I needed to hear."

"About the blog." Sol cleared her throat. "It's been hard meeting my deadlines with all the soccer practices and games. And there are special senior events I'd like to do this year if I had more time. But—" She paused and tucked the notebooks into her backpack. Sucking in air, she slouched back.

I waited. As an introvert, I understood the need for time to collect your thoughts.

Finally, Sol lifted her shoulders. "Remember our pact to try new things? I love soccer, but ... do you ever think about quitting?"

You could have slapped my face with a live trout. "No! Why would you say that? We've played soccer forever."

"I've also sung in the shower forever and sketched forever and written poetry forever and—" She paused. "Look, it's our senior year, and you were right. There are things I still want to try before I graduate and head to college."

A good ribbing might lighten her tone. "Please tell me one of them is *not* pep squad." I inched the car forward in line. "I may have to disown you if that's the case."

Sol laughed, her giggles bursting like spray from a blue whale's blowhole. "No. Not unless they're interested in leading cheers like, 'Be pertinacious! B-E pertinacious!'" She clapped as she chanted.

"Pertinacious?" I rolled my eyes. "I don't even know what that means."

"It means persistent." If a voice could flounce, Sol's did. "Sorry, but you know that's the writer in me indulging in ostentatious words. Anyway, I started thinking about our deal, and I realized there are career days and Senior Tag and yearbook nominations and a lock-in and all sorts of nov-el—pardon the pun—activities we can do. In fact, last week Harper asked me to help decorate for the fall dance, and I said no. Now I want to say yes. What do you think? We could both do it. It would be fun."

"Harper?" I searched my memory and drew a blank. "Do I know her?"

"Probably not. She's in my third hour journalism class."

Sol and I didn't share any classes at school. She planned to be a journalist one day and maybe write a Pulitzer Prize–winning essay. My goal? Someday, I wanted to be on a field. Not a soccer field, even though I'd love to play on a rec team. A science field—animal science, which could branch off into everything from genetics to entomology, a fancy word for the study of bugs. So my schedule had more advanced math and science classes, while her courses fell in the reading and lan-guage arts arena.

I frowned. "I hate that our schedules are so different."

"We solved that problem." Sol swatted my shoulder. "I play soccer so we can be together for the best part of the day. *After* school. Besides, we have the same lunch period."

"True." *Thank goodness for that!* "But words have multi-ple meanings, which confuses me. I can't believe they excite you. Give me a straight up math problem and a logical an-swer any day."

"You want straight up and logic? Straight up, I'd like my coffee intravenously," Sol said. "And logically, helping with the decorations gives us a chance to hang out more."

Ugh. Who cared about confetti and balloons? But it would push me to grow socially, and the opportunity obviously mat-tered to Sol.

Her feelings were something to consider, at least.

I rolled down my window and leaned toward the metal speaker. "Hello?"

"It's a good day at Coffee, Tea, and Glee. How can I help you?"

"A cranberry tea, one sugar. And a large caffe mocha." I raised an eyebrow at Sol.

"And one of those blueberry scones," she sang.

"Sol!" I frowned at her.

She shrugged. "We can't have the coffee and tea without the glee, right?"

"And two blueberry scones," I said, completing our order.

"No energy bar?" Sol gasped and put a hand to her mouth. "You're trying something new? Could it be the pact influence? I'll tell Harper we're in."

As we edged toward the payment window, something close to panic swept through my nerves. I swallowed hard. "No. Pact or no pact, I've got a lot of calculus homework this week. You can do it, though."

Sol quieted, so I glanced her way. Her eyes narrowed in a scrutinizing gaze. "Are you backing out?"

My tongue froze like it always did when an uncomfortable situation arose. I covered my awkwardness by handing my credit card to the cashier. Sol would thrive in a crowd, but not only would it drain my energy, I'd also be an extra wheel if I joined that crew with a bunch of strangers.

At the same time, I didn't want to let her down. And I was the one who floated the idea of trying new things in the first place.

Sol clicked her tongue. "Don't worry about it." The disappointment in her voice broke my heart. "It was a stupid idea. I've got a lot of homework to do too."

A mixture of relief and guilt flooded my veins. I pulled

forward to the next window, still unable to verbalize how I felt. How much I longed to talk and joke with an ease I'd never possessed like Sol did. How many times I'd launched outside my comfort zone and into the social scene—inwardly kicking and screaming—just so I could feel like I belonged. How uncomfortable it felt to sit with strangers and know from their subtle reactions my attempts at conversation weren't cutting it. I wanted to be someone who dove into the fray of people or drew attention like a magnet. Someone who didn't dwell on problems or difficulties but brushed troubles off their back.

Sol started humming "Without You" from *Rent.* A subconscious slip?

Dread pulsed through me, and I tightened my grip on the wheel. Maybe I should upgrade my personality. If I had to, I could hang out with new people to support my friend. Get over my shyness. Even if it killed me.

"I'll do it." My words came strangled.

"Yay!" She exploded so loud she practically made the interior of the car go supernova with her excitement. My discomfort didn't register on Sol's receptive scale.

"You'll need to carve out time for both dates," Sol said.

"Dates?" I accepted our food and passed it to Sol. "It's not a one-time deal?"

"No." Sol's face lit up as she placed our drinks in the cupholders and handed me a scone. "We'll need to dedicate a lunch period today to plan and Thursday evening to set up the gym."

"Oh joy," I mumbled, uncertain if my stomach would be able to handle a scone after all.

CHAPTER FIVE

ACTOR

At noon, Sol waved at me from across the lunchroom.

Heart pounding, I pushed my way past clusters of students. My anxiety had nothing to do with food and everything to do with the crowd.

Extroverts don't understand my reaction. In their minds, everyone looks forward to lunchtime. They view the midday meal as a chance to relax, recharge, and catch up on—or create—gossip. They feed off chain reactions to comments, movement, and noise.

But introverts like me? Not so much.

It's not that I'm antisocial. It's just that small talk drains my energy. As much as I long to understand the extrovert vibe, I'd rather listen to elevator music or solve a crossword puzzle.

By the time I made it to Sol's table, chatter about the latest social media trend or the newest video game or the next installment of a reality show buzzed in my ears. I let the babble wash over me.

A dozen people already crowded the chairs. Some of them looked familiar. I recognized one from a poster advertisement for a student council election. With popular people like that involved, chances were pretty good I'd run across them at some point during my three-and-a-quarter years at Eastwood High School.

There were no openings by Sol, but she gestured me over anyway. "Share my seat. You're skinny. You can squeeze in."

"Thanks," I said, relief giving my tight muscles a temporary reprieve.

With a little maneuvering, I wedged myself between Sol and a girl who could have passed as a model with her bright blue eyes and skin so pale that I suspected a computer screen might be the only source of light in her life. She held a glitter-encrusted iPhone with the name "Ashley" bejeweled on the casing.

"Everything good now?" Sol whispered.

"Yeah," I whispered back. "But if all these people are helping with the dance decorations, why do they need us?"

She pushed my shoulder, which nearly unseated me. "Why not? We said we'd try new things. Hey guys!" She raised her voice. "This is my friend Dani. She's a soccer beast."

"Hi, Dani," someone called.

I gave a vague nod in the general direction of the outburst.

"So," Sol leaned close, "want the scoop?"

I picked at the beans on my tray—a glaring deviant from the Deli Bar sacks filled with gourmet turkey or ham sandwiches and potato chips with trendy names like *Hot Flash* and *What a Good Dill* that many of the other students had laid out in front of them. "Nah, just the highlights."

"Our theme is *When in Rome.* We're fighting over the color scheme." The light in her eyes danced.

I attempted to mirror her excitement. "What a thrill."

"I know, right?" Sol gave a breathy giggle, then latched her attention on Harper, who sat across from us.

"What's wrong with a black-and-white color scheme?" Harper had a determined bent to her jaw and a distinct whine to her voice.

Sol shook her head. "Black and white is perfect for the Colosseum and the Pantheon, maybe even the chocolate fountain aqueduct. But that doesn't mean the rest of the gym should look like an old television set. Color did, in fact, exist in ancient times."

Color. I tried to imagine the dance without it. Sol was right. Black and white presented a certain classy look, but color would brighten the gym.

Ashley interrupted my thoughts. "Are you going?"

She gave me an expectant look, and I realized she must have been talking to me. I totally missed the conversation. Much as I hated to ask, confusion won over pride. "Going where?"

She blinked at me. "To the dance?"

Heat filled my cheeks. "Maybe. I don't know."

Beside me, Ashley tapped French-tipped nails on the table and shot me a sidelong glance. A tiny frown tugged at the corners of her mouth, as if her lips were undecided about which way to point. Was I distracting her from something?

Lowering my gaze, I stabbed a fork into my green beans. I felt her stare linger on me.

"Sol said you might have a few good ideas for the dance," Ashley said. "Do you have any?"

We made brief eye contact, during which, instead of saying something brilliant like 'we should rig a zipline across the gym,' or 'let's hire elephants to transport people from the parking lot,' or 'instead of hiring a DJ and dancing, we should hire a magician and just kick back and enjoy,' I shook my head.

"Oh." Ashley grabbed her phone. Her face lit up, and she leaned to the girl next to her, showing her whatever was displayed on her device. The two of them broke into laughter.

Sol nudged me. "What do you think? Is Harper right?"

Squaring my shoulders, I shook my head. "Nope. Go with your gut. A little bit of color never hurt anyone. Unless they're allergic to ink."

She laughed and went back to her animated conversation.

Tuning them out, I took another bite of food and swallowed over a growing lump in my throat. I think I mumbled something about Rome needing a disco ball before I gave the dance any serious consideration.

I recognized where this lunch was headed. I felt like I wasn't even there, and except for Sol, people treated me like I wasn't there too. Sitting with a group who already had established relationships kept me an outsider. They'd be polite, like Ashley with her forced conversation, but I wouldn't share their inside jokes. They might ask for my opinion but wouldn't care what it was. To make matters worse, all the noise made it difficult to focus on one discussion. And I didn't want to be that annoying out-of-place kid who always asked, "What did you say?"

Instead, I ate in silence and pretended to have fun. Like I understood what was going on and heard what was being said.

Like I belonged.

I couldn't let Sol believe otherwise. She wanted to hang out with these girls, and I didn't want to hold her back from doing something she was obviously passionate about.

And even though I had never felt so alone than while sitting in this crowd, I still desperately wanted to be part of it.

A cheer erupted from Sol, startling me. She stood, pumping her fist in the air. "Google cast the deciding vote." She held up her phone and read. "Romans wore garments dyed in vibrant purples, reds, greens, and yellows. When in Rome, we've got to add color, people!" she announced to the group.

She spread her arms, pulling everyone into her excitement. "Anyone up for Tyrian purple streamers, the favorite color of every aristocratic Roman including, most likely, Julius Caesar?"

A chorus of yeses burst around her.

I half expected Sol to break into song. Instead, she rotated her shoulders in a decent pop move. "Yay! No more monochrome decorations! We set up the gym in two days. Clear your calendars for Thursday night."

Like Ashley and the girls next to me, I clapped and hooted. Sol would have been proud of my performance. Now all I had to do for the next twenty minutes was act interested, nod a few times, and ignore the empty ache growing in my heart.

CHAPTER SIX

PLIGHT OF THE LIZARD

T oo much time interacting with party planners and insufficient time alone to recharge was like caging a bearded lizard with monkeys. The monkeys won't care. But the lizard's personal burnout was inevitable.

CHAPTER SEVEN

DRILLS

After school two days later, Coach Hering gathered the team together. "Warm up, Speed of Play, ten minutes," she said, which sent us scrambling to an assigned spot on the field.

The Speed of Play drill helps improve teamwork, communication, passing ability, ball control, and reaction times. Cones marked each corner of a number of invisible squares on the field. Teams of four stood one player at each corner with the first player in possession of a ball. Player one passed the ball to player two, who passed to player three, then player four, then back to player one. The idea was to be the first group to pass the ball around the outside of the square three times without a miss.

"And don't forget to call the name of the player you're passing to." Coach Hering rolled a loose ball to me, but not before her hard look told me the words were aimed at me. "It's only half a pass if you don't communicate."

My face heated. "Yes, Coach!"

After our assistant coach—a silent but intense relic of a woman about forty years old named Coach Lofton—passed out the rest of the balls, Coach Hering paced the field, eyes laser-focused on our footwork. "Sol, remember, two touches on the ball. One to control, one to pass."

A mortified look shot across Sol's face. "What?" she squawked. The ball bounced past her, and she raced after it. "I need more touches. I'm a touchy-feely kind of girl."

Snorting, Coach strolled past, flanking us. "Sandy!" She paused and modeled a pose with her shoulders squared and feet spread. "Open your body to receive the ball so you can pass with the next touch."

"But I'm a goalie!" Sandy complained.

Coach glared. "You never know when we'll need you on the field."

Worries about Sol's social ambitions and my parents' hectic work schedule faded as I concentrated on executing each move. The smell of the grass, the sun kissing my face, the beat of my heart—each singular stimulation helped shed the barriers always keeping me in check. Here, sweating on the field, pushing myself harder and harder, life made sense.

After we finished the drill and stretched, Coach Hering called a water break and circled us up. This was typically when she gave us her analysis about the last game while Coach Lofton stood in the background with a scowl on her face.

As I slurped down my lukewarm lemon sports drink, I braced myself to take a few verbal blows. I glanced at Sol. How would she react to criticism when, outside of warmups, she hadn't set foot on the field? But from the distracted look on Sol's face, I doubted she'd even notice if Coach upended a bucket of ice on her head.

Dance fever. Sol must have visions of the streets of Rome on her brain.

Not me. I prefer grass stains and sweat over a corsage and perfume.

Coach Hering cleared her throat. "Ladies, last game ended in a loss. It could have been a win. But in sports, mistakes happen. No one gets a play or a shot right every single time." She frowned as if remembering past errors. "The goal is to make fewer mistakes each time, and that happens when decisions are made and acted on with quick, lethal force. Tactical toughness comes with the territory. So does tenacity."

Nudging me, Sol leaned over and whispered, "It sounds like today's lecture is sponsored by the letter T. That's a capital T. Which rhymes with C. Which stands for C'mon."

I recognized the tune from *The Music Man*. Sol and her nerdy fascination with the arts! I pressed my lips together, hoping Coach hadn't heard her comments.

"When passing is a better option, trying to dribble the ball out of trouble is a judgment error." Coach pinned her gaze on Reb and then me. "Going offsides is a mistake of awareness. Missing a pass is a communication blunder. All these areas can be improved with discipline."

"I only counted two T words that time." Sol's voice was muffled by her shirt, which she'd pulled up to cover her mouth. "Guess I made a literal alliteration mistake."

The blood drained from my face. I put a finger to my lips to shush her.

Coach Hering continued, apparently unaware of our inter-action. "While it's frustrating to misplace a pass or over-kick a goal shot, the important thing is to identify those problem spots and iron them out of your game. Making those adjust-ments sets a good team apart from a great team." Coach lifted her chin. "And we aim to be a great team. A team others fear. A team that makes it to playoffs at the end of the season. A team that—"

"Dominates," Coach Lofton said.

"Yes!" Erika pumped her fist in the air, and the rest of the players chorused agreement.

Coach Hering held up a hand, quieting us. "We can solve some of our issues with simple communication. When we trust each other, talk on the field, and know each other's strengths and weaknesses, we will perform better. But—" she paused, her eyebrows pinching together, "other issues involve technique. Ball control. Timing. Positioning. That's what got us in trouble yesterday. And that's what we'll work on today."

While we hopped in line for the next drill, Sol grabbed my arm.

"Harper wants to meet at six. Can we skip out of practice a few minutes early?"

"How early?" I snagged a ball with my foot and dribbled down the line.

Sol kept pace as we hustled to the nearest cone. "Five forty-five."

"What? No!" I lost my focus and flattened a cone with the ball.

"Dani!" Coach Lofton bellowed. "Exercise control!"

Wincing, I slapped the marker back in place. "Soccer comes first," I hissed to Sol.

She didn't mention the meeting for the rest of practice, but

I could tell the delay bothered Sol. The later it got, the longer she lingered on the sidelines during water breaks, checking her phone and frowning.

Near the end of practice, we scrimmaged three-on-three. Sol was on my team, but her mind still wasn't on the game. She missed passes, tripped over her own feet, ran out of position—let's just say she committed practically every mistake Coach Hering had targeted.

I bet Sol didn't even have her eyes set on playoffs anymore. I half expected her to weave a grass crown and wear it while she danced the macarena. Parties, prima donnas, and promising popularity might become her new norm.

All brought to you by the letter P.

That's a capital P, and that rhymes with T, and that stands for Trouble.

Great, now my *life is a musical.*

Practice ended with Killer Conditioning, which involved interval sprinting up and down the field. It wasn't exactly what Sol or I or anyone with a heartbeat would classify as fun, so the two of us always went as the last group and raced each other to spice it up a bit.

This time, Sol put in as much effort as a plucked chicken. Which is to say, she ran raw and spastic.

When we completed the final set, I hunched over, head spinning, hands on my knees, sucking in air.

Sol sprawled on the ground next to me, chest heaving, a pinched expression on her face. She checked her watch and groaned. "Six fifteen," she said between gasps. "We're late. We'll have to. Hurry up. Right after. I catch. My breath."

Reb tapped my foot with her cleat on her way past the bench. Grass stains marred her socks and sweat slicked her face. "Good job, Dani. Strong finish. See you tomorrow."

Without lifting my head, I nodded. It's hard to talk when you can't breathe. Still, the compliment seared my ears. When you spend most of your life being invisible, it's nice for someone to notice your hard work every once in a while.

Sol pulled herself into a sitting position and snagged her water bottle. She sloshed a swig around in her mouth and spit it out. "I thought. That practice. Would never end. You?"

Me? I *hoped* that practice would never end. Because now it was over, and I had to force myself to hang decorations with a mob of people I didn't know well.

But as much as I dreaded the interaction, I didn't want to disappoint my friend.

Steeling my nerves, I straightened my back. "I'm ready for action."

I was careful not to specify what action—like fleeing, curling up into a fetal position, or rending my clothes biblical style. Let Sol draw her own conclusions.

CHAPTER EIGHT

TORTURE

For the record, running interval sprints in a tight bikini with a stampede of water buffalos bearing down on me would be less torture than decorating a gym for a dance with a squad of socialites.

CHAPTER NINE

UCA

When I picked up Sol for school the next morning, she popped open my car door like a cork. "I can't stop thinking about last night. I know you don't normally like meeting new people, but"—she pinched her fingers— "didn't you have a little fun?"

Typical extrovert, energized by the crowd scene. I had to drag myself out of bed this morning after that whole ordeal. Still, it could have been worse. I cocked my head, considering my mixed emotions. "I guess it wasn't as bad as I thought it would be."

A smile burst across Sol's face. "I'll take that as a win!"

I matched her smile. "Okay, I'll admit, outside of a few dozen awkward interactions, the decorations turned out well. I guess we did good."

"Good?" Sol gave an exaggerated sigh. "We had strings of white lights framing the doors and crisscrossing the ceiling to represent Roman constellations in the night sky. My personal favorite was your attempt at building Capricornus."

"Who could resist making something whose name meant 'The Sea Goat'?" I asked. "I got to use lights to create a pirate version of Tom Brady on the ceiling."

"Stop!" Sol laughed. "That's why you picked it? Oh, that's a hoot."

I grinned. "Why not? You took liberties. Like the balloon arch. How is that Roman?"

"Someone didn't do their homework." Sol raised her brows. "The balloons mimic the Arch of Constantine, a foundational Roman architectural masterpiece."

"How do you explain the disco ball then?"

"Ever hear of the stray cannonball lodged in the Palazzo Colonna?" Sol's eyes danced.

I scoffed. "You just wanted an excuse to add a disco ball, didn't you?"

"Yup," she said. "But that cannonball really does exist. I've got a screenshot of the website if you want me to prove it."

Shaking my head, I waved her off. "No, I'm good."

"I can't wait until Saturday night. Did you know Barrett asked me to the dance?"

"Yes. You've told me a half dozen times, remember?" My heart warmed at her contagious enthusiasm. "You met in English class, he's on the cross-country team, his favorite color is red, and you share the same passion for music and movies." Slowing for a stop sign, I laughed. "I was listening."

"You always listen." She pushed my shoulder. "That's what I appreciate about you."

"And you always talk," I said, flicking on my turn signal. "Or sing. That's what I appreciate about you. Except for the singing part. I have an entire catalog of musicals permanently lodged in my brain thanks to you."

"No thanks necessary. I'm awesome that way."

I snorted. "And you're awesome for your willingness to be a few minutes late so I can buy some desperately needed coffee."

"What, no herbal tea this time?" She gave a high giggle. Well, higher than usual.

Imagine a hyper kitten pouncing on multiple pointer lights and you'll get the picture.

"Who are you and what have you done with Dani? Never mind, I like this version too. Order me a large coffee with three sugars and a cream. I'll pay this time."

She opened her purse, but I held up a hand. "No, my treat."

"You always treat." Her hand hovered in midair.

"Maybe I like having you in my debt." I arched a brow.

Shaking her head, she thrust her card into my hand. "Even without the free coffee, I'm always in your debt. I got this one."

I blew a raspberry at her, but I let her pay. This time, anyway.

After parking at the high school, we rushed into the building for our weekly United Christian Athletes, or UCA, club meeting before first period. It wasn't a large group, which I appreciated. Our school sponsor, Ms. Brown, always brought donuts or muffins or sausages wrapped in croissants for breakfast. She led prayer and shared encouraging stories and Scripture.

I suspected Sol had another reason to attend. Barrett was one of the athletes in the club.

Donuts and boys and Jesus. A win-win-win situation.

Because of our coffee stop, Sol and I straggled into the room right after the opening prayer. I took in all the faces staring at me and plastered on my best smile, although by the stiffness in my cheeks, I'm pretty sure I looked more like a teeth-clenching emoji. Ducking my head, I slid into one of the chairs near the front.

"Sorry we're lay-ate." Sol sang her apology. She grabbed two donuts from a box at the front. She tossed one to me, which I caught with one hand. Then she waved at the crowd and winked at Barrett before giving an exaggerated bow and plopping into the chair next to me.

"Thanks," I whispered, frowning at the chocolate frosting and sprinkles squishing through my fingers.

Making a face, Sol nibbled the corner of her own glazed pastry. "Don't be so picky. Ugly donuts and pretty donuts taste the same." The playful tease in her voice was undisguised.

"Truth!" Barrett yelled from the back.

Ms. Brown arched a brow. "Welcome, ladies. Glad you could make it. I've got more truth for you, but I'm not going to sugarcoat it like your breakfast."

A chorus of *oooo* made me slouch further in my seat, even though both Ms. Brown's comment and the room's reaction were meant in good fun.

"Truth," she repeated, voice carrying over the teasing. Leaning against the desk in the front row, Ms. Brown turned on the smart TV and pulled up an image of a volleyball player diving after a ball. "With fall sports in full swing, I thought this would be a good time to address a key factor in our success."

The screen changed, showing a muscular football player lifting weights. "In athletics, we often focus on the physical aspects of the game. Our stamina. Our strength. Our technique."

A new picture appeared. A soccer player, with muscles taut and eyes squeezed closed, heading a ball toward a goal. "These skills and abilities are good. But do you know what else is equally if not more important to our success?"

Murmurs tickled my ears as people behind me shared their thoughts.

Ms. Brown advanced the presentation. The new image captured a tennis player sitting on the bench with his head between his hands. "Our mindset."

The room quieted.

"Competition brings pressure. Ace the serve. Win the race. Make the goal. Catch the ball. Win." Ms. Brown pinched her lips together and let her gaze travel the length of the room. "Expectations are high. The coach might be hard on you. Your teammates might snap at you. Your parents might scream from the sidelines. You might be hard on yourself. Sound familiar?"

It did. Pressure was a constant but unwanted companion. Why did I let it dominate me? At least I kept my circle of victims to one—myself. Unlike Nick, who dealt with pressure by taking risks with everyone, including himself. Pushing boundaries in school and at home. Letting impulses rule him. And behind each ten-second thrill he earned stood a truck-load full of consequences, like the hazing incident that got him suspended from the soccer team.

At least when the heat of pressure bore down on me and I failed to rise to the occasion, my only consequence was personal disappointment flavored with a touch of guilt.

A quick glance around me revealed athletes with hard eyes and lips drawn in straight lines. Guess I wasn't the only one facing that issue.

"All that critical talk undermines your confidence, makes you second-guess your abilities, slows your decision-making," Ms. Brown said. "Even the most capable athlete will fail if they lack the proper mental preparation for the game. That's why it's important to believe in yourself."

Sol frowned and raised her hand.

Ms. Brown inclined her head. "Yes, Sol?"

"I wish it was that easy. Believe. Achieve," Sol said, wiping chocolate off her fingertips on a napkin. "I'd have won three marathons if life worked that way. But my experience says just believing isn't going to change anything."

Several students muttered in agreement, but Ms. Brown held up a hand. "You're not wrong. But here's the thing about believing you can succeed. Actions typically follow. You believe you can win, so you work harder to make it a reality. You believe you can get an A in biology, so you study longer to increase the probability of it happening."

"So how is our mind connected to our performance?" Sol asked.

"Let me ask you this." Ms. Brown paced across the front of the room. "You have two players who possess equal abilities and powerful bodies. What pushes one toward greater success?"

"Their motivation." Sol nodded. "The mindset."

"Yes." Ms. Brown paused and planted her fists on her hips. "And the truth is, no matter how shrill the roar of the crowd, the loudest voice we hear is the one inside our heads. Every great athlete faces doubt. How we respond, well, that's the measure of our mettle."

"Medal? Like gold, silver, or bronze," someone called out.

Sol turned around in her seat. "No, mettle. M-E-T-T-L-E. Like your courage, determination, or grit." She grinned.

"As in, if you have enough mettle, you can download a dictionary app!"

Laughter peppered the room. Sol wielded tease like a tickling feather duster.

"Exactly," Ms. Brown said, without missing a beat. "I'm sure your coaches have addressed mental toughness." She strolled down the row toward a senior named Elijah. "What do you think?"

Elijah's eyes darted side to side, and his ears pinked. His obvious discomfort made my heart go out to him. Not everyone likes the spotlight.

As silence dragged on, Elijah cleared his throat. "Coach Campbell is big into positive self-talk and visualization. Before each game, he has us imagine ourselves dribbling and shooting the ball. 'See the win, claim the win,' he says."

Licking a sprinkle off my finger, I let Elijah's words sink in. How many times had I deflected compliments? Downplayed my successes? Dwelt on stupid mistakes? I'd played long enough to know when athletes got shook up or upset, it threw off their game. But it was hard to avoid negative thoughts.

"Good answer." Ms. Brown nodded. "Athletes can train their minds to rebuke doubts. But here's a final thought. When you face pressure to perform, when you face challenges that test your strength, when you doubt yourself, it's important to not just believe in yourself. It's important to believe *beyond* yourself."

Ms. Brown clicked the remote and dropped it like a microphone.

She read words covering an image of a grassy field. "'*The weapons we fight with are not the weapons of the world. On the contrary, they have divine power to demolish strongholds. We demolish arguments and every pretension that sets itself up against the knowledge of God, and we take captive every thought to make it obedient to Christ.'* 2 Corinthians 10:4-5, ESV. Bam! That's a truth you can use." She pointed at her heart. "On and off the field."

You could have heard a ladybug fluttering its wings.

The bell rang, breaking the spell. People joked and chatted and texted while gathering their supplies. Hefting my backpack, I waited for Sol. "Great message."

"Agreed. I guess that's why Coach makes us do those pregame visualization exercises. Except I keep imagining myself sunbathing in Florida, and I haven't scored that one yet."

"Ha!" I smirked. "Now I understand why you carry a beach towel in your duffle bag."

"I carry a book in my duffle bag."

"I was kidding," I said.

"I wasn't." Sol laughed. "I'll catch you at lunch, all right? Barrett's walking me to class."

I stepped back as Barrett pushed forward as proud as a Clydesdale.

Sol put a hand on my arm and gave me *mwah, mwah,* pretend kisses on the cheeks. "Later, Squirrel. Enjoy your three point one four one five nine." She quirked a grin at Barrett. "That's pi. It's a calculus joke."

They left, side by side, leaving me by the donuts.

I swallowed. The chocolate frosting from my earlier indulgence left a sticky-sweet flavor on my teeth.

But I could do all things on and off the field, right? Like walking to class alone.

To be fair, I always did that anyway.

My class was on the other side of the building.

CHAPTER TEN

ENCOUNTER

actually enjoyed people. I just needed them in small doses, which didn't happen often on a typical school day because the rooms and hallways were crawling with people.

And I didn't mind conversations. I just hated small talk. So hearing "How's it going, Dani?" three dozen times got old quick.

Practice—an open space with fewer than thirty teens—couldn't come fast enough today.

For warmups, I partnered with Sol, as usual. My friend was a hummingbird, flitting here and there, and I was an owl on silent wings. During the breaks, she talked about her next blog, something we both enjoyed. But she also talked about the upcoming dance, a topic that reminded me why I preferred the field.

Physical activity finally filtered away lingering anxiety. Drills and footwork reclaimed my body. Tips and teamwork reclaimed my mind. And exhaustion reclaimed my Sol—pun intended.

By the time we got to the small-sided scrimmage at the end of practice, my shirt clung to me, my muscles ached, and all was well with the world.

Coach split us into two teams. "We've got a game on Friday, but we still need to work on a few areas." She pointed. "Sandy."

Our keeper straightened, a soldier receiving marching orders. "Yes."

"Remember what I told you to focus on during the free kick drill?" Coach folded her arms, a challenge in her gaze.

Sandy widened her stance. "Trust the wall."

"That's right." Coach nodded. "When your teammates line up to block the attempt, trust they'll do their job and put yourself in the most vulnerable spot. You keep sneaking forward. Stop. Remember, it's hard for an attacker to shoot over the wall and under the crossbar. Got it?"

Sandy nodded.

"Dani." Coach Hering gestured. "Concentrate on field awareness. You're still going offsides."

My inner critic flared, a knife deflating the tire of my confidence. Despite my best efforts, I was still surging past the defense? I'd worked hard on field, ball, and especially player awareness. Just ask me what flavor of gum Erika was chewing!

"Coach." Sol's hand shot up like a rocket. "Want me to grab the bottom of Dani's t-shirt and hold her back like a dam blocking water?"

Coach Lofton grunted, the closest thing to a laugh I'd heard from her.

"Maybe." Coach Hering quirked an eyebrow, a smile tugging on her lips.

The good-natured exchange helped stifle my doubts. Determination settled in its place. After all, to improve in soccer, you've got to be coachable. With struggle comes progress.

Or sometimes disaster and then more struggles. I once saw a brown house moth try to struggle its way out of a spider web. Didn't work too well for the moth.

I gritted my teeth. "Thanks, Coach. Will do."

"This is the only time I'll ever hold you back. Literally," Sol whispered to me in a singsong voice before sprinting to her spot. "You're welcome."

"Thank you, oh wise word wizard," I shot back with a slight bow.

Sol stuck her tongue out, but in a way that let me know she appreciated my humor.

I worked hard after that. By the time Coach blew the final whistle, I had a cramp in my side. Doubling over, I engaged in what I call gasping. Sol called it diaphragmatic breathing, a method that fully expanded your stomach, lungs, and diaphragm. She'd researched the science behind it to help her recover after sprints.

Or so she could throw around another big, fancy word. Could be either with her.

After the pain passed, I looked for Sol. She stood on the sidelines flanked by Erika and Reb. When the three hooked arms and headed for the locker room, the urge to close ranks almost overwhelmed me. I started their way, but hesitated. Sol wouldn't mind. But how would Erika and Reb react to me butting in?

Indecision decided for me. By the time I mustered the courage to join them, the trio was halfway to the building. Nothing is more embarrassing than a tagalong running to catch up.

Well, actually, some things are more embarrassing. Like smiling at a cute guy with broccoli stuck between your teeth. Or having a coughing fit in the middle of study hall. Or someone knocking on the bathroom door, and you have to answer to keep them from barging in.

But chasing after people who've left you behind without a backward glance definitely ranks high on the list.

To save face, I grabbed the ball bag and slung it over my shoulder Santa Claus style before trudging off the field. I could catch up later. After all, I was Sol's ride home.

The boys' practice was still going on, so I sat on the second row of the aluminum bleachers. I didn't think I'd stand out too much since there were others watching. Students like me, no doubt checking out a certain athlete on the team.

I quickly pinpointed Elijah, the poor guy Ms. Brown put on the spot at our last UCA meeting. We shared one class, science, but I'd known him since middle school. Sweet, but plain vanilla. And kind of cute. He'd filled out a little more this year.

Or maybe a lot more this year. Hmmm.

Did he find quiet math-and-science-loving soccer girls attractive?

A middle-aged man slid into the front row, blocking my view. He wore an average Joe kind of look with faded jeans and maroon state t-shirt. He used his phone to snap a few pictures of the players and then turned the camera to snap a selfie. I sat in the background like an accidental photobomb, uncertain if I should smile or turn away. Was he a college recruiter? Or maybe a proud freshman or sophomore dad waiting to drive a player home?

Eyeballing the guy, I scooted farther away.

Another player caught my attention. Hayden. I'd seen him in the hallways. Dreamy brown eyes and long hair. Fidgety, like he was hot-wired for action. He was like an anime character with an edge. Wish I knew him better, but that would require initiative on my part.

His neon yellow jersey made him easy to spot. I tensed as a wingback charged at him from an angle. The only way to stop Hayden would be a slide tackle, which didn't always end well for the person on offense. But when the defender initiated his attack, Hayden used an inside touch to tuck the ball behind his other leg. The defender slid into a space the ball no longer occupied. And Hayden ended up three steps farther down the field.

I sucked in a breath. "Nice move," I murmured.

"That was tricky, wasn't it?"

It took me a moment to realize the voice was addressing me. "Excuse me?"

The maroon-shirt guy flashed a smile. "The play. It was tricky." He bit a piece off the top of a red licorice stick and pointed at Hayden with the remainder of it. "That player really put the moves on that defender, didn't he? Highly effective."

Drawing my legs close to my body, I nodded. It was a great play—one I should add to my repertoire. I'm sure Nick could do it on the fly. If he still played. Maybe this Hayden kid would teach me sometime. *Yeah, in my dreams.*

Leaning back, the man sighed. "Watching these boys scrimmage makes me miss my coaching days. I see you've got shin guards. You must be a player too."

"Yes." An odd desire to share my soccer status gripped me. "Starting midfielder on the varsity team."

"A tough position. Takes more energy than I care to think about at the ripe old age of forty. But if you can't play, coach." He chuckled.

I risked a sidelong glance. Just my luck, sitting next to a talker. You know, the type who struck up a conversation with everyone he met, including garden gnomes. A chatterbox who cornered people on airplanes, in elevators, or in grocery store lines and showed you a billion pictures of their spoiled dogs or the fifty-seven ways they grilled hamburger. The ones who could talk until hair sprouted from your ears with the passage of time.

I positioned the ball bag between us.

He seemed harmless enough though, like a nosy neighbor, and I didn't want to be rude. Finally, I couldn't help myself. "Did you play in college?" I asked.

The man laughed. "Oh, no. I was good, but not *that* good. Still, I love the game." He cocked his head. "How well do you know the players on this team?"

"Not too well. At least not as well as I'd like." A rush of blood heated my face. Did I say that out loud?

The man raised a brow. "I've been watching practice on and off for the last few weeks. Oh, hey!" He raised a hand, and I turned to follow his line of view.

The boys' coach lifted a hand in response.

I straightened my back. "Do you know Coach Campbell?"

"Yep." The man bit off another piece of candy. "We went to the same high school. Course he went off to Purdue University and came back a bigwig high school history teacher."

Was there a hint of smirk in his voice? A protective fire stirred in my veins. "A well-liked history teacher and a hard-working soccer coach who took his team to state last year."

The man shook his head. "Hey, sorry, I didn't mean to sound disrespectful. Coach Campbell and I are old friends, so I get to tease him about anything I want." He extended his hand for a handshake. "My name is Jay."

"Hi." I waved, not willing to touch him.

He let his hand drop. "You know, Cliff—you knew his name was Clifton, right? Clifton Campbell."

I nodded. "Not sure what his parents were thinking with that name."

"Right?" Jay released a belly laugh that made me smile. "Well, C.C., he's still my man. Anyway, one time between classes, Cliff tripped on the steps and grabbed the closest thing to him to keep his balance. Which was, in fact, a cheerleader's backpack. And not just any cheerleader. The prettiest one on the team. Not only did he end up in a tangled heap at the bottom of the stairs, but he dragged the poor girl with him. The entire cheer squad shunned him for weeks. You've got to admit, that's grounds for a good ribbing."

Despite myself, I grinned. Simply knowing Jay had connections with someone I respected made me let go of my angst. "How embarrassing. I can't even imagine it."

"Don't tell him I told you," he said, tone serious.

I zippered my lips with my fingers. "Our secret."

Grunting, Jay turned his attention back to the practice.

"I haven't seen you at school before. Are you visiting Coach Campbell?" I asked. It was a bold move, reopening the conversation since it seemed to finally dwindle. But curiosity had a way of pulling me out of my shell.

Jay spat a nub of red licorice onto the ground. He wiped his mouth before answering. "I am, in fact, scouting for him. I let him know who looks like a player and who he might want to bench. At least from this spectator's point of view. What about you? Any player stand out?"

His question caught me off guard. Why would he care what I thought? Unless he was looking for intangible things, like character and discipline—things an observant person like myself might notice while navigating the hallways at school. Then my input might prove valuable. Or maybe even help someone get more playing time. "Elijah's a solid guy." I pointed him out. "Smart. Disciplined. Kind of a quiet leader, so you might overlook him on the field, but he knows his stuff."

He scanned the field. "How about that golden boy?"

"Hayden?" My voice rose, even though I tried to keep it neutral.

Jay studied me for a moment, as if gauging my reaction, then nodded. "Hayden."

"He's a senior. Moved here last semester. I heard the upperclassmen didn't like how he earned a starting spot on the soccer team since he was an outsider."

Hayden elbowed a defender and broke away. When the coach blew the whistle to stop the play, Hayden's face clouded and his fists clenched. He crowded close to his defender and barked some sharp-toned words I couldn't quite hear. Coach Campbell held up a hand, and, just as quickly, Hayden's scowl faded.

"The guy's scrappy," Jay said. "And he doesn't seem to like losing."

I lifted my shoulders. "Who does?"

"Good point."

Jay asked me a few more questions about the players. Like, did the seniors hang out with the underclassmen. Who started last year. Did they have a winning season.

A squirm lodged itself in my spine. "If you want to find

out more, you can probably look up everyone's stats on our school's website," I said.

"The tab next to the advice column? Been there already."

Then he should have known the answers to some of his questions. Which meant this conversation was faltering into small talk, and I didn't have the energy for it. I pulled my hoodie over my head and tightened the strings.

We watched in silence for several plays. Him, taking in the field as if memorizing the players' faces. And me, fighting an unreasonable urge to pick up a soccer ball and prove my prowess. To prove girls deserved the same respect when it came to competition. But all we had for extra support was Coach Lofton, who played rec soccer a billion years ago and communicated with grunts. We were lucky our uniforms were made in the twentieth century. No, Jay didn't ask a single question about our program. Instead, he was helping the boys' team strategize, and they already had two legit assistant coaches. As I simmered about the inequity, Sol emerged from the locker room and cupped a hand to her forehead. She was probably scouting for me. Time to go.

I couldn't take off without at least putting a plug in for our female athletes, so I stood and cleared my throat. "It was nice to meet you, but I gotta go. You could always come to one of our games sometime and root for the girls' team. We've got some amazing players."

His eyes widened. "I could. Sometime. If I'm not too busy scouting."

When I made it to Sol, I glanced back. The boys' practice was coming to a close. And Jay still sat hunched in the bleachers, studying them with the eyes of a hawk. If only we could be so lucky.

CHAPTER ELEVEN

SAME OLD STORY

Friday was game day. My favorite day of the week.

The only problem? Our team faltered against the Greenville Hornets. When the ref signaled the start of our fifteen-minute half-time break, the score stood tied—not because of the Hornets' stellar play, but because we stunk up the field.

I collapsed onto the bench. Chest heaving, I passed Reb her water bottle before uncapping my own. My skin blazed in the late afternoon heat, slicked by sweat and grime. I scooted to make room for Erika and then gave up my spot for Wren, our other forward. Everyone needed a breather, and I could rest standing up.

Squatting in front of us, Coach Hering pinched her lips as tight as a square knot around an elephant. Her glare cut down the line. "Ladies, do you fear a zombie apocalypse?" Her voice had a raspy scrape, evidence of the yelling she'd done. "If so, don't worry. You're safe because apparently, you've all left your brains in the locker room. I saw a lot of desperation out there, but very little thought."

Coach had called it true. We'd made mindless blunders. I'd earned two offsides calls. Reb took three shots, each preceded by a poor set-up touch, and she missed each goal by a solar system. Wren kept turning into her defenders and losing the ball. Erika missed tackles, looking like a misplaced baseball player stealing second base in the middle of a cornfield. And Sandy allowed the solitary goal against us when she was late to challenge a charging player in the penalty area.

"They're cheaters." Reb sat with a stiff back, her chin lifted and eyes hard. "Whenever I go after the ball and barely touch the defender, she flops to the ground, moaning and cradling her fake injured leg. Then as soon as the ref calls a penalty, wham!"

I nodded. "She's up in everyone's faces again like a horsefly at a picnic."

"Don't use someone else's underhanded tactics as an excuse for your own mistakes." Coach Hering stared at Reb, fire matching fire. "Channel that frustration into your game instead. Use it as motivation to work harder. Right, Rebecca?"

Oooo. Coach used her full first name. Not good.

"Sure." Reb glowered, anger obviously still eating at her.

Sol put a hand on Reb's knee. "Hey. Let it go." She

channeled her inner Disney by singing a snippet of the tune from *Frozen.* "Let it go. You can beat that girl, my friend."

Even though the girl had pipes, I was glad she didn't finish her rendition of the song.

"Trust me, number eleven isn't half the actor I am, and you can handle me just fine." Sol thrust her hand forward and skewed her face. "Oh! My poor *hangnail.* Whatever shall I do?" Her voice rose to a dramatic sob. "Call the doctor! Or no! Call the pet store. I need a litter of sweet golden retriever puppies to lick away my pain."

Her antics burst the tension. Reb let out a hiss of air. Erika's shoulders shook in silent laughter. And I took a deep, calming breath.

Grinning, Coach Hering nodded at Sol, as if to say, *And that's why I keep you on the team.* "Ladies, it's time to put the grit back in the game. We're switching to a three-five-two formation. That will give us better stability on both the attack and defense of the ball at midfield. Dani, this will give you more options to penetrate the back line. But for heaven's sake, don't go offsides."

I nodded, mentally kicking myself. *Always jumping ahead.*

Grunting, Coach Lofton folded her arms across her chest—a gesture I learned was her way of communicating full agreement with the assessment and a touch of disgust.

Coach Hering moved on. "Outside players, you'll have to work harder, or they'll beat us on the wings. But given their tendencies, I don't anticipate that being a big problem."

As Coach ran down her list of adjustments, I scanned the crowd to see if my mom was at the game. If she didn't have time to change after work, her light blue scrubs would stand out among the spectators.

My stomach tightened. What if she didn't make it again?

Maybe I shouldn't have craved her time. I knew she loved and supported me, but Mom was busy. Still, her actual presence at the game brought comfort in knowing someone came specifically for me. Someone who rooted for me no matter how many times I failed.

I scoured the crowd until I finally spotted the telltale patch of blue. Once I saw it, my nerves settled in time for Coach Hering's final remarks.

"Stay constantly aware of your position across the goal face, who's controlling the ball, and the passing options. Be ready to make your move if you spot an opening." Coach Hering thrust her hand into the middle. "We got this. Team on three."

We circled around Coach Hering and piled our hands on top of hers. Coach Lofton squeezed her blocky body in there too, the way a goat might jockey for position on a mountain.

"One, two, three," we chanted. "Team!"

As I set my water bottle down, Sol cornered me. "Don't worry about the first half. It's over. You got this, Squirrel. And I'll treat you to a pretzel after the game. With cheese."

They had pretzels? Smiling, I lifted my hand to high-five her and glanced at the concessions stand.

And froze.

A maroon shirt. Had Jay decided to attend an Eastwood girls' game after all?

Blinking, I zeroed in on the person. Whoever it was, he was too far away to identify for certain. Besides, it's not like I'd memorized Jay's features. We'd only talked for maybe twenty minutes, and I'd split my time between avoiding eye contact and bragging on my team.

Sol's hearty slap on my raised palm brought me back to

reality. "Go get 'em." She folded her arms across her chest. "And stop eyeballing my boyfriend."

"Barrett? He's here?" I frowned. "Why would I—"

"Don't you see who he's standing next to?" She elbowed me. "Hayden, who has an ambrosial charm about him—"

At my blank stare, she grinned. "Ambrosial, meaning exceptionally pleasing."

"Uh-huh," I said, remembering his long hair and square chin. I couldn't disagree.

"Anyway"—Sol drew out the word like honey—"Ambrosial Hayden asked about you yesterday and decided to tag along with Barrett today. So you better play like a beast in the second half. Because your fan club just grew by one." The tease in her voice made light of the fact she hadn't played at all.

The blood drained from my face. Hayden asked about me? Had he caught me watching his practice with my messy hair and sweat-stained shirt? How could I possibly compare to the bubbly cheer squad I'd overheard crushing on him in the hallway?

I swallowed. "Then I hope I don't make a fool of myself."

"Just be you." Sol tightened her ponytail. "Dani the unstoppable. The Soccer Star. Let me worry about the fooling around."

Pulse racing, I squashed down thoughts about Hayden and jogged to my spot on the field. I had a game to win. With or without a Dani fan club.

Luckily, Coach Hering's new formation strategy worked.

Reb scored two minutes into the start of the second half and, with a Hulk-ish kind of primordial pose, shouted, "Take that, you overdramatic actor!" in number eleven's face.

And was promptly benched for two minutes by Coach

Hering for poor sportsmanship. Although, from the slight curl of Coach Lofton's lips, she, at least, approved of the outburst.

I got into the action too, timing a header on a corner kick from Wren just right to knock one into the net. I ran the length of the bench, screaming and slapping hands, secretly hoping Hayden saw my goal.

When the whistle blew to end the game, I rushed the toward the bench, arms spread wide. Sol met me halfway.

"We have another tally in the win column," Reb yelled. "If we keep this up, we'll make playoffs!"

Chest puffed out like a Persian cat, Coach Hering quieted us. "Smart playing, ladies. You capitalized on your strengths. I only have one word of warning for you." She paused and leaned in. "Watch out for the zombie horde!"

As one, we leapt to our feet and cheered. It was short-lived though, because Coach ordered us to pack our bags so we could head back to school.

The task took me longer than Sol. I had to change my shoes and slip out of my stained jersey, and she was still fresh. By the time I zipped my front pouch, she'd already stepped over to Barrett and Hayden. From her animated gestures, I could tell Sol was in her element. Was she gossiping, flirting, or telling jokes? Probably all of the above.

I would have followed right away, but Mom hovered behind the bench with a few other parents. Her face lit up when I bounced my way over to her. "Way to go." She gave me a shoulder squeeze. "A win. I'm proud of you."

I beamed. "Thanks. I'm glad you saw our comeback."

"I'd have been here sooner without rush-hour traffic." She puffed her lips to blow a stray hair out of her eyes. "I'm drained. See you at home?"

"You bet." I rolled my neck, working out some of the

stiffness. "Is it okay if Sol and I stop for a milkshake on the way back?"

"Only if you pick up something for me too," she said.

Behind Mom, Sol looped her elbows to place a boy on each side. The girl had no fear. But I had plenty enough for both of us.

I swallowed and forced myself to smile. "Of course. What do you want?"

"Surprise me," Mom said.

After we loaded the bus to head back to school, Sol pulled out her latest advice column to share with the team. "Listen to this one. 'Dear Heart—'"

Erika's eyes widened. "Nice! A relationship one."

"You wish." Sol made a face. "It's kind of borderline. Both personal and interpersonal. Listen. 'On social media, I see a lot of pretty girls with thousands of followers. I feel the pressure to live up to a higher standard of beauty than I can pull off. What should I do?'"

Wren leaned closer. "Tell the girl to use a camera filter. Those things could make a potato look like a Greek goddess."

"Nah." Sol shook her head. "Doesn't address the underlying issue of self-comparison."

"Think body positivity," Erika said.

"Lame." Reb slapped Erika on the arm. "What your girl needs to do is focus on female power. Tell her, who cares what you look like? It's the guts that matter. So show some—guts, that is—and put yourself out there."

"What would you say?" Sol asked me.

"I totally get how she feels." My stomach churned. "I think everyone has something about their looks that they don't like. Like their nose or their teeth. And I know being pretty has its perks. People are more likely to pay attention to a good-looking boy or girl." Hayden's face flashed in my mind.

I covered my sudden crush moment by offering Sol a granola bar. "Here's the thing that gives me hope. My grandma is the most beautiful woman I know, and she wears polyester, and she's ten pounds overweight with a face full of wrinkles. Tell your reader not to apologize for her uniqueness. Her so-called flaws are what makes her beautiful."

Sol laughed, high and musical. "You should listen to your own advice sometime. That's perfect."

"How is that any different than my idea?" Reb demanded.

Shaking her head, Sol grinned. "It's not, really. But it's all in the delivery, my dear Rebel. All in the elocution."

"I'm not sure what elocution means." Reb huffed. "But I hate it. Unless it means zapping walking dictionaries with electricity. And then I love it."

"It means it's all in the way you say it." Sol tilted her head.

Reb frowned. "Then I hate it."

The rest of the trip crawled by as more and more people pressed around Sol and I pulled away for air. How does the girl keep her sanity being surrounded all the time?

It was just as well. I had Let's Shake on It on my mind, a stop Sol and I would not make alone on the way home. Barrett and Hayden would meet us there. And I had Sol and her fast-talking magnetism to thank.

CHAPTER TWELVE

LET'S SHAKE ON IT

oud music and crowds can overwhelm me. But since my pact was to try new things, like meeting new people, I decided I could handle mixing in a large group as long as I stuck with Sol and left early.

Still, my throat went dry on the drive to Let's Shake on It, and I maintained a death grip on the steering wheel. "How long are we staying?"

"My curfew is midnight." Sol checked her makeup in the visor mirror. "But if you can't stay that long, I can hitch a ride with Barrett."

I sucked in my cheeks, thinking. Mom would be waiting for me at home, but I was sure she wouldn't mind me staying. She might even encourage this social outing.

More likely, she was already asleep on the couch and wouldn't want me to bother her. Came with the territory. Nursing took a lot out of her.

"I'll play it by ear," I said.

Sol dotted her mouth with cherry-colored lip gloss. "That works for me."

When we arrived, the boys sat under a red umbrella outside the restaurant. Barrett waved, holding up a French fry like a flag, and Hayden raised his cup.

Immediately, some of the butterflies in my stomach calmed. If they'd already ordered their food, this was a more casual encounter than Sol led me to believe. Hard to call it a real date when you paid your own way, right?

"There they are!" Sol pointed, not realizing I'd already spotted them. Her energy level ramped up from firecracker to nuclear bomb. When she threw open the car door, I was surprised she didn't rip it off like a charging rhinoceros.

I shifted into park and shut off the motor. "I'll order for us and meet you outside," I said. There would be no holding Sol back anyway, and the extra alone time would give me a chance to steel my nerves. "What do you want?"

"Get me a cookies and cream milkshake." She unfastened her seat belt and jumped out of the car. "Medium sized. Yes, a cherry and whipped cream. And a spoon in case it's chunky."

Inside, I stood in line behind a few middle school girls and scanned the menu. Was I brave enough to try strawberry? Or should I go with my usual?

"Good game, Dani," a voice behind me said.

Heart in my throat, I whipped around. "Elijah! You scared

me." Catching my breath, I relaxed. "I didn't know you were at the game." I'd been too fixated on Hayden to notice anyone else.

"Yeah, I was in the student section." His cheeks dimpled into a smile. "Blending in."

No kidding. The guy was cute, but low-key.

"Well—" Awkward! I shifted, wondering what I should say next. "Thanks. And I liked what you said at UCA. I need that positive mindset sometimes."

"I think we all do. I read an article once about the mental toughness of athletes. It said the level of success you have depends on it. A can-do attitude can work wonders for your game."

He chuckled at his own joke, which was sweet in a nerdy way.

"Well, that explains Reb's success then," I said. "She's mental all right."

"No kidding." He looked down and toed the floor. "I sometimes pull a Bible verse for motivation during the game. If I make a mistake on the field—"

"When, not if," I said. "No one is perfect."

He grinned. *"When* I make a mistake, I focus on the inspiration behind those words instead of beating myself up. Takes the pressure off. If you want, I can send you some pregame verses." The eager pup raised his brows.

Was Elijah flirting with me?

I glanced out the window behind me. Sol seemed to be in her element with both boys sporting enthralled looks. A compulsion to hurry spiked through me. What was I missing? "Yeah, sure." I licked my lips. "That would be great."

His ears pinked. "Cool. What's your phone number?"

Ready to move on, I handed him my phone. "Put in your number and shoot me a text. I'll add you to my contacts."

"Great." He typed a message, then handed it back.

I checked my device. He'd texted, "Hello" and a soccer ball emoji.

"I can't wait for our school season to start," Elijah said. "This club team rocks, but I'm ready for conference matches, you know?"

"I know." The girls in front of me finally made their selections. *C'mon.*

I replied to his text with a smiley face, then waved my phone. "We're all set now. It was nice talking to you."

Elijah touched his forehead like a salute. "See ya."

A few minutes later, I joined Sol outside. Crumpled wrappers littered the round table, and a splotch of ketchup stained the concrete underneath. The boys had finished their meals. Not surprising. Most teenage boys inhaled food in less time than it took to pop a giant pimple.

Sliding into the only open seat, I passed Sol her cup.

"Finally!" Sol accepted her drink and pushed a straw into it. "What took so long?

I pressed my lips together and jerked my head toward the next table. "I got stuck behind those two middle school girls, who insisted on sampling every flavor of ice cream before deciding to go with rainbow sherbet."

"I hate when that happens." Barrett leaned forward, keeping his voice low.

"Me too," Sol said. "But I don't know how you stop ice cream samplers. I mean, is there a rule somewhere that dictates the correct number of flavors you can try before it becomes a nuisance?"

"I feel like three is the unspoken magic number here, especially when there's a massive line waiting to order." I shrugged. "But who's going to enforce that?"

The two girls in question chose that moment to burst into shrill giggles comparable in volume to the screech of a howler monkey. One of them turned up the music on her phone and started singing. Badly.

Sol blew a raspberry. "They don't divertimento well, do they?

"Divertimento meaning ..." Barrett cocked his head.

"Serenade," Sol said.

I frowned. "Meaning?"

"Sing. The girls don't sing well, people!"

The songster must have overheard her because she glared in Sol's direction before huddling with her pal in relative silence.

Sol flipped her hands in the air. "So much for talking in code."

Guilt swept through me. They were just kids acting like kids after all. "I didn't mean to make them feel bad," I whispered, twirling my straw.

What would Hayden think? I glanced at him. He had a crooked grin on his face, hinting that he found the conversation amusing. Or else he had an uneven gumline, which, based on his other heart-throbby features, I doubted.

"Don't worry about it." Sol pushed my shoulder. "They could use a few manners." She took a slurp of her shake, then held the cup at arm's length. "The black and white Oreo chunks remind me of the rejected color scheme for the dance. Did you know Dani and I helped decorate for it?"

"Ugh." I groaned. "No offense, Sol, but that decoration session was worse than having a wart removed. Not that I have any experience with that."

Hayden scoffed. "What, you don't like to put up streamers?"

"The streamers were fine." My nostrils flared. "It was the piece-by-piece assembly of the Pantheon using 183 recycled Styrofoam dinner trays that did me in."

"Dani!" Sol's voice rose an octave. "That decoration shows off modern ingenuity."

"Yes, well, so does chewing gum, but you don't see anyone creating sculptures in the shape of sticky blobs. Can we talk about something else?" With a surge of unexpected bravery, I pulled a move out of Sol's playbook and poked Hayden on the shoulder. "Like that trick footwork you pulled in practice the other day, Hayden. You smoked your defender."

"I smoke other things too, but no one applauds me for that." He paused, as if waiting for a reaction.

When I didn't take the bait, he cleared his throat. "Which move?"

Wait. Not *when did you watch my practice?* I expected him to ask me that, but he must have noticed me watching from the sidelines. A strange thrill shot through me. Score one for the introvert! "The spin move, where your defender tackles an empty space and ends up looking like an idiot while you're halfway down the field ahead of him."

"Oh, that." He waved his hand as if it were nothing. "It's called a Cruyff Turn. You've probably seen it before. The pros use it."

Sol held up a hand. "Stop. You know I love soccer, but if you're going to talk sports, Barrett and I are getting some more fries. I need something to dip, and we still have details to discuss for the dance tomorrow."

"We do?" Barrett scrunched his face.

"Yes." Sol stood and pulled Barrett to his feet. She maneuvered behind him and pushed him toward the door. "And I need fries to do it with."

Hayden gave a low chuckle and watched their exit. His jeans had a convenient hole above the knees. If he wanted to, he could probably slip a team flyer in there. "Guess Sol's pretty excited."

"She is."

I needed to contribute more to the conversation than two-word answers. Something like panic—or whatever you want to call the overbearing urge to flee screaming—filled me. Outside of soccer, I didn't know Hayden well enough to know what interested him. When Sol made new friends, how did she gauge the right tone of voice to use? Or the perfect moment to crack a joke? What would Sol say?

She'd tell a story. Or she'd ask questions.

The first one posed a challenge. Did I know any interesting stories? Not unless Hayden had a burning interest in World Cup statistics, the plight of polar bears in the warming arctic regions, or luna moths, which, unbelievably, had a ridiculous amount of hair on their insect bodies. Those facts were things someone like Elijah would enjoy, not Hayden.

But I could handle asking questions. I asked myself questions all the time. Like, would someone from Egypt who adjusted your spine be called a Cairo-practor? Or why do we call the television controller a remote when we try to keep it as close to us as possible? And why do runners call a switch between sprinting and jogging a fartlek? It sounds like a gassy trek down the road.

Shoring up my courage, I looked Hayden in the eyes. "Do you think you could teach me that Cruyff move? I have a ball in the trunk of my car. There's enough light from the buildings and streetlamps to see. And the Dry-Cleaning Guru parking lot is empty next door."

A seductive smile curled his lips, which curled my toes. "You're on."

Chapter Thirteen

THE CRUYFF TURN

bounced to my feet, totally up for the challenge. Three quick slurps finished off my shake, and all our trash went directly into the garbage can. I paused to text Sol so she'd know where we were.

Hayden waited for me at the curb, and I scrambled to catch up. "You don't happen to have cones, do you?" he asked.

"No, but I have empty water bottles on the floor in the back of my car." Two pairs of last week's stinky socks and a wadded practice jersey were crammed there too, but he didn't need to know about them. I clicked the button to unlock the doors. "How many do you need?"

"Two." He held up his fingers. "They'll mark the goal."

While gathering supplies, we chatted about the game that night, our favorite soccer players, and the weather in Chicago, his hometown. Like dribbling the ball down the sidelines, the words flowed easily. Naturally. Unforced.

In fact, I was downright gregarious—a word Sol used to describe herself when she got excessively talkative.

Insects fluttered against the streetlights as we set the water bottles as goalposts.

"This is Betty," I said, handing him the black and blue paneled soccer ball I kept in the car. "I've had her since forever. Be nice to her. She gets kicked around a lot. Although she does roll with the punches."

Hayden's eyes danced, but he took Betty without comment and dropped her on the ground. He didn't even ask me how I came up with the name. I guess some mysteries weren't meant to be revealed.

"I'll do it in slow motion and explain the steps first," Hayden said. "All successful Cruyff Turns are made when the attacker has enough awareness to know there's space behind him—or her—to turn into."

"Coach Hering is always on me to be aware of my surroundings." I shrugged. "If I followed her advice better, I wouldn't get called offsides so much."

"The movement is swift. Controlled. Smooth." Hayden quirked a brow. "Like me."

"Demonstrate." I cracked my knuckles. "I'll defend."

He pressed his hands on the small of my back and guided me like a dance partner. A shot of lightning traveled the length of my body.

"Pay attention." He cupped my chin. "You want your defender on the opposite side of the foot you're doing the skill with."

Face flushing, I nodded, adjusting my stance. His musky scent lured me closer to him, a moth to flame. Heat spread down my neck, and I hoped I wouldn't break into a sweat.

As soon as I pushed against him, Hayden lunged, then pulled back when I moved to intercept.

"It's two moves combined, really. A shoot and a scoop," he said. "Watch me."

How could I not?

Fast as a bee sting, he modeled the Cruyff Turn full speed, leaving me stranded on the wrong side of the ball.

"You make it look easy." I folded my arms across my chest. "Break it down."

"Okay." He rolled the ball back in place. "You start by making a fake shot, but you stop your foot as it goes past the ball." He demonstrated, moving the ball to his right. "Make a quick change, angling so the inside of your foot is flat against the ball." He stopped Betty with his foot. "Continue the momentum, scooping the ball straight backwards." It went behind him, out of my reach. "Then rotate 180 degrees so you can dribble the moment you flip."

He executed the whole maneuver in slow motion, then sped it up. "That's it. Keep your body tight to the ball. But you gotta sell that fake shot. If the defender sees it coming, they'll adjust. Once they bite, run the steps quickly, and the two moves will blend into a single fluid motion. Try it."

He booted the ball my way, and I herded it to a spot in front of the water bottles. Step, fake shot, scoop, turn. "Like that?"

"Almost." Hayden stepped closer and put one hand on

my shoulder. He pulled my arm to the side with his other hand. The skin under his touch burned. Well, not burned, but I had some type of hormonal reaction to his presence. Maybe a rash?

His breath warmed my neck. "Raising your opposite hand helps you keep your balance when you turn."

Goose bumps peppered my arms.

When he stepped back, I buried my surging emotions and tried again. "How about now?"

"That's better." He nodded. "Not polished yet though. The turn requires good timing and flair. You want to deceive your defender, so don't give it away."

Sagging, I ran my fingers through my hair.

"It's better if you start slow," Hayden said. "Get used to the move first. Practice making a lot of small but smooth 180 degree turns over and over. You'll get faster too."

"Good to know." I swatted away a mosquito and squinted back at Let's Shake on It. Sol and Barrett had their heads bent together, paying us no attention. "Those two are still sitting at the table. Want to play some one-on-one?"

"I'm in." He clapped his hands and rubbed them. "We'll need two more water bottles though. Or beer bottles if you've got them. For another goal."

Beer bottles? I wrinkled my nose. "Very funny." His sense of humor needed tweaking. Alcohol and all its problems were no joking matter. "That's not my scene. Will a sports drink do?"

"Oh, sure." Hayden's face reddened. "Not mine either."

After we set up, Hayden let me start with the ball. He stole it quickly, and I shoved him, laughing. "No fair. I wasn't ready."

"Too bad." He relaxed his stance, and I leapt at him. He

protected the ball with his body, effectively blocking me. But like I'd been trained, I continued to pressure him, staying light on my feet at enough of an angle to be able to shift in front of him when he changed direction.

At one point, I booted the ball away. He jogged after it as if he had all the time in the world. I beat him to it and kicked a goal. "You'd better not hold back on me," I warned.

His mouth dropped open. He snapped it shut, meeting the challenge in my eyes. "Wouldn't dream of it."

Soon we were pushing and jostling each other, battling across the asphalt. He'd sometimes taunt me in a good-natured way, but I could give as good as I got.

"Enjoying yourself?" He grunted, feigning left.

I spun and flashed a smile. "The last time I had this much fun, it involved a food truck and a trip to the dentist."

We kept at it, easy talk and hard play, until Sol marched over waving her phone. "Your mom texted me since you didn't pick up. She was a little frantic."

"Oh no!" I cringed, breathing hard from exertion. "I forgot to let her know I'd be out longer than a drive-thru time frame."

"Well, she knows now. I love your mom. Don't make her worry like that." Sol frowned. "Good thing she knows my number. I told her you were fine, but she says you need to go home now."

Using the bottom of my shirt, I wiped sweat off my forehead. "What time is it?"

"Ten forty-five," Barrett said, coming up behind Sol. "The restaurant is about to close, so we'll probably leave soon too."

"But not go home yet." Sol held up a finger. "I have until midnight. You, on the other hand, have got to—" She swayed and broke into the chorus of "Ease on Down the Road" from *The Wiz.*

Hayden leaned into me. Heat radiated off his body. Or maybe it was sweat. It was hard to tell under the circumstances. "You put up with this?" he whispered.

"All the time," I whispered back. "She has quite a musical repertoire."

"I meant your parents. Giving you a curfew," Hayden said. "You're eighteen, right? Old enough to vote?"

"Uh …"

Sol's phone buzzed again, and she glanced at it. "Your mom says not to forget her ice cream. Should I answer?"

Sighing, I collected the closest water bottle. "Tell her I'm on my way."

"Hey." Hayden bent down next to me, retrieving the ball. "That was fun. We should do this again sometime."

I froze mid-step. "You mean the four of us meet at Let's Shake on It?"

"No, just us." His eyes held mischief. And redness.

I thought he was joking about smoking before. Now I wasn't so certain.

Better to know now.

"Why are your eyes red?"

He rubbed them. "Cat allergies. You got one?"

"No, but Sol does." I relaxed. "I'll keep her away from you."

"Thanks." He swiped a sleeve across his forehead. "And our date?"

I smoothed a stray hair away from my face. "Okay. Sure."

My hands shook and I probably looked like a half-drowned sheepdog, but Hayden didn't seem to mind.

"I need your cell number." He fished his phone out of his back pocket and I typed in my contact information. "Are you going to the dance?" he asked.

"Nah." I bit my lip, debating with myself. Did I admit the

thought of being on a crowded dance floor sounded about as appealing as eating pickled cow tongue? Not if I wanted to project confidence. So I left it at *Nah*.

"Want to go to a movie then?" he asked.

I wasn't sure if I'd heard him right, so I just nodded and stumbled off like Cinderella at the ball, except with a soccer ball instead of a dance ball and I kept both shoes on my feet. And my clothes weren't transforming into rags. And the clock wasn't chiming midnight. And I wasn't going home in a pumpkin.

So maybe only the stumbling off part of Cinderella.

"I'll pick you up at six. Wear something sexy. Like a clean t-shirt." His voice carried the same light tease Nick always used with me.

The streets were dark on the way home and the traffic sparse. I didn't turn on music, preferring the quiet hum of the car motor and the stillness of the night. My heart was still soaring when I turned on my street and accelerated toward home.

A porchlight on the corner caught my attention. It cast shadows on a solo figure sitting on the front step. When I drove past, I recognized the slight girl who had spooked me in my driveway earlier in the week. She looked even younger than I first thought. What was she doing up so late? Probably gazing at the stars. That's what I'd be doing.

No, there was a glow in her hands. She was texting. Or maybe flipping through social media. Both were addicting.

"You sure keep strange hours," I muttered, putting on my turn signal. "Does your mom know?"

Chapter Fourteen

MACIE

A dinging notification from my phone woke me up Saturday morning. I groaned and blinked my eyes open. The clock on my desk said seven o'clock. The only teen I knew who'd rise and shine this early on the weekend was Sol. But she was totally worth waking up for.

As I rolled over to grab my phone, my calf muscle spasmed. I stiffened my leg, hoping to avoid a cramp. Our bodies need lots of water after exercise to avoid dehydration, and I'd put in an extra workout with Hayden. I should have drunk more liquid before I went to bed last night.

The room was still dark when I checked Sol's message. She'd sent me a gif of a dancing monkey in a pink dress.

Cute. I dictated my answer. *I see you're already dressed for the dance tonight, but you might want do something with your hair.*

A moment later, my phone lit up again. *Guess I could chimp it. Instead of crimp it.*

LOL, I typed. *Why are you up?*

I decided to get my nails done this morning. Want to come?

Last time we went to a nail salon, Sol kept her polished gems for a month before they wore off. My decorative claws only lasted one day on the soccer field.

How many ways could I say no? There was the yuck emoji, thumbs down, clenched teeth, big eyes, the scream. I settled on thumbs-down. *Hope that's okay,* I added.

No worries, she texted. *I'll get Harper to go with me. I'm bummed that you won't be at the dance, especially after all the time you spent on the decorations. But I know you'll have more fun with Hayden. I'm super excited for you. I want details tomorrow.*

I sent a smile emoji. *Have fun with Barrett. Send pics.*

Now fully awake, I contemplated my day. With this early start, I could finish my homework and read a book before my date. But what I wanted to do most of all was perfect that Cruyff Turn so I could impress Hayden. I may not be much for conversation, but actions speak louder than words, right? With enough practice, I could give him an earful. Instead of going back to sleep, I jumped out of bed and headed downstairs.

Dressed in a fuzzy plaid bathrobe, Mom sat at the kitchen table with her Bible in front of her and a cup of coffee cradled in her hands. No matter how busy she was, she always seemed to have time for morning prayers. And coffee.

"You're up early." She took a sip of her brew, her way of inviting me to fill in the blank.

"Sol texted." I shuffled to the refrigerator and poked my head in. Mom kept low-fat cheese, tortilla wraps, veggies, fresh fruit, and nuts on hand. After last night's junk food, I needed a healthy breakfast to replenish my energy. As an athlete, I knew this. As a teenager, I'd kill for a donut. Even a squished one thrown at me by a friend. "Do you want eggs?"

"Are you offering to make them?" Mom arched a brow.

"After my glaring lack of communication last night, it's the least I can do." I pulled out the carton, a frying pan, and butter. "Besides, I know your shifts have been crazy this week."

"You got that right." Mom yawned and rubbed the heel of her hand into her eyes. "I can't wait until your father flies back tomorrow afternoon. Of course, then he's got a series of board meetings and a Rotary luncheon." She sighed. "We need a vacation."

I nodded. We did. "Scrambled or over easy?"

"Over easy with a slice of toast." Mom set down her mug. "Do you want help?"

"No, you've had a long week. I can do it." I cracked the shell on the counter's edge and dumped the translucent, gel-like egg into the pan. Now add a little salt and pepper, and all I had to do was time the flip.

Timing. Hayden said the Cruyff Turn took flair and timing. I imagined the move and tried the footwork by the stove. Without Betty, it felt weird. I wadded a sheet of tinfoil into a ball and dropped it on the floor. This time my foot rocketed the shiny orb across the room. I'd have to get it later.

"Sol told me you have a date tonight." Mom rested her chin on her hand, oblivious to my wayward shot. "I'm surprised I didn't hear it from you."

"She gets up earlier than I do." I shrugged. "I didn't have a chance yet."

"You were working your way up to it?"

"Something like that," I said, turning down the heat on the stove. "It's not really a big deal."

"What do you mean?" She straightened her back. "It's the first crush you've had since Captain America."

I snorted. "Mom!"

"Do I get to meet the guy?"

"Yes, you can meet him. He's picking me up at six, and we're going to a movie." I used a spatula to lift the edge of the egg. If I flipped it too soon, the yolk would break.

"Which movie?" Mom leaned back, finger tracing the rim of her mug. "And are you going to dinner first?"

"I don't know. About either." The egg stayed intact as I eased it over. "We can figure it out when he gets here. What kind of bread?"

"Wheat. I have a gift card to Papa Pasta if you want to use it." She couldn't disguise the eagerness in her voice. And I thought I was supposed to be the excited one.

Frowning, I pressed the lever on the toaster. The inside glowed red as it heated. "Thanks, but that's too fancy for tonight. We'll probably order pizza or something."

The rest of breakfast went that way—with Mom asking questions about Hayden and me doing my best to answer them. The truth was, I couldn't tell her much about him. He moved in spring semester last year. He seemed popular enough. A smooth talker, but charming. I wasn't sure if he went to church, but he had a quick smile. A little rough on the edges, but that could be how kids acted in Chicago.

No, he wasn't as easy to figure out as the boys I'd crushed on before. Freshman year, it was Tommy. He had a brain on him, shared five classes with me at Eastwood, and loved sports, especially baseball. And we got along great … except for the part where he dated a cheerleader named Lilly and never noticed my puppy-dog eyes.

Sophomore year was all Brandon. He was homeschooled, but he'd been in my Sunday school class since third grade. But an hour on Sundays and Wednesdays at church didn't give this shy girl enough time to formulate a complete sentence around the guy. Hard to form a relationship based on small talk.

And junior year I devoted so much time to soccer, I didn't have time for a love interest.

Until now.

"Well?" Mom said. "Will I like him?"

I sucked in a breath. "I hope so. You'll need time to know him better. We both will."

"Caution." Mom spooned the last bite of egg into her mouth and pushed away her yolk-streaked plate. "I like that."

After I cleaned up the dishes, I packed a snack and a water bottle in my backpack, grabbed Betty from my car, and headed to the empty lot down the street. I needed practice if I wanted to pull off a Cruyff Turn, and I aimed to show Hayden I was a fast learner.

A quarter mile later, I lowered my bag onto the edge of the property. The short, yellow grass stood as a testimony to the lack of rain. A mound of dirt curved upward from the street like a brown strip mall with three concrete steps leading nowhere. The remains of an old chimney marked the outline of a house that had burned to the ground years before I was born. Other than that, and a pair of old tractor tires stacked by the wooden fence line, the property was clear of obstacles. Perfect for me.

Twenty minutes into it, the late-night girl from down the street walked by. She lingered by the stairs, her dark eyes following my every move.

The athlete in me noticed her physical appearance. She wore a long-sleeved shirt, too warm for this kind of weather, and tight jeans. Hand-me-downs perhaps?

I ignored her at first, but curiosity got the better of me. Who was she? And why was she always wandering around by herself? I resolved to find out.

After five smooth Cruyff Turns in a row, I left Betty resting in a patch of dandelions and strolled over to grab my water bottle. I nodded at the kid, and she nodded back. Then I tilted the container, rehearsing what I would say.

The girl spoke first. "You're good."

With a sidelong glance, I swiped my mouth. "Thanks." I capped the lid and sat just beyond arm's length next to her on the top step. "Do you like soccer?"

"No. I hate sports." She lowered her gaze. "My dad says I'm terrible at them."

"Oh." I frowned. So much for my grand opening. "How old are you? Twelve? Thirteen?"

"I'm eleven."

"Eleven." I leaned back. "That's good. You still have plenty of time to learn. Do you want me to teach you a little?"

"I can't." She slouched. "I'll never be as good as you."

I bit the inside of my lip. Why did this kid even bother talking to me if she was going to be so negative? Still, her awkwardness reminded me of my fourth-grade year when Sol was sick from school for a week and I needed a friend on the playground.

Taking a big breath, I tried again. "Then what do you like to do?"

"Nothing." Her face clouded over, and she tugged on her overlong sleeves.

Time for a new approach. "I've seen you around before. You live in the house on the corner, don't you?"

Narrowing her eyes, she nodded.

"That makes us neighbors. I'm Danielle. Dani for short. What's your name?"

"Macie." Her voice came out timid, like a fawn finding its legs for the first time.

"I bet you're better at soccer than you think." Whether or not this was true, a little encouragement never hurt. I patted my hands on my knees and straightened my back. "I'll tell you what. I'm going to practice my shooting, but I need someone to play goalie. Will you do that for me? It's simple enough. All you have to do is keep the ball from passing between my backpack and the chimney over there." I pointed, and she followed the line of my finger with her gaze. "You can stop it with your hands. Your feet. Your head. Anything. The goalie is the only one on the field without real limitations."

"Okay." Reluctance laced her words, but she trudged after me and stood where I directed her to go. Then her brow wrinkled, and she licked her lips. "Can you give me a few tips?"

"Sure." I rubbed my hands together, thinking. How did Sandy defend the goal? "Stay on the tips of your toes, so you'll be ready to move. Keep your eyes on the ball. Don't wait on me to shoot. Instead, move to the ball. And spread your arms so you look as big and intimidating as possible."

I wasn't sure if that last suggestion was legit, but if animals like the blowfish puff themselves out to look more threatening, so could people.

"Got it?" I asked.

She nodded. "Got it."

And then, for at least the next thirty minutes, we talked.

Well, technically, we played, but actions speak louder than words. And I hoped my efforts told her she could do it. And that I was someone she could trust. For some reason, it seemed important to me.

When I paused for water, my stomach protested with a loud grumble. "Macie," I said, dabbing my forehead with the bottom of my shirt, "my internal clock is telling me to go home and have lunch. My body needs fuel. I bet yours does too."

"Okay." Macie studied the ground for a moment, then she threw her arms around me in a hug. "Thanks, Danielle."

Unsure about how to respond, I patted her back. "Any time."

After I gathered Betty and my backpack, we parted ways. I scanned the street when I got home to see if I could spot her from my driveway.

She was too far gone.

CHAPTER FIFTEEN

NOT THE DANCE

For my date that night, I selected comfortable slim fit jeans and a red button-down shirt over a white tank top. I debated between cowboy boots and sneakers but opted for blue-strapped wedge sandals instead. They accentuated my height.

When I slipped the sandals on, my plain old toes peeked from under the strap, and for the first time all day I wished I had taken Sol up on the trip to the nail salon.

But this was not the dance. Casual worked fine.

After applying eyeliner and mascara, I checked myself in the mirror. My skin was a little splotchy, but passable. The static in my hair lifted the strands on top of my head but made the ones around my face cling to my cheeks. Meh.

Frowning, I dug around until I found an old bottle of vanilla fragrance and misted myself. Sweet smells improved everything.

I checked the time. 5:55. Sol would head to dinner about the same time Hayden came over. I had bugged her to send pictures earlier, but she only texted a snapshot of herself in a bathrobe with her hair wrapped in a towel and a green mud mask on her face.

By now she should be ready. I patted my hair in place, thinking. Sol would probably reciprocate if I sent her a picture, so I held up my phone, flashed a selfie, and pressed send.

Two seconds later, my phone buzzed twice, both from Sol. A message. Nice. And then a picture of her wearing a tight red cocktail dress and high stilettos. I zoomed in to get a better look. Her makeup and nails were perfection. But how in the world did she walk in those four-inch stilts? I wiggled my toes, grateful for my more practical footwear.

You look gorgeous, I texted.

I know, ha-ha, she texted back. *I'll send more later. Gotta go!*

The doorbell rang. Hayden, right on time.

Heart racing, I sent a quick thumbs-up to Sol, then stood and smoothed my shirt. I couldn't explain why I could face down a dozen fierce-faced opponents dressed in jerseys and cleats, but my knees went weak for one smooth-talking boy.

I stuffed my phone into my purse, flew out my bedroom door, and took the stairs two at a time.

Voices made me slow when I reached the bottom. Mom had already pulled Hayden inside. Her bright smile and animated gestures indicated she'd wasted no time diving into the meet-and-greet stage.

"I think that's a great dinner plan." She put a hand on his arm, a tactic I knew she used to draw people in. "Dani loves Taco, Taco, Taco."

Hayden avoided eye contact, a signal he wasn't completely at ease in this situation. I sympathized with him. After handling Nick on a regular basis, Mom often asked pointed—and sometimes embarrassing—questions. How would I feel being interrogated by his parents on a first date?

I cleared my throat. Did I imagine it, or did Hayden's face light up when he saw me? Heat rose to my cheeks. "Taco, Taco, Taco sounds perfect."

"Hayden was telling me about Chicago." Mom shifted her gaze to me. "It can be a rough place to grow up."

"I'm sure it has its perks too. Like its awesome zoo." I pulled at the collar of my button-down. Was it hot in here? "Wish we had one. I could watch the animals all day. Besides soccer, animals are my jam."

"I love the platypus," Mom said. "Such a weird mish-mash of creatures. God had a sense of humor when He made that one."

Head bobbing, Hayden tucked his thumbs in his pockets, a move I would have copied myself if my jeans were looser. But "slim fit" didn't lend itself well to acting cool.

Taking a play out of Sol's book, I gave Hayden an opening to talk about a subject he loved. "Hayden is on the club soccer team at school too. He taught me the Cruyff Turn yesterday. What were the steps again?"

Perking up, Hayden looked around the room. "Do you have a ball I can use?"

"Yes." I clomped in my wedges over to the entry table

where we kept the keys and reached behind it. "Will this work?" I asked, displaying the aluminum ball I'd kicked out of the kitchen that morning.

He laughed. "Toss that baby to me."

With quick confidence, he modeled the play. It wasn't quite the same since the foil didn't roll, but Hayden didn't seem to mind. He gave me a chance to show my improvement—I had to take the shoes off—and offered to help my mom get the steps down too. We had a good fifteen minutes of hilarious chaos until Mom bumped the coat rack and sent it smacking to the floor.

"Oof! That's enough." Mom straightened the pole and replaced the fallen jackets. "It's time for you kids to get going. Midnight curfew, Danielle, unless you text, and then I might give you a little more wiggle room."

"Thanks, Mom." I gave her a tiny wave as Hayden opened the front door, and we left.

"Nice muscle car," I said, running my finger over the jet-black hood. His family must come from money to afford this beauty.

"A 2022 Dodge Viper." Spoken with the proud tone of a matador showing off a prize bull. He opened the passenger door for me. "And she runs great."

"She?" I arched a brow.

"Black Ivy," he said as I climbed in.

"Wait." I held up my hand. "You named your car?"

"Says the girl who has a soccer ball named Betty." He quirked a grin as if he'd just scored a rebound goal.

"Touché." I smiled to myself as he flicked the door shut.

Taco, Taco, Taco was everything a fast-food Mexican restaurant should be. I almost ordered my go-to meal—crispy tacos—but changed it to a burrito because I feared spilling meat and tomato guts all over myself when I took the first bite. Those hard shells were unpredictable.

When we sat, I rifled through potential talking points in my mind and picked animals. "Do you like dogs?" I asked.

He unwrapped a fajita and spread salsa on it. "Love them. I'm not really a cat person. Allergies, you know. And they're too needy. Plus, those things will try to kill you. My uncle owns a tabby and it's mean. Always hissing and tripping people on the stairs."

"Mmm." I took a bite of rice. "So which dog do you think is the hairiest?"

"I don't know. A Lhasa Apso maybe," he said.

"Those tiny dogs?" I wrinkled my nose. "No way. Have you ever seen an Afghan hound? Their hair is so long, they're like the supermodels of canines."

"Really?" He pulled out his phone. "Let's see which one the internet says is the hairiest."

After some digging around, he uncovered the Komondor, a dog so hairy, Hayden released a four-letter word when he saw it.

"Better not say that around my mom," I said.

"Well—" And he said the word again, as if I'd find it funny.

I didn't. "Potatoes." I firmed my voice, letting him know I meant it. "Substitute the word *potatoes* instead. Please."

"Okay." He shrugged and flipped to another video. "Look at this." The reel showed the hairy dog running in slow motion.

I nearly snorted soda out my nose laughing. "That dog is a humongous mop. If someone spilled five gallons of milk in my kitchen, I'd borrow one of those mutts and plop him in the middle of the room, and in seconds all the liquid would be soaked up."

"Not just the milk on the floor, whatever juice you had in the refrigerator just, swoosh! Gone." Hayden spread his arms like an umpire calling a runner safe at home. "Potatoes!"

We picked a movie afterward. I steered him away from horror to a comedy spoof, explaining I'd rather howl with laughter than fear.

Usually, social outings drain my energy. But when we pulled into my driveway ten minutes before midnight, my nerves buzzed with adrenaline. I didn't think I'd ever had such a perfect night. What was so different about Hayden? Was it the fact he seemed to find everything I said fascinating? Or his alluring charisma?

He shut off the motor. "I had fun tonight."

"Me too." I fiddled with my seat belt, uncertain if I should get out.

"And I like you. A lot. We should do this again sometime." He put both hands on the steering wheel. "You know. When we're not avoiding dances."

"I'd like that." I decided it was a safe time to tease him. "But you should know, if I have to choose between you and soccer, I'm sorry, but soccer wins."

"You took the words right out of my mouth." He drummed his fingers, tension flickering across his face as if debating with himself. Finally, he let out a pained hiss of air. "I like you. But you're too nice. I—I can't do this. I can't do this to you. I don't think I should see you anymore."

What? My heart sank. Was he breaking up with me before we were even a couple? How exactly did that work anyway? I swallowed the lump forming in my throat. "So … friends?" I asked, keeping my tone light. Noncommittal.

"I—" He tightened his grip and bowed his head between his arms. His ears burned fiery red, as if he were wrestling a bear and losing. "Yeah. Fine. Friends."

What had he been about to say?

Ashes filled my veins. I guess it didn't matter.

Sucking in a quick breath, I unbuckled and let myself out. "I had fun. Thanks."

As I shut the passenger door, he mumbled, "See you, Dani."

Mom was reading on the couch when I let myself in. She marked her place with her finger and looked up. Bags lined her eyes. She hadn't recouped her sleep from the stressful week, but she waited up for me anyway. It was sweet. "Congratulations. You're back on time. Did you have fun?"

"It was the best night ever," I said in all honesty. I left the rest of the sentence unspoken. *And the worst.* I leaned over and kissed her cheek.

"You want to tell me all the details?" she asked.

My stomach churned. "No, I'm tired. I'm going to bed now."

I must have seemed exceptionally droopy because Mom accepted that answer at face value. Ten minutes later, I crawled into my bed with only my tank top and underwear on. I hadn't bothered to grab my pajamas or brush my teeth.

My phone lit up the room from under the purse I'd dumped on the floor. Hayden?

No, he'd played the friendship card. It had to be Sol.

I'd begged her for pictures, but I was having such a fun time with Hayden, I didn't bother to look at any of them.

Shivering, I slipped from the covers, grabbed my device, and pulled up the images she'd sent.

A happy-faced Sol pinning a boutonniere on Barrett.

The two of them laughing, hand in hand in front of a Roman city backdrop.

That's it? Two pictures? She had to have more. With something like anger coursing through me, I pulled up her social media and scrolled through what she had posted there.

Sol and Barrett under the disco ball.

A close-up selfie of Sol and Barrett, photobombed by Harper.

Harper and her date arm-in-arm with Sol and Barrett.

The four of them posing by the Pantheon I'd assembled.

Then just Harper and Sol, tongues, thumbs, and pinkie fingers out in a rock-and-roll pose.

Sol and Harper doing their "bad girl" pose.

Sol and Harper laughing.

Sol and Harper …

When Hayden left, I thought my self-esteem couldn't drop any lower.

I was wrong.

CHAPTER SIXTEEN

WHY?

"Dani!" Mom pounded on my bedroom door. "It's almost time for church and you haven't had breakfast yet."

Groaning, I pulled my pillow over my head. "I don't feel good. Go without me."

A creak announced my bedroom door opening, then my mattress trembled, and a hand lifted my pillow fortress. Mom, dressed in khaki slacks and a silk blouse, sat on the edge of my bed. Eyebrows drawn, she pressed her hand against my forehead. "I'm sorry to hear that. You don't feel warm. Maybe Taco, Taco, Taco didn't agree with your stomach."

"Maybe," I said.

"Are you going to be okay without me?"

I stared straight ahead. "Yes. I just need to rest."

She sat a moment longer, rubbing my back. Finally, she sighed and rose. "I'll be back around two. I promised Ms. Clark I'd meet her for lunch after church. I hope you'll feel better by then. Your dad will be home by four."

"I'll be okay." I wished she would leave.

Instead, she leaned against the doorframe and folded her arms. "Did you have a good time last night?"

She was fishing for more information about my date. But how could I answer? Or explain how I felt? It was too humiliating to verbalize. "It was okay."

"Do you like him?"

I pulled the bedsheet to my chin and answered honestly. "Yes."

That one simple word peeled back the protective layer I kept firmly around my heart, making it vulnerable like a hermit crab outside its shell. I quickly deflected any question she might ask next. "He seemed nice. But I'm pretty busy with soccer right now. Gunning for playoffs. Maybe too busy to date right now."

"Okay." She stood there a moment longer, as if waiting for me to elaborate.

I didn't.

Closing my eyes, I pretended to sleep.

A few minutes later, the garage door rumbled open and closed again. Now it was just me and an empty house. And an empty heart.

I rolled onto my back and stared at the ceiling. My body, lethargic and achy from lack of sleep, protested. My mind wrestled with emotions.

Hayden and I had a blast last night. True, I'd started with get-to-know-you questions I planned ahead of time. But once we got talking, it was like I'd known him forever. And he felt the attraction too—I could tell. His flirts, the touches, every laugh and wink he taunted me with? Genuine.

What was wrong with me? Hayden said I was nice, but nice wasn't good enough for a second date? It made no sense.

At least he agreed to be a friend. I enjoyed being with him too much to close that door. But why did he bother asking me out in the first place if that's all he wanted? He'd executed an emotional Cruyff Turn on me—leading me one way, then going 180 degrees in another direction. Was he too naïve to recognize the impact of his rejection?

Tears brimmed and my throat tightened. I reached for the tissue box on my nightstand. My phone sat there too.

My phone, with all its pictures.

As if embracing a self-inflicted wound, I scrolled through Sol's posts again. Even though I knew what I'd see. Even though I knew how her success would make me feel about my failure. I mean, of course Hayden dumped me. I could never measure up to Sol's level of simple beauty or easy confidence or contagious charm.

No, I was just nice. And that wasn't good enough.

My heart was a coyote trying to claw its way out of a bear trap. I let the phone drop out of my hand and sobbed.

The logical part of my mind viewed my breakdown as a classic fight-or-flight response. Our bodies process deep sensations, like sadness or anger, as signs of danger. Adrenaline courses through our veins. The brain signals a gland connected to our nervous systems, which releases a chemical to make us punch or cry or scream. Or pray.

Like David did when he wrote the Psalms, I reminded

myself I wasn't completely alone. *My flesh and my heart may fail, but God is the strength of my heart and my portion forever. God, please be my strength, for I have none of my own.*

I found more comfort in the Bible verse than I did in the purely academic approach.

Eventually, my choking teardrops faded to sniffles, and my sniffles quieted to deep sighs, and my deep sighs simmered to anger. What kind of game was Hayden playing?

And why did I want to keep playing it?

Finally, my body, weakened after purging my emotional roller coaster, urged me to get up, use the restroom, and find something bland to eat. With new purpose, I climbed out of bed.

After eating wheat toast with butter, I felt physically better, but tension still lingered in my gut. I needed a physical workout to relieve the stress.

Not bothering to change out of my crumpled tank top, I slipped on a pair of shorts and laced my sneakers. Betty waited for me in her resting place. I grabbed her and a bottle of water and headed for the empty lot.

Last time I was here, I worked on the Cruyff Turn. Today, I would perfect it. Then I'd use it on the field and show Hayden what he was missing. I wasn't just nice. I was tough. And talented. And tenacious. And—

It sounds like today's lecture is sponsored by the letter T. That's a capital T. Which rhymes with C. Which stands for C'mon.

Sol's tease came to mind, and the memory tugged my heart. She and Harper seemed to have gotten close over the past few days. I'd show her too. I didn't need her friendship. I didn't need anybody.

I threw myself into the drills. Fake shot, foot flat, scoop the ball, turn around, dribble in the new direction. I repeated the steps until my tank top clung to me and my hair plastered to my face and my salty tears blended with salty sweat. I pushed myself with such fierceness, I didn't see Macie until Betty landed near her feet and she picked her up.

Wincing, I wiped my face with the bottom of my shirt. "That's my ball."

"I know. Betty." She held it over her belly like a baby. "You introduced me to her a few days ago when we played soccer. Do you remember me?"

"Yeah. I remember. Macie." My voice came out gruffer than I'd intended, but I still hadn't worked out all my demons. The kid would live. Fighting irritation, I held out my hand, expecting her to hand me the ball and leave.

She didn't budge.

"Thanks for showing me how to play goalie." She took a big breath as if steadying herself. "I joined a group of kids playing after school. I remembered what you told me and blocked a few shots."

A sliver of sunshine cracked through the turmoil in my mind. "Great. I'm glad I could help. Soccer is the perfect way to make new friends."

"Yeah." Macie gave a wistful smile. "It was nice."

Nice. That word brought a wall of hostility slamming back down. My lips twisted into a frown. "Well, good. Keep it up." I snatched Betty out of her hands. "Guess I'll see you later."

It was a clear dismissal, but Macie trailed after me. "What are you working on today? I could play goalie again." The hope in her voice called to a tender spot in me, but I ignored its plea. Macie would be fine. I was the one who needed space. I didn't have time to babysit.

I dropped Betty in front of me and folded my arms. "Look, Macie, what are you—fifth grade?"

Wide-eyed, she nodded.

"I'm busy. Why don't you go find friends your age to play with?"

Her face crumpled. "Never mind. Forget I asked."

I could almost hear her facial muscles tightening like cable being winched.

There was no mistaking the pain behind her words.

My pulse spiked. Encounters with Macie flashed through my mind. Her walking the streets alone. Staying up late. Isolated on her porch. And now, rejected by me.

What had I done?

I extended my arms, trying to calm a storm of tears before it started. "We can kick the ball around next week maybe. I just need some time by myself right now to sort things out."

"You hate me." Macie's lower lip quivered, and her body trembled.

That went south fast. Hormonal reaction? I cocked my head. "No one hates you, Macie," I said in what I thought was a reasonable voice.

"You hate me. Everybody at school hates me." Her voice hardened, lashing like a whip.

I connected the dots. "Is someone bullying you at school?"

"Everyone is mean. Including you." She glared at me. "Trey was right. He's my only friend."

Trey? I froze, remembering Jay. Had he befriended more than me? "Did you say Jay?"

"No. Trey. Like you care."

I frowned, mind racing, gut clenching. "Are you sure? What does he look like?"

"Better than you." Macie's lips curled.

Okay, maybe Trey was the one friend she still had and

clung to. I could relate. Lord knows my own circle of friends was small.

I frowned. "Macie, you're in middle school. It's a confusing time of life, and you might doubt yourself. And trust me, finding and making good friends can be hard. You've got to be encouraging and honest and supportive and—"

Squeezing her eyes shut, Macie screamed. Before I could react, she ran toward her home.

I should have gone after her. I was faster and stronger. And I knew what it was like to feel like an outsider. But my muscles and my heart, which had already been through so much this morning, stayed locked in place.

As I watched her flee, a dread I couldn't fully understand flooded me. The adrenaline rush sent trembles through my body. I needed to go home, hole up in my room, find my center. If only I could shut off my curiosity. What was I missing that had turned my conversation with Macie into a disaster?

CHAPTER SEVENTEEN

SHORT-LIVED PEACE

By the time Mom returned from her luncheon that afternoon, I'd explained Hayden's rejection this way. He had a goal, maybe soccer, but he found me so alluring, he feared I'd sidetrack him from pursuing it. With that mindset, I could accept his friendship. Count it as a win, even. Would I love a more romantic relationship? Yes. But at least the self-imposed distance he'd erected between us took the pressure off trying to be girlfriend material, which came with its own set of unspoken rules—like,

I might be expected to wear perfume or eat lunch with him or write sappy love poems in my free time. Hopefully, this arrangement would prevent any more blows to my ego. Like confusing a Komondor with a mop. And Sol had always been an extrovert. She fed on high-energy events like the dance. Of course, she'd throw herself into the middle of all the action. I still felt a twinge of jealousy toward her connection to Harper—I wasn't sure I could avoid that completely. But Sol and I were best friends.

Macie though? Something still didn't sit right with me. Maybe she was simply going through hormonal changes. Those cause wild mood swings. Or maybe she was struggling with bigger issues. Not that I could do anything about it, except maybe being more aware of her insecurities and being more encouraging around her.

I stayed shut up in my room until midafternoon working through those thoughts. After praying, my mental war eased enough to let things rest.

Unwilling to leave my nest, I opened my computer and read Sol's most recent *Heart and Soul* blog. "Unrequited Love" had a crush on a senior who only loved her back when he partied. "College Bound" was freaked out about school applications and wanted coping tips. And "Sugar Daddy" wanted to know if dark chocolate was good for you. Sol had witty answers for each.

A slamming car door caught my attention.

I peeked through the window. A ride share driver had popped the trunk. Dad waited nearby. A USA soccer cap crowned his head, in stark contrast to his crisp gray business suit. Mom stood by his side.

I rushed downstairs to join them.

When I burst through the front door, Dad's face broke

into a huge smile. "How's my girl?" he said, sweeping me into a bear hug. He smelled like Old Spice and coffee.

For a moment, I was three years old again, burying my face in his broad chest. Then he tightened his grip. Laughing, I pulled out of his embrace. A girl needs to breathe, you know? "We won our last game. And I scored."

"Wonderful. Sorry I missed it. Maybe I'll catch the replay this week." He squeezed my shoulder before turning his attention to my mom. "And how about you, dear?"

A smile played on her lips. "Exhausted. We're short-staffed at work, and you know how that goes. Extra shifts."

He nodded, rolling his suitcase ahead of him as we walked toward the house. "You're tough. I'd buckle under that workload."

"You would not." She scoffed. "You're a regular work horse."

"Okay." He made a goofy face. "You're right. I'm awesome." He parked the suitcase in the entryway.

Mom grabbed his arm and drew him to the couch. "Tell me about your trip. With my schedule, it's about the closest thing I'll get to a vacation this year."

I squeezed in next to them. I don't care how old you are, nothing beats family moments like this.

As I listened to my parents banter back and forth, a warm peacefulness filled me. Things would be all right. Macie would find her group. Nick would make peace with Mom and Dad. Hayden would realize his horrible mistake and fall madly in love with me. And Sol would be my best friend forever.

Things were safe. Back to normal. Comfortable.

My eyelids grew heavy. Dad's deep storyteller voice, the pressure of my mom's warm body next to me, and the soft cushions lulled me to sleep.

I awoke in my bed at 3:32 a.m. How and when I transferred

there, I didn't know. I was still dressed in my clothes. A sour taste fowled my breath, a gaping hunger filled my stomach, and nature called big time.

Guided by hallway night-lights, I tiptoed to the bathroom first, then down the stairs to the kitchen. I found a pizza box with three slices of thin crust pepperoni left in it. Mom and Dad must have ordered delivery for an easy dinner last night.

Stuffing one piece into my mouth, I grabbed the other two slices and a bottle of water and carried them upstairs. Mom might not approve of food in my room, but I didn't want to turn on any lights, and the shadows and darkness left in the kitchen made it too creepy to stay.

Instead, I enjoyed the pizza at my desk so I wouldn't get crumbs on my covers. My phone sat on its charging pad, tracking the minutes. I checked my notifications in case Hayden had texted again. He hadn't, but Sol had. Six times. My heart lifted. Harper hadn't upset the balance between us. Good. *What's up?*

Are you there?

Don't tell me you turned off your phone again.

Did you see the news report on this girl in Indiana? Here's the link.

I just called your mom. Good night. Hope you're not sick. Read the article.

Are you still asleep? I guess I'll see you in the morning.

Wiping my fingers on my shirt, I scrolled back to the link and clicked to open the website. The more I read, the more my stomach churned.

I should have waited until the sun was up to read that article. Even when I finally pulled the covers over my head, I couldn't block the words or images. By 4:17, with sweat slicking my body and the bedsheet twisted around me, I gave up trying to sleep, squeezed my eyes tight, and prayed. Gut-wrenching words uttered between choked sobs. My mind played tricks, exhausted and drifting in and out of focus.

God. Please. Protection. Strength. Courage. Justice. Free. Restore. Help.

I don't know if my prayers made sense or not. I only hoped the Spirit could fill in the words I could not find.

CHAPTER EIGHTEEN

THE NEWS

Worry and disgust soured my stomach the next morning. I packed my soccer gear for practice and slipped a taser into my bag. Mom had bought it for me three years ago and told me to carry it in my purse, but I'd stuffed it in a drawer and forgotten about it instead. Last night reminded me why she gave it to me, so I'd charged it while attempting to sleep.

Mom and Dad were already at work. That left me alone getting ready for school.

The clock in the living room ticked a steady beat, marking

the empty passing of time. To drown out its grating rhythm, I played the soundtrack to *Mamma Mia!,* one of Sol's more outlandish birthday gifts to me—even though I secretly enjoyed it. Then I closed every open door in the hallway and turned on all the lights.

I've never rushed outside faster in my life. Well, except maybe the time I was five and Nick told me Santa was stuck on the rooftop. That wasn't fun either. Just wetter. And colder.

Nausea swept through me when I drove past Macie's house. She was only a year younger than the victim in the article. If I saw her again, I'd take more time to find out how she was doing. What she was up to. If she was being bullied, that might make her more vulnerable to sex traffickers.

But though I slowed and strained my neck, her home looked deserted.

Sol, however, was waiting on her front porch when I pulled into her driveway.

"Did you read the article I sent you?" she asked as she plopped into the front seat.

I shuddered. I'd done more than read it. I'd pulled up every newsfeed I could find on it. "Yes. It sickens me."

The girl was attending an Indianapolis Colts game with her father and had excused herself at halftime to use the restroom.

She never returned.

The father contacted the police on site, but they directed him to another county. An out-of-jurisdiction kind of thing. After the parents filed a report with the city, detectives treated it as a runaway case instead of an abduction. Knowing better, the desperate family hired an outside agency. Nine days later, the investigator located their child being prostituted on a website in California. The police arrested five people in a human trafficking ring.

The predators included both men and women.

"Who would grab a twelve-year-old girl in the bathroom?" I asked.

Sol pressed her lips together. "I can't even imagine what that poor girl went through. And they grabbed her in a public place! Video showed the girl leaving with an older woman." She clenched her fists. "Didn't anyone notice something was wrong? It makes me furious. Women preying on other women and the men behind it all."

"Me too. Mad. Upset. Confused. Scared." I narrowed my eyes. "What I don't understand is why the police would treat her as a runaway. If my dad spent the money to take me to a professional sporting event, then logically, I would go home with him. It doesn't make sense for the police to believe she ditched her dad to leave with someone else."

"Yeah, but that's the rub." Sol held up a finger. "It does make sense in a roundabout way. If you had a bad homelife or were a rebellious teen and wanted to escape, it would be easier to get lost in the crowd."

I frowned, chewing on that thought. "True. I still don't like it. The police should err on the side of caution." I put on my turn signal and eased around the corner. "You know what? I like my privacy, but I'm glad I've got a tracking app on my phone so my parents can always locate me."

"Really?" Sol tugged on the seat belt, then sighed. "I didn't activate mine. I don't want them following every move. When I go to a store or stop by a friend's house, they'd be watching. And no doubt questioning me when I got home." She waved her hand, as if dismissing the idea. "Anyway, enough of this depressing conversation. You didn't answer your phone yesterday, so I don't know how your date with Hayden went. I want details. C'mon, I'm dying here. Well?"

I stiffened.

Sol reacted immediately. "Oh. That bad? I'm sorry. I thought you were a cute couple."

"No, it's not as bad as that," I said, throat tight. "It was actually fun and we got along great."

"But?" Sol prompted.

I sped toward the flashing speed lights marking the school zone. "No sparks for him, I guess. When we got home, I expected a kiss or at least a peck on the cheek. Instead, he said he's got too much going on right now. So we're friends." I kept my voice casual.

"Friends?" Sol lifted a brow.

"Yep." I had to change the topic. "Tell me about the dance instead. I saw a bunch of pictures. The food line missed the mark—should have served Caesar salad. But my Pantheon sculpture was a hit, wasn't it?"

Sol squeezed my shoulder and leaned back. "Everyone loved your masterpiece. And the dance was so much fun! You saw my video of the matching boutonniere slash bouquet exchange, right? The cat steals the show. The saga of the rose?" She used air quotes around the last phrase. "It got 3K views on social media. After that fiasco, we went out for sushi and ..."

I listened and nodded as Sol motored her way through as many details as she could cram into the amount of time it took us to park and walk into school. She highlighted who came together, which couples got out of hand, which girl wore the most scandalous dress, you name it. She was probably trying to lighten the impact of my failed date by filling the gap with noise. And in a way, it actually did help. It reminded me there were still people out there I could connect with, even if I wanted to do it only one at a time.

"Elijah was there too, and he asked about you." Sol lifted her brow. "I told him you hated dances. Didn't figure I'd mention you were with Hayden. You know. Just in case Elijah was interested too."

I laughed. "Elijah's sweet, but I'm not sure Plan B is a reason to crush on someone."

"Maybe he'll give you a better reason sometime." Sol checked her phone. "Another notification. I am totally getting a new crop of submissions to *Heart and Soul.*" The whole prospect seemed to excite her.

"I can see it now." I swept my hand across the air like a headline. "'Dear Heart, my boyfriend's cat ate my bouquet and then I accidentally stabbed him when I pinned on his boutonniere. He claims I did it on purpose to get revenge on the cat. Now, the cat is staring at me in a way that makes me question my future. How do I convince my true love that it was all a big misunderstanding? Signed, Cat-astrophe.'"

Sol smirked. "So you *did* watch my video."

"Of course." I cocked my head. "And I only laughed about your tragedy once. Or twice. Politely. When the cat knocked over your purse. And when you drew blood."

She groaned as we walked down the hallway. "It was only a few drops."

"Sol!" I shook my head and lowered my backpack in front of my locker. "He had to change his shirt."

"No, he wanted to show off his chest."

"And that huge grin on your face says you didn't regret that." I spun the combination on my locker and shoved my soccer gear into the narrow space. When I slammed the door shut, Harper stood on the other side.

I nearly screamed in my surprise. Heart pounding, I scowled at her. "You scared me."

Her lip twitched, as if amused by my reaction. "Boo."

The five-minute warning bell rang, sending my heart racing again. Flustered, I hefted my backpack. "I'll see you at lunch, Sol." I turned to leave. "Save me a seat."

"About that …" Sol winced and glanced at Harper.

Harper wagged her pointer finger between Sol and herself. "We're going off campus with the theater group. I have some Kickin' Chicken gift cards burning a hole in my pocket. But I have room in my car. You can come if you want."

Her body language clearly stated this was only a perfunctory invitation. And I didn't want another repeat of the dance-planning lunch, where I sat with a group of girls but wasn't really part of it.

"No, I'm good. I'll just—" I waved my arm, trying to find a plausible excuse but coming up empty. Lowering my arm, I glanced at Sol. "I'll see you after school at soccer practice."

Sol flashed me a thumbs-up and left, walking side by side with Harper with their heads bent together.

They must have the same class. I didn't even have one with Hayden. Who rejected me but called me a friend too.

CHAPTER NINETEEN

HARP SEAL

I once saw a nature documentary about harp seals. When the mama gives birth, she protects and feeds her baby for the first twelve days of the pup's life. In fact, she's so attentive, she doesn't feed herself. But after time elapses, the mama abandons the young seal on the ice to fend for itself. The mama doesn't even consider the impact this will have on the child when she leaves.

This puts the youngling in a dire situation. It can't swim until it's eight weeks old. The poor thing is stranded for the next forty-five days, unable to catch food.

Reports say thirty percent of harp seal pups die during this isolation period.

As I stood in the lunchroom after my third period class, I commiserated with the baby harp seal's predicament. Sol had abandoned me, and the idea of fending for myself, even with my own teammates, threatened my can-do spirit.

After an anguishing scan of the lunchroom looking for a safe harbor, I dumped my tray in the garbage can, hid in the restroom, and scrolled through videos of soccer tricks until the bell rang to start fourth period.

Stress about the changes on the soccer team and embarrassment over my friend status with Hayden ate at my emotional reserves. But I survived.

CHAPTER TWENTY

REFRAMED

Sol rushed into practice ten minutes late. "Sorry," she announced, gulping air. "I had a blog deadline."

"I see." The way Coach Hering said the words—flat toned with her arms folded and brow wrinkled like a hairless cat—made me highly suspicious about the truth of her statement. That and the fact Sol had to run extra laps.

Her tardiness and punishment forced me to warm up with Erika and Reb.

Not forced. Let's reframe this. Sol's actions provided me the opportunity to expand my warmup routine by joining my teammates Erika and Reb. And it was a good thing because it gave Reb an extra challenge—two against one.

After the humiliation of my solo lunch, I determined to keep a positive attitude. Expand my horizons. Tap into my potential. Sol wasn't my only friend, just my best friend. I needed to develop those other connections.

What had Ms. Brown said?

I can do all things through Christ, who strengthens me.

Including bonding with my teammates.

Soccer made an easier channel for me to interact. Total immersion in the competition combined with heightened awareness of my mind and body broke down some of the barriers holding me back.

Erika and Reb let me listen to them strategize during one water break. Sandy and I laughed together as we set out cones for a drill. I raced Wren instead of Sol during conditioning and then handed her a water bottle when she stood doubled over, chest heaving.

By the end of practice, the pent-up anxieties of the day had faded, cast aside by physical exertion and sweat. Strands of hair had worked loose from my ponytail and stuck to my face. I had grass stains on my socks and a smile on my face. Coach often claimed that with difficulty came improvement. Right, as usual.

I volunteered to collect the equipment so the rest of the team could get to the locker room faster. Sol joined me, humming a tune from—I paused to listen. The melody came from *Toy Story.* I shot her a sidelong look. A hint of a smile curled her lips and mischief colored her eyes.

In a soft voice, I put words to the "You've Got a Friend in Me" chorus—only two octaves lower than an elephant and three keys flatter than a dime.

Sol cringed, squeezing her eyes shut. "Stick with soccer. Leave the singing to me." She opened one eye, face still scrunched. "Your voice reminds me of the dying calls of a foghorn. No offense."

"None taken. And foghorns don't die. Their sound slowly fades." Cradling my orange stockpile, I bent and scooped up another cone. No reaction to my poor attempt at a joke usually meant Sol had something on her mind.

"How was lunch with Harper?" I asked. Even though my stomach tightened, I kept my voice light.

"You should have come with us." Sol stacked another cone on top of my growing collection. "We read a few *Heart and Soul* submissions. Your ideas would have helped."

"Maybe next time," I said.

We walked side by side, hauling the equipment between us. She didn't ask about my lunch, and I didn't offer any details. I didn't want to burden her with my angst. I'd try harder to fit in.

"Thanks ladies," Coach Hering called from the sidelines. "Put those things in the golf cart, please. I'll take them in. And rest up tonight. We've got a big game tomorrow."

"You got it!" Sol yelled back.

Coach Lofton looked on, as stone-faced as ever. I saluted her, and she snorted.

The sky mellowed to stripes of pink and purple as Sol and I approached the boys' practice field. Dusk came earlier with the fall season. The air carried a chill and a few faded leaves blew past on the ground like yellow and red mice. Hugging my arms around my middle, I slowed, scanning for Hayden. If he truly wanted me as a friend, he should welcome the attention.

I put out a hand to stop Sol. "Want to watch the boys for a few minutes?"

"Sure." Sol gave the slightest flicker of her eyebrow. "It's always good to support a friend. And maybe you can still help me come up with ideas for the blog."

The metal bleachers gave a hollow clang as I climbed into the second row. "You really should cut back on your newspaper responsibilities."

"And leave all my heartbroken classmates without"—she pointed to herself—"a Sol to turn to?"

"Hmph." I grunted.

Sol clambered into the space next to me. "You're right, though. I probably should share my duties. But I get too much insane pleasure out of it."

On the field, Hayden toyed with Elijah. I tracked his movements, recognizing some of the same tactics he'd used in our parking lot match. But when he tried to force a play up the sideline, Elijah made a tackle, and the ball rolled out of bounds toward the bleachers.

As Hayden ran to inbound the ball, he caught my eye and waved. It only lasted a split second, but there was no mistaking the electricity shooting off his fingertips.

I raised my arm to wave back, but he'd already turned around. I recovered quickly, twisting my hand to scratch my chin instead.

"Was Hayden swatting away a mosquito, or was he flirting with you?" Sol's tone suggested a good ribbing was headed my way.

"We're friends," I said, lacing my fingers and setting them on my lap. It was a small move I'd learned to create space. I didn't have the emotional energy for teasing, so I focused on the field and let the silence grow between us.

"Fine. Be coy." Sol slapped my leg. "Let's focus on me for a minute. You owe me a listen." She fished her phone out of her bag and woke the screen. "'Dear Soul'—"

I held up a hand to stop her. "I thought you already talked about these with Harper."

"I did. And she had some great ideas. But I miss yours."

"Thanks. You're loyal. Like a goat. Those kids don't mess around." I smiled and stretched my legs forward. I could force myself to concentrate for Sol. *Not force. Reframe it.* Listening to Sol might boost both our spirits. *Better.*

I gave a thumbs-up. "What have you got?"

"'Dear Soul.'" She bent her head over the phone in the dying light. "'I love broccoli, but it gives me terrible gas. I don't eat it at lunch anymore, but I want to. What should I do? Signed, Vain Vegetable Vagabond.'"

"How did you respond?" I kept my eyes forward, narrowing the stimulus by targeting one player. Hayden. Across the field, another man seemed to be tracking his movements too. He had to be a recruiter. Or wait—was he tracking me? If I didn't know better, I'd swear he was staring at me like those dead trophy deer heads hanging on the wall in a hunter's log cabin.

Tensing, I squinted. The man flagged down Coach Campbell, who paused to listen and then waved a kid off the field. A sophomore. Maybe getting picked up early from practice. Yeesh, that human trafficking article was playing tricks on my mind.

"I told her to cook it." Sol's voice broke through my haze.

Wait—what? Had I spaced out? "Cook?"

"The broccoli." Sol frowned. "Stick with me, Squirrel. I said to cook the broccoli because raw broccoli is harder to digest. That's why you get gassy." Shrugging, she dropped the phone into her lap. "It's true, but my answer lacks zing. Can you help?"

"Tell her to warn people she might spontaneously combust,

so they need to clear the room." I raised a brow. "And if they ignore your warning, they don't get to complain when you introduce a symphony of sounds and smells into the environment. And if your reader isn't willing to take that bold approach, she should cook the broccoli instead."

Sol's face lit up. "I'm totally stealing that. It's in-your-face but still has the practical advice at the end." She flicked her finger on the phone. "Next one. 'My friend smacks her lips when she chews and it's driving me crazy. I don't want to embarrass her by confronting her. But if I keep hearing that smacking, I don't think we can be friends. Help! Signed, Chew Blues.'" Sol threw up her hands. "I didn't actually come up with an answer for this one."

"You should have." I quirked a grin. "It's an easy solution. If you don't like to hear her chewing, buy her a smoothie."

"I can work with that. It's an amusing non-answer that will force the reader to realize how you eat isn't as important as the friendship itself." Sol lifted her eyes as if searching the clouds. "Although I do think talking to her friend about her feelings should be included. A true friend can take the criticism without getting bent out of shape."

"Hmm." I gave a noncommittal grunt. Was Sol referring to my own refusal to open up?

Coach Campbell blew a whistle and called an end to their practice.

An odd reluctance filled me. "It's getting late. We should go." I stood.

"Sure." Sol tucked her phone away and grabbed her bag. She clanked down the rows after me. "Thanks for your help. I can't wait to share these with Harper. She's going to get a kick out of them. And she promised to come to our game tomorrow. Barrett's coming too. We can all go out afterwards."

Her suggestion syphoned away what remained of my energy. More crowd time. But I couldn't let her down. Saying no? Not my superpower.

"Perfect." I kicked a stone lodged in the grass. "Just perfect."

Sol flashed a thumbs-up, and I forced a smile.

Let me rephrase. I *chose* to smile to make my friend happy. And actions spoke louder than words.

That night, when I dragged myself to bed, my phone buzzed. Heart pounding, I snatched it. *Hayden?* No, not him. A number I didn't recognize.

"Therefore, since we are surrounded by so great a cloud of witnesses, let us also lay aside every weight, and sin which clings so closely, and let us run with endurance the race that is set before us." Hebrews 12:1, ESV

Another buzz. *Good luck with your game tomorrow.*

It took me a moment to remember Elijah said he'd send me a pregame verse. I smiled. It was a sweet gesture. Regardless of his motivation, it came at a good time.

Thanks, I texted back.

His words lifted a small measure of stress from my heart.

Chapter Twenty-One

HOME GAME

ome games rock. You play on a field where you know every dip, dirt patch, and anthill intimately. A cheer squad stirs up school spirit. The smell of popcorn and roasting hotdogs broadcast that the concession stand is open for business. When the hometown MC announces the starting lineup, they pronounce everyone's names correctly. And a soloist from our school choir performs the National Anthem, making the whole experience legit.

After school on Tuesday, we were already on the grass going through our pre-match warmup routine when the

Gainsville Raiders arrived. Adrenaline pulsed through me, matching the beat of the song blaring over speakers set between the benches. Every nerve tingled in anticipation of the upcoming battle.

Between kicking and sprinting to the next position, I peeked at the gathering crowd. My mom and dad sat near a group of other soccer parents in the upper section of the bleachers, and I waved at them. A few students had arrived to cheer us on—some popular boys who might have been there for the cheerleaders instead of us and a handful of underclassmen I couldn't name.

And—hello? A maroon t-shirt stood out in the midst of our turquoise and white school colors. Jay, back for more? I knew he'd be impressed with our team. Maybe he'd get Coach Campbell to recruit more help for us.

"Lady Eagles!" Coach Hering called us into a huddle while the opposing team set up. We crowded together, a sea of determination and sweat. "We need this win, girls," Coach said. "You've been working hard on ball control and passing. Now you've got to execute. Believe you can. Then do it."

A few rowdy hoots peppered the air.

Coach held up a hand. "Coach Lofton scouted this team last week."

The stiff-lipped assistant gave a firm nod.

"Here's the breakdown. Gainsville is 8–2 on the season." Coach Hering pointed at a tall girl wearing silicone gloves. "The goalie runs a tight ship. She's had six shutout games this year. She approaches the ball aggressively and uses her whole body to defend. So don't dribble too close to her. She'll block you."

Coach shifted, opening her body and sweeping her arms outward. "Avoid playing the ball too wide. That will narrow the area she has to defend. Instead, try altering the angle prior to taking the shot. Or feint. You might unbalance her enough to create extra space to aim."

She directed our attention toward a quick-footed girl juking and diving through a drill. "Their striker scores a lot on rebounds, so watch for that."

Jaw set, Erika gave a crisp nod. "Got it."

Sandy frowned. "How many goals do they average per game?"

When Coach Lofton held up four fingers, Sandy's eyes widened. "That's a lot."

"And they're tall too. Number eleven played club with me last year." Reb recapped her water bottle. "She's the real deal. She got recruited as a sophomore." She shook her head. "She's great to have on your side. But not someone you'd want against you."

"Reb, if I didn't know better, I'd say you were nervous," Sol said.

Reb pressed her lips in a line. "I have a healthy respect for her, that's all. She should be eyeballing me too. No one wants to play opposite my powerhouse kick either."

"Nervous," Sol whisper-sang to me, pinning her lips immediately afterward at Reb's glare.

"I heard she takes people out like a kid popping bubblegum," Erika said.

"Opponents like her sharpen their elbows every night and then dream up ways to threaten players with them without committing a foul." Wren ducked her head. "Like a soccer ninja."

"They have strengths. Doesn't matter." Coach Hering's gaze hardened. "They have weaknesses too. We have to expose them and then capitalize on them."

Erika narrowed her eyes. "What weaknesses?"

"They're aggressive and exceptional at dribbling," Coach said, "but not as effective passing. Be suffocating on defense, and they won't have space to move or time to attack. Look for openings to steal the ball. And sometimes they're impatient. If you play your cards right, you can draw them offsides."

That wasn't much to go on. I glanced at Coach Lofton.

Her nostrils flared, and she shrugged. Not exactly a vote of confidence.

From the way Sandy shifted her feet and Wren pinched her lips and Reb kept peering over our heads to watch the Raiders' warmups, I could tell this would be more than a tough physical battle. It would be a tough mental battle. As a senior, I'd survived matches where the opponent looked un-stoppable. How could I boost the team's confidence?

Before I came up with a plan, Coach Hering thrust her hand into the center and the rest of us piled our hands on top. "Believe and achieve, ladies. Eagles on three."

"One, two, three. Eagles!" we shouted.

Back on the field to complete warmups, Sol pulled me aside. "Look who's here! I invited my own personal cheer squad." She fingertip-waved at the bleachers.

What was Sol up to now?

Stomach dropping to my knees, I turned.

Like the wildebeest stampede from *Lion King,* a group of raucous boys bumped chests and howled on the sidelines. Barrett was the ringleader with Hayden close by. Elijah hov-ered on the fringe, a typical fish out of water, the poor guy. Harper, dressed like a belly button model in her cropped shirt, hovered in a group of girls behind them. Wasn't she cold? Yeesh! And I recognized bling-a-ding Ashley and other girls from the dance-planning lunch table.

"Good grief!" I smacked my forehead with the palm of my hand. "Did you recruit the whole senior class?"

"Why not?" Sol winked. "Can we hit Let's Shake on It afterwards? Everybody's going."

I swallowed. "Everybody?" *Hayden?*

"Everybody." Sol grabbed my hand and squeezed it. "It's just what you wanted. Another chance to talk with your friend"—she gave extra emphasis to the word—"Hayden and hang out with"—she pointed both thumbs her way—"the cool kids."

"Sol and Dani!" Coach Lofton barked. "Quit standing around!"

"I think she means business." Sol tore her eyes from the crowd. "That was the longest speech I've ever heard from her."

"Are you kidding?" I pushed Sol. "Coach Lofton talks nonstop. It's called body language. And right now, she's screaming something I'd rather not repeat."

I grabbed the nearest ball and joined our passing drill.

Now that I was more aware of the audience, I had trouble focusing. Should I show off my new Cruyff Turn? Would Hayden notice and realize what a fool he was for putting me in the friend zone? No, forget that line of thought. The kid had reasons. And I had soccer.

When Erika and Reb went over for the coin toss to determine which team would kick at the center of the pitch to start the match, our PA announcer sidled over to Coach. "I know you insisted we make everything perfect tonight for this crucial game, but"—the man cringed—"the soloist didn't show up to sing the National Anthem."

Coach Lofton's pug-eyes bulged.

Baring her teeth, Coach Hering glared at the man. "Be a problem solver. Turn your phone up to full volume and play a YouTube version of it."

"Or—" Sol scrambled next to Coach Hering with all the eager expectation of a dog playing fetch. "I could sing it for you."

I stepped next to her and put my arm around her shoulders. "C'mon, Coach. Sol sings all the time. She's really good. Besides, having one of our very own players nail a song this colossal makes a statement."

Coach Lofton widened her already huge eyes and held up a finger. "Talented."

That seemed to convince Coach. Blowing a raspberry, she inclined her head toward the microphone on the score table. "Fine. Be awesome."

"Victory!" Sol whispered to me as she flounced past. "This is the first time I've been grateful for Lofton's succinct wording."

After she positioned herself by the table and whispered something to the announcer, the speakers sparked to life. "Ladies and gentlemen, welcome to today's match between the Gainsville Raiders and"—here his voice exploded—"your Eastwood Eagles!"

Like a bomb, our sparse crowd burst with screams. Two cheerleaders landed back handsprings all the way across the front of the unruly mob.

"Singing our National Anthem, please welcome Eastwood's very own senior Sol Garcia!"

Either we all shrank or Sol grew taller as she lifted the microphone with swan-like grace and glided to center field.

Murmurs swept through the bleachers and ballooned into a buzz. Students bent their heads together, whispering and pointing. A few of the girls cheered. Barrett called out, "Go Sol!"

After nodding at the audience, Sol bowed her head as if collecting energy from her surroundings.

The crowd hushed, and my stomach clenched.

I couldn't stand the pressure of a hundred eyes on me. Could Sol?

CHAPTER TWENTY-TWO

GOOSE BUMPS

Like my teammates, I tucked one hand behind my back and placed the other over my heart.

Maybe for dramatic effect, Sol let the silence drag on for three long seconds before she lifted her head and raised the microphone. "Oh, say, can you see …"

Goose bumps raced up my arms.

They say few voices compare to the enchanting melody of the nightingale.

Sol's did.

I never realized until the moment those notes crossed her lips the kind of magic her voice could inspire.

I'd heard her before, obviously. Because of her consistent outbreaks of song, I owned an impressive knowledge of show tunes. Which, trust me, was not something your typical teen bragged about. But since she often added an accent or some other goofy twist, she disguised her talent.

When the last vibrato sounded, our fans in the bleachers erupted.

With a broad smile and her face flushed with the same intense sheen you'd see after kicking the winning goal, Sol passed the microphone back.

Our teammates swarmed from the bench, offering Sol high-fives and slapping her back.

I tagged along behind them, a proud hen.

I couldn't devise a way to boost my team's morale, but my best friend had effectively energized our team with a single song.

Now all we had to do was tap that momentum to win the game.

Swallowing hard, I wiped sweaty palms against my shorts and studied the hard faces of my opponents.

I glanced once more at the crowd.

At Hayden.

Here we go.

CHAPTER TWENTY-THREE

GAME ON

For the first five minutes of the game, my mind flailed like a catfish caught on a line.

On one side of my brain, distraction ruled. I kept checking the bleachers to catch quick glimpses of Hayden. The crowd's movement made him hard to track. He sat near the center of the action, engaged in much of what I recognized as testosterone-driven horseplay, but several notches calmer than his rowdy counterpart Barrett.

As if he enjoyed being near the spotlight, but not actually in it.

The other side of my brain screamed at me to challenge

players, push myself, focus on winning the position and the ball.

I needed this side of the brain to win. Because if it didn't, not only would my performance sour my abilities in Hayden's eyes, but also, my team might lose.

And the only thing worse than losing while Hayden watched would be doing it with broccoli stuck between my teeth. Which, luckily, wasn't going to happen since we didn't bring any vegetables to the game.

As time ticked away, Coach Hering shot out instructions like bullets. "Cover the center!" or "Watch the trap!" And we scratched and scrabbled and surged to obey.

When the timekeeper indicated three minutes remaining in our 0–0 game, we ratcheted up our intensity. So did they, pulling their defenders forward to create a short field and putting more pressure on our backfield.

Their all-star player gained control of the ball.

"Someone press her!" Coach yelled, pacing the sidelines. "Move, move, move!"

Like an angry chihuahua on steroids, I battled the girl, slowing her.

Hair flying, Erika swooped in from the side, almost tripping us both.

When the striker tried to shoot it to the wing, Erika got a piece of the ball, deflecting the pass and sending the ball behind their player.

Shoving their striker to gain an advantage, I switched directions. She fell and moaned, probably trying to draw a foul, but her acting was too bad to be believable. Streaking past, I pumped my arms, straining to chase the ball.

Wren beat me to the spot. When she trapped the ball and took off, I changed my trajectory again. Their defenders adjusted too, moving to block the path upfield. Just before they crashed on her at midfield, Wren kicked the ball my way.

As if in slow motion, a breakaway stretched before me.

Time snapped back into place. Pouring all the steam I had left, I raced toward the goal. Their keeper responded to my approach, spreading her arms and bending her knees.

A few steps more. Close enough to the penalty box to shoot.

Defenders converged on me, fighting for position, forcing me to turn and protect the ball. My heart pounded in my ears, and my breath came loud as a jet.

A scream. My name. A waving hand. Reb. "I'm open."

I should have passed. But I didn't.

Instead, my body, trained by hours of practice, shifted into a Cruyff Turn. I dribbled past my defender, faked the shot, stopped my foot, and moved the ball to my right. Keeping my momentum, I scooped the ball straight backward … right into a player trailing behind me. I'd forgotten to check for space to turn. When I spun the 180, it was directly into a girl who stole the ball from me.

My stomach plummeted. And after tripping on my own shoelace, so did my bottom. I hit the grass hard enough to shake a tree fifty miles away.

I slapped the ground. *I blew it again!*

A blur of motion raced past me from the side. Erika slid, a viper striking. Her clean tackle popped the ball toward a waiting Reb. She made a quick pass to Wren. The two split the defense with a smooth give-and-go.

When she regained possession, Reb, master of improvisation, twisted her body. With impossible grace, precision, and power, she shot low to the side corner of the goal.

It happened so fast.

The ball spun like a hurricane.

Their all-star goalie dove and stretched her fingertips toward the ball.

And missed.

The net snapped as the ball slammed into the goal. Score!

"And that's how it's doooooooooone!" Reb screamed, racing back toward our teammates, eyes lit, mouth open, hands flung wide.

The crowd erupted. Cheerleaders waved mini poms. Erika and Wren threw themselves into Reb's arms, jumping together in a threefold hug.

My error mostly forgotten, I scrambled after them, fist-bumping and high-fiving the other players on the field.

As we settled back into our starting positions for the kick-off to restart the match, Reb sauntered over and gave me a hawk-eyed stare. "Next time I'm open like that, you'd better pass."

Face heating, I nodded. With all eyes on Reb, they were sure to be on me too. Judging our interaction. *My error, not forgotten at all.*

Relief washed through me when the final whistle blew. For the last minute of the game, we fought them off to win 1–0.

CHAPTER TWENTY-FOUR

THE AFTERMATH

Coach Hering, sporting a rare smile, pulled us together. "Ladies, I'm proud of you. You played as a team. Keep this up, and we'll be in a position to make playoffs."

A few hoots interrupted Coach, which made her smile even bigger. When it quieted again, she said, "Now get some rest, and we'll see you tomorrow."

Since it was a home game, my teammates and I could leave any time we were ready. As I gathered my gear, the stands emptied, and a handful students made their way to the field. Several crowded around Reb, who broke into an impromptu dance, quickly joined by her fans.

Sol had her own fan club surrounding her, with Barrett and Harper at the forefront. The quick banter and broad smile on Sol's face indicated she might be talking about something besides soccer. Her singing debut perhaps?

Elijah clustered near the edge of Sol's clan. A silent rock, with his hands tucked into his pockets as people flowed around him. Sweet of him to come. When he looked my way, I flashed him a thumbs-up, and he lifted his chin. His solid presence was a nice fill-in for my missing brother.

My focus shifted to the person standing behind Elijah. Hayden, with his arms folded and his hair wild as black-crowned crane.

So adorable. And also looking my way.

I almost raised my hand to wave, but then I remembered my failed Cruyff Turn and stopped. What would he think about my blunder?

Not willing to find out, I plopped on the bench and slipped my cleats off. A moment later, a hand touched my shoulder, and I looked up into my dad's face. My mom stood behind him, talking to Sandy's mom, probably about concession stand candy options.

"Good game, Dani," Dad said. "Your mom and I are picking up pizza on the way home. Want any?"

"No, I'm good." I rolled my neck until it popped. Sol's laughter carried over the general buzz of the crowd. After hesitating, I added, "I might go to Let's Shake on It instead."

"Are you asking or telling me?" He raised a brow.

"Asking." I smiled. "Of course."

He nodded. "Home by midnight then. And call if anything comes up."

"I will." I stood and gave him a quick hug. "See you at home."

After my parents left, I scanned the remaining people. Some students talked to clusters of my teammates. A handful of adults milled around the bleachers. Others closed down the concession stand. The refs packed their gear.

Clutching my Eastwood Soccer hoodie around my face, I sought Sol.

It didn't take long. She stood, laughing with Harper, Barrett, and her dance-decorating crew. As if she sensed my stare, she glanced up and waved at me. But then, Harper snatched away her attention by pulling her into a group photo.

"C'mon, Dani!" she called. "Get in the picture."

I waved her off. "No, thanks. I'm sweaty."

"That's how you should look after a tough game. It shows your effort." She planted a fist on her hip. "I'm the one who looks too clean to be a champion."

"Still no." I made a show of sniffing my armpits. "You'd never survive the smell."

"I love you, smell and all." Sol stomped over, grabbed my arm, and dragged me to the camera.

I plastered on a smile and hoped I wouldn't look like a pigeon in a bevy of swans.

After that, I sat on the bench and pretended to talk on my phone. Better to look busy than lost. I kept my voice low and paused long enough between statements so it would appear like a real conversation.

This is ridiculous, Dani. You should have stayed with Sol and joined the conversation. But what if they remembered how I almost lost the game with the failed execution of a trick play? What if they gossiped about something I don't know anything about? Blah!

Someone sat next to me, and I jumped. My pounding heart slowed when I recognized Jay. I remembered his licorice smell. Behind him, Sol still held her animated discussion. She didn't look like she'd be leaving any time soon.

A wash of relief swept over me. If I talked to Jay, I wouldn't have to pretend anymore.

"Hey, Jay." I lowered my phone and clasped it to my chest.

"Don't you need to hang up?" Jay quirked a brow. Amusement danced in his eyes. My grandpa once gave me the same teasing look when he caught me stealing a cookie but didn't rat me out.

"Oh, sure." I fumbled with the device so he wouldn't see my blank screen and then sighed into a slouch. "So you came."

He shrugged. "I told you I might make it to one of your home games, and I did. Being honest here, I enjoyed the match, but I had an ulterior motive for coming. Coach Campbell likes to keep tabs on his boys, and several of them turned up here. Talking to you gives me a legit reason to be here, so they won't know what Coach is up to. Not that I saw anything alarming from them. Not even social media worthy."

I tried not to scoff. They were in high school. They didn't need babysitting.

Behind me, I heard a loud belch. I turned to see a broad smile on Barrett's face, Harper plugging her nose, and some juniors hooting in laughter.

Then again, maybe they did need babysitting.

"What did you think of the game?" I asked. "The girls' team rocks, doesn't it?"

He nodded. "Not bad. I think your cheer squad over there"—he jerked his head toward the cluster of boys—"certainly enjoyed the show."

The show? There was that underlying lack of respect for

women again, as grating as the *you run like a girl* insult boys threw out so often. I gritted my teeth. "You mean they enjoyed the *battle.*"

"No, I meant the show. That Reb girl? She schooled the defense. Toyed with their emotions in such an entertaining way. Never seen a player with such ferocity. One wrong move, and she'll rip your face off with a glare. I would not mess with that girl."

I relaxed into a smile. Maybe Jay wasn't one of those patronizing men after all.

"Reb's not so bad. She's actually nice." I winced at my word choice. *Nice.*

"Did any of the boys' team come to watch you play?" Jay asked. "Say ... Elijah? Or Hayden maybe?"

Was my attraction to him that obvious? I squeezed my hands into fists. I didn't know Jay well, and he might be exactly who he claimed to be, but my research into the Indiana event showed that sex traffickers looked for people who acted shy. As if shyness somehow made you vulnerable.

So just in case Jay had a shady side, I refused to show any weakness.

If I could help it, that is.

"If you're interested in either one, you can talk to them yourself."

Jay sniffed dismissively and leaned back. "Maybe I will." He pulled a crumpled sack from his back pocket. "Care for some licorice?"

The guy was probably shooting for polite, but he missed the mark. Red flags shot up. I mean, what parent hasn't told their child not to take candy from a stranger? Even if he wasn't technically a stranger. "No, thank you."

He laughed and pulled off a single strand. "Suit yourself." He took a large bite and tucked the rest away.

Licking my lips, I chanced another look over my shoulder. My heart lifted. Sol was striding my way, and the others looked to be walking to their cars. I bolted to my feet and shouldered my bag. "Sorry. I gotta go. Thanks for coming."

"Yeah, sure," he said. "Maybe I'll catch you next time."

I nodded and walked away. Maybe that news story got to me. Made me see villains behind every well-meaning action. After all, Jay had an overly friendly neighbor appearance and attitude. But the question about the boys who might have come to watch me rubbed me wrong. Not a lot, but enough to make me decide I needed to exercise caution around him until I made up my mind if he was safe.

"You looked like you needed a rescue," Sol said, reaching for me.

I let her pull me into a hug. "How did you know?"

"A big crowd, lots of small talk, and you cornered by someone's dad. Probably one showing you pictures of his cat." She let me go. "That's not your scene."

I let her pull me into a hug. "Thanks. Are we heading to Let's Shake on It soon?"

"Right now." She grabbed my hands in hers. "And guess what else? Remember how they cancelled the fall play because the theater teacher had to take care of her mom?"

I remembered Mrs. James had taken a leave of absence, but since I'd never taken her classes, I didn't pay much attention.

"Anyway, she's back now. And she's determined to put on a fall musical." Sol grinned. "The cast will have to follow an ambitious schedule to pull it off, but auditions are Saturday."

"And I care about this because …?"

"We made a pact at the beginning of the year to try new things. This could be our chance to do something outrageous our senior year, either on stage or behind the scenes."

My jaw dropped. "What?"

"I'm talking about taking a risk like we discussed. And I know this may not be what you had in mind, but it could work."

"It's unexpected," I said. "I was thinking more like trying every kind of cafeteria food or taking a college tour with a group of random people."

"Think bigger. I know it's kind of crazy, but after I sang the National Anthem, everyone kept going on about what a good voice I have. Then Harper tells me about the fall musical, *Into the Woods,* and how she thinks I'm a good enough vocalist to land a lead." Sol gestured, her flailing hands contributing to the conversation. "You know how I'm singing all the time. How much I love it. But I never had enough electives to do both soccer and choir. So let's audition. What have we got to lose? And if it helps you make new friends too, that's a win for both of us."

"What about soccer?" I asked. "How are we going to do both?"

She shrugged. "We'll find a way. I mean, who needs sleep? And I know being on stage in front of a crowd might seem scary, but you could be in the chorus. Or maybe on the lighting crew. I heard they have some cute juniors running tech. And—"

"Sol." Gritting my teeth, I imagined myself center stage, the torture of a thousand eyes crawling on me like fire ants. I imagined my lines forgotten, or words lodged in my throat like a crushed can of empty soda. Or me, fumbling around backstage, tripping over wires and makeup and trying to find an outlet for a wayward plug.

"I don't want to be in a play."

She frowned. "Why not?"

"I know I should branch out. Overcome my nerves." I lifted my shoulders. "But I need to take baby steps into that new reality, not a headlong plunge. Like maybe picking a seat in the front of the room instead of hiding in the back. Or making eye contact with a cheerleader."

Sol shook her head. "The Dani I know is bolder than that. I've seen you stare down a defender."

"That's different," I said. "I could race down the sidelines in Wonder Woman pajamas and not bat an eye. The field is like my home."

Sol folded her arms across her chest. "Time to add a new wing."

She had a point. Maybe this would be good for me. Maybe I could discover a new talent. Then again, maybe I'd fail.

My indecision must have shown because Sol nudged me. "If I don't do it, I'm going to regret it. So I'm going for it. With or without you."

I squeezed my eyes shut.

I forced myself to reach beyond my comfort zone and consider Sol's point of view.

And I realized friendship sometimes required sacrifices. Sol supported me in soccer. I could do the same for her in theater.

Pressing my shaking hands against my stomach, I gulped a huge breath and released it.

"With me. We'll do it together." I buried the fear threatening to derail me from my decision. "But I am *not* dressing up as the backside of a horse costume."

Like a bolt of lightning, Sol perked up. She cupped her arm around my neck in a strangling head-hug. "Thank you, thank you, thank you! You're the best. I mean, I know it's hard for you, but it means so much that you'd still do it, and

I can't wait to see what happens and wow, just wow. Are you going to audition then or volunteer to work backstage? No, don't tell me now. Let's go to Let's Shake on It and plot the next move."

"My next move," I choked out, "is to breathe again."

Laughing, Sol released her grip. She led the way over to the bleachers, side-hopping half the steps to where Barrett waited for her. I was so numb, it didn't even phase me, being swept into the crowd. All I could think was—what had I gotten myself into now?

CHAPTER TWENTY-FIVE

A DIFFERENT KIND OF SHAKE

B y the time I walked into Let's Shake on It, it was crowded. *Stupid traffic lights!* I hadn't wanted to be the first one there, but being one of the last ones to arrive was almost as bad. Tables already overflowing with people in deep conversation made approaching anyone difficult. I'd stand out like a white cockatoo trapped in an aviary of peacocks. Everyone would recognize which bird didn't belong.

Sol waved me over, and I squeezed into the chair with her.

It was tight, with Barrett and Harper and Sandy and Reb and Erika and Wren and a random cheerleader all cozied up like sardines, but I made it work with only half my body hanging in thin air.

Holding my strawberry shake like a shield, I poked my straw into the icy cream but didn't sip. So much stimulation. How could I swallow anything past the lump in my throat?

Instead, I nodded and smiled at all the appropriate pauses.

Maybe Sol was on to something, having me try out for this theater audition. Bet I could make it big on stage. I'd done my share of acting.

"Hey."

I jumped, my inner drama interrupted by Hayden's voice. Hands shaking, I tucked a strand of hair behind my ear and turned, leaning back on Reb to keep from falling out of my seat.

A mixture of emotions churned in my stomach. Relief, having someone address me with interest. And distrust, not understanding exactly how that person felt about me.

Oh, well, I made it this far. What did I have to lose?

I kept things simple. "Hey."

"You look squished. Come sit with me instead. I've got a table outside."

"Sure." I twisted to glance at Sol. "I'm going to hang with Hayden for a little while. Text me later."

She winked and gave me a thumbs-up.

Time to add a new wing to my home.

I followed Hayden through the side door and into the area of picnic tables gated in with a white fence. Instant relief flooded me. "You saved me," I said. "I needed some air."

He snort-chuckled. "Yeah, you looked like a deer in headlights."

I glanced back at the large glass windows separating us from the inside. I saw my classmates in full swing. Elijah stood by Sol's table. She was pointing my way. Or maybe showing him a dance move.

"Want a fry?" Hayden offered me a half-empty container. "Still warm. They taste good dipped in milkshakes."

"Thanks." I snagged a long fry and uncapped my cup. "Like this?" I asked, soaking the fry in the creamy drink.

He watched my technique. "Close. But you've got to get the right ratio of fry to shake."

"Hmm." I lifted a brow. "Show me."

After hesitating, he pressed closer to me and skimmed a crispy potato across the top. "See?" He held it up for my inspection, then popped it into his mouth, as if sealing the deal. "You just might be able to execute the dipping dive move better than the Cruyff Turn."

"Oh." I slouched. "You saw that."

He grimaced. "I saw you attempt it." He sniffed and rubbed his bloodshot eyes.

"That bad? Don't sugarcoat it." I handed him my napkin. "Allergies?"

"Yeah. Thanks. I sat next to someone with cats. Dander gets me every time."

"Sorry," I said. "That's miserable."

"Tell me about it." He pulled his chair closer with one hand and swept his other in an arc. "Look, no lying. The problem with the Cruyff Turn is, you've got the move down, but you've been practicing on your own. The footwork is fine, but you've gotta sense the space behind you for the turn. If you had another person to practice with, you could develop that awareness."

I pressed my lips together. "Thanks, Coach."

"I wasn't criticizing." He cleared his throat, his movements jerky. Did I make him nervous? "That's actually why I'm here. As your instructor, I feel obligated to make sure you get it right. When you're done with your shake, we can find an empty area in the parking lot and try again. I wouldn't want Betty to think I failed as a teacher."

Lifting my gaze, I searched his face. Was he teasing me? From my observations, he didn't seem to be a prankster. But Nick was a sweetheart too, and he'd trick me all the time.

"Um—" I stalled, stretching my words. "Maybe?" My heart rate rose, and I tensed. Would he pull the *just kidding* line from his back pocket or not?

"Never mind." He half-stood as if to leave. "It was a dumb idea."

"Wait." I grabbed his arm to stop him. "It was a dumb idea for you to help me out of a sense of obligation. But if you want to fix my footwork as a *friend*"—I paused until he met my gaze—"then I'm all in. After you help me polish off this milkshake."

The strain lining his face relaxed. He settled back into his seat. "Deal. We can't disappoint Betty after all."

"Of course." I scooted closer. "But I'll need access to those fries."

The side door clanged open, and footsteps sounded on the concrete. I turned to see Elijah making his way over.

"Hi, Dani," he said, stopping next to the table. "I wondered where you disappeared to. I didn't get to congratulate you after the game. You did a great job."

"Except for the Cruyff Turn." Hayden sat up straighter. "Which we're going to work on. Right, Dani?"

"Yep." I pressed my lips together. "Gotta fix my colossal fail."

"Ah, nah, don't be so hard on yourself." Elijah made a dismissive wave. "You'll get it soon. I'm impressed you tried it."

His easygoing attitude made me smile. This guy could encourage a snail to explore skiing. "I appreciate that," I said.

Something flickered across Hayden's face. Irritation? Jealousy?

An idea tickled my mind.

Maybe Hayden needed a little competition to get out of the friend zone.

What would he do if I flirted with Elijah a little?

Wait … was I capable of flirting?

I guess if I could go to a theater audition, I could at least try. But what would capture Elijah's interest? Besides soccer.

Ah. Physics. I felt certain that might be Elijah's love language. Like a defender on the field, I could draw him in.

I hesitated, twirling my straw. I knew Elijah had to like me at least a little bit. Why else would he seek me out just to congratulate me? His interest made my whole idea seem manipulative. Almost slimy. At the same time, part of me wanted to know if I could pull it off. It's weird how our minds and hearts tell us different things.

I listened to my mind. "So. Hayden. Do you have physics?"

"I think. Yeah," he said.

I raised a brow. "What did you get on the last assignment?"

He blinked as if struggling to remember. "I don't know. A seventy?"

Elijah slipped into the seat next to me. Perfect. "You guys talking about the class with Jones? I got a ninety-one."

Hayden's posture stiffened, a wild dog on high alert.

"I got a ninety-one too." I wiped my hands on a napkin. "I messed up on the question about wave particle interactions." I wagged my finger. "Got them confused with how a particle wave fails in large football stadiums."

"Hmm. Nice dad joke." Elijah shook his head, the corners of his lips curling ever so slightly. "I missed the question about black holes."

I narrowed my eyes. Could I make Hayden jealous? "We should get together and compare notes next time."

"Sure." Elijah's ears pinked. He sucked on his straw, as if hiding his excitement.

Hayden crushed a fry between his fingers. "Who cares about black holes anyway?"

"You probably don't understand the true nature of them." I twirled a fry in my shake. "Everyone knows what they are."

His face darkened. "Huh?"

"Everyone knows"—I grinned—"that black holes are what you get when you wear your black socks across rough concrete without your shoes on."

"Ha!" Elijah choked on his drink. "Dani, really? Two lame dad jokes in a row?"

"Yeah," I admitted.

"I feel your pain." Elijah swiped shake froth off his chin. "My dad told me one yesterday, and it's just as bad." He lifted a finger, imitating a professor. "Why should you never take electricity to a soccer game?"

"Wait, don't tell me. Let me think. I'm pretty good at figuring these out." Despite my objective of drawing him into my flirtations, he'd drawn me in instead. I'm pretty sure it wasn't supposed to work that way, but I had to solve the riddle.

I rifled through electricity-related words, searching for a connection. "Spark. Charge. Electron. Proton. Neutron. Voltage. Conductor. Watt. Grounded. Circuit. Current." I clapped and pointed. "Because it never knows watts up."

Elijah shook his head. "No, it—"

"Stop!" I said. "I'm still guessing. How about you don't ask electricity to a game because it's not well grounded in sports? Or it hates running circuits. Or maybe it doesn't know the current rules."

"Wow. No. But those are good answers too. Keep trying." He reached for one of Hayden's fries and got a scowl in return.

"How about—?" I squinted, thinking. "Electricity doesn't like change. It likes to keep things static."

"No." Elijah leaned back in his chair. "Not even related to soccer. Give up?"

"How about shut up and go away?" Hayden glared at Elijah. He actually used more colorful words, but nothing I hadn't heard before.

I put a hand on the table, trying to at least end on a positive note. Give both guys a win. "Nah, this is fun. Let me figure it out." Counting on my fingers, I sorted through a dozen more. Then it hit me. I snapped my fingers and pointed at Elijah. "Electricity doesn't know how to conduct itself on the field!" My words tumbled out in a rush.

"Yes!" Elijah gave a belly laugh this time, and something warmed in my chest. The emotion confused me, like a mouse caught between two choices of cheese and drawn equally to both. You know—I thought I wanted cheddar. But this Swiss sure was tempting too.

Chair scraping across the concrete, Hayden stood. "Dani, you owe me a one-on-one match in the parking lot. I'd like to collect now."

Ignoring the odd twist in my stomach, I crumpled my napkin and tossed it into my cup. "Okay."

Elijah made to rise, but Hayden pinned him with a stare. "One on one. Any more than that, and it's a different game. And this game's mine."

Hayden hooked my elbow and escorted me away. I barely

had time to grab my phone. "Quit being nice," he hissed in my ear. "You'll just encourage guys like him."

So my ploy worked. Hayden *was* jealous.

Then why did I feel so horrible?

I turned to wave at Elijah. One look at him reminded me of my manipulation. What was I thinking, using his friendly banter to further my own agenda? When had I learned to play with fire and not get burned?

And yet now, because of Elijah's overtures, Hayden, who could win the affections of anyone, chose me. I won, didn't I?

No. That wasn't fair to either boy. It was wrong to take advantage of Elijah's feelings. I'd made it worse by toying with Hayden's emotions.

Somehow, I had to make it up to Elijah. And Hayden.

Right now, probably the only one who didn't like me was me.

Because I knew better. And I did it anyway.

Just like Nick.

CHAPTER TWENTY-SIX

CURFEW

Outside of the gnawing guilt I felt about Elijah, the hour Hayden and I spent in the parking lot kicking Betty back and forth went as fast as a cheetah's blink. We stayed well past the time the last high school student left to haunt other grounds.

Maybe things would work after all.

As he climbed into his car, I sent him a text. *I had fun. Good night!*

Standing back up, he caught my eyes and texted a heart emoji.

A warm tingling spread from my head to my toes. I didn't

even remember the drive back. But it was the first time I ever came tumbling home seconds before my curfew.

I rushed in, breathless, and slammed the door behind me.

My parents watched a movie on the couch. Dad smiled at me over his shoulder, and Mom turned. "Have fun?" he asked.

"Yes." I stood, gulping air, not willing to elaborate. *Ask me to vacuum the house or clean the garage, but please don't press me for details about my night.* I had no words to describe how I felt. And no control over my heart.

"Good." Mom raised an eyebrow, allowing me space to talk if I wanted to. I didn't.

Operating on the vapors of my remaining adrenaline, I rushed upstairs to shower before hitting the sack. After throwing my sweaty clothes into a pile, I hugged myself, basking under the cleansing burn of hot water and the scent of lavender soap. Hayden was exciting and magnetic and charming and ...

Hayden was a friend.

Or was he more?

CHAPTER TWENTY-SEVEN

REMINDER

"You sound like you just woke up." Sol's voice chirped over the phone.

"I did." Blinking away the last dregs of sleep, I squinted at the clock. Seven thirty. I had no idea why I needed to be awake at this ungodly hour on a Saturday morning. Unless—

I bolted upright, heart pounding. "Wait, do we have soccer practice today?"

"Very funny. You promised to go to theater auditions, remember?"

"I thought it started at nine." I yawned. "Don't we have a whole hour and a half?"

I had hoped Sol would forget about my rash bargain and it would go away like a dead fish down the toilet.

"Yes, but I'm too excited." Her words tumbled faster and faster. "Can we get there early? I need to practice my monologue. Luckily, I know just about every line from a dozen musicals, so no big deal, right? Did you decide what to do? Audition or work backstage? Whatever you decide is fine. No pressure. I'm proud of you for taking a risk. How many people do you think will show up? I wonder if—"

I fumbled with the earbuds on my dresser and inserted them into my ears, just in time to hear the rest of Sol's sentence. "… you'll catch the theater bug too?"

"We'll see." Frowning, I leaned toward the mirror and examined myself. A tangle of hair in dire need of braiding. A new pimple on my forehead. Circles under my eyes. Great. I flashed my teeth, half expecting to find broccoli lodged there. "Can you just tell me when I need to leave?"

"Can you be here in twenty minutes? Is that enough time?"

"Don't worry. I'll be there," I said.

"Good. See you soon." A beep, beep, beep announced Sol had hung up.

The rush of throwing on a wrinkled t-shirt and stressed jeans salvaged from my laundry basket while raking a brush through my wiry hair kept my mind off where I was heading.

To the stage. Where I'd either make a fool of myself or discover a thrilling new talent for Broadway that I never wanted to use. I sniffed my armpit.

Meh. Not too bad.

The smell of pancakes, eggs, and bacon greeted me when I stampeded downstairs.

Mom must have heard the thunder of my footsteps because she stuck her head out the kitchen doorway. I wasn't sure how she could have missed it since the whole house shook.

She held a spatula in her hand like a sword. "Dani! You're up early. I didn't know you had practice today."

"I don't. I'm going with Sol to auditions for the musical. And I'm going to give it a shot too." I grabbed a warm cake off the plate and took a bite. "Wish me horrible luck. I don't want to get cast."

Mom let her arm drop. "Then why are you doing it?"

"I want to try something new. Plus, I promised Sol. And I try to keep one hundred percent of my promises to others." *Promises to myself, not so much.* "I should be back by noon." I stuffed the rest of the pancake into my mouth, hoping its sheer volume would prevent any further discussion.

My phone pinged. Sol. *Did you dress for success?*

If my intent was to sabotage my chances, I had dressed perfectly.

"Yep," I dictated into my phone as I rushed out the door to my car.

After throwing my phone on the passenger seat, I revved the engine.

Ping. *Remember, if you decide to audition, you have to sing. I brought sheet music because Harper said they would have a pianist. I should have asked earlier, but do you want me to print something for you in case you decide to audition?*

What, like "Row, Row, Row Your Boat"?

Grunting, I snatched the device and clicked the microphone again. "I have the vocal range of a frozen jellyfish. I'd never match a piano key. I'll sing a cappella. Now stop texting. I'm on my way."

My hands shook as I gripped the wheel. My Mother Goose was about to be cooked.

Out of habit, I checked Macie's house as I zoomed past. The grass needed mowing, and weeds lined the driveway, but the porch stood empty.

Worry churned my stomach sour. I hoped the tween didn't take my brush-off personally. She must have recovered by now. Kids were resilient. At least she had sense to sleep in this morning instead of willingly putting herself on the executioner's block—I mean, putting herself on stage. Even though I was hurtling through space doing exactly that. Going to my own funeral. Or no, reframe that. Going on an adventure.

My phone pinged again. Sol, no doubt.

I gunned the engine, even though I knew Mom would disapprove of me speeding toward my imminent humiliation. Or success. *I guess we'll see.*

CHAPTER TWENTY-EIGHT

AUDITIONS

Dressed in a short floral-print dress and white Converse, Sol entered the auditorium like she owned it. As we made our way to the front row seats, she waved or hugged or chatted or high-fived everyone in the room. Including the poster of young Zac Efron hanging on the wall.

"How do you know these people?" I crowded my friend like a shadow. "I only recognize Harper." I had, in fact, given her a firm nod, which she returned after checking behind her, perhaps to see if I might, in fact, be having a seizure instead of saying hello.

"You forget I have different classes than you do. And these are my people. A lot of them are like me. Nerdy." She sang the last word, then leaned in and whispered, "Although I'm a jock too. Best of both worlds. I'm the nerd and the preferred. An actor and an athlete. I love everybody, especially my geeks, but we don't get to hang out much. Soccer, you know."

With the number of words Sol was stringing together, I feared her dramatic side might dominate her loyalties. Luckily, her train of thought got sidetracked by a boy who could have passed for a Hobbit.

A grin split his face and he grabbed her into a side hug. "You made it. Excellent. Because … you, Sol—" He hummed the rest of whatever show tune he had pegged.

"Nice, Michael." Sol squeezed her eyes shut. "From *Waitress*, 'You Matter to Me,' right?"

"Right!" He beamed. "It's my audition piece. I hope I get cast as the Baker."

He struck a heroic pose, and I couldn't help thinking, *That's one saucy chef. Bet he makes super gyro sandwiches.*

"I'm hoping you get it." Sol gave him a thumbs-up.

"Was Michael gushing?" I whispered as we strolled away. "It sounded like gushing. Why was he gushing? Are you gushing? Oh great, I see that smile. You *are* gushing. Is everyone else going to gush? Should I gush? I'm not sure I know how to gush. It sounds like a fish thing."

"Relax." Sol smiled. "I've done junior plays before when we were in grade school, and everyone helps each other. I remember it being a close-knit community." She stopped and put a hand on both my shoulders, squaring me up to her. "Did you decide what to do? I think you should at least try for the chorus. What do you think? Ready to take a chance?"

The look in her eyes, the shine on her face, and her chattiness all pointed to one thing.

Hope.

She really hoped we'd do this together. And honestly, I hoped we could too. Despite my apprehension. If I came out of my shell a little, it was worth testing the waters.

"Yeah." I swallowed my fear. "I got this."

Some lady wearing a Hawaiian shirt and pink-framed glasses sang three notes, high, low, high.

My heart nearly jumped through my chest when all three dozen students surrounding me echoed the notes. "What was that?" I whispered out the side of my mouth.

"That's how the director gets our attention," Sol whispered back, lips barely moving.

What a weird way to get us quiet. Instead of using a whistle like Coach Hering or just barking out "Team!" like Coach Lofton, she sang. I'm not kidding, like, la, la, la sang. What was I supposed to do with that?

The buxom woman patted several people on their heads, singing, "There's a friend and there's a friend and there's a friend and there's a friend …" She stopped by me, grabbed my hands, and twirled me around. "And here's a new face. I'm Mrs. James. What is your name?" She sang the whole thing—low, low, high, low.

My cheeks burned. "I'm Dani," I mumbled, voice flat as a tire.

A brief frown flashed across her face until the toothy smile won out again. "Welcome, Dani." Again, she sang, low, low, high, low. She turned to Sol. "Another new! Another new! Who have we here?"

"My name is Sol." Sol mimicked the four notes perfectly. "Nice to meet you."

Mrs. James's eyes lit up, and she gave a nod as if Sol had scored a goal in her singsong game. "Hello, Lovey." She continued down the line until everyone had introduced themselves.

Once done, she made us sit in the front rows. "Since this is a musical, it's imperative we sort out our singers before we go too far into casting. You will have piano accompaniment for the singing portion."

I eased back in my chair, fighting the feeling the only accompaniment I needed was an escort out the door and back to the soccer field.

"When I call your name, please approach the microphone on stage and tell us what musical number you are going to sing," Mrs. James said. "You will then have thirty-two bars to impress me, and another minute to present your monologue. Once finished, please return to your seat. Questions?"

I wanted to ask if she had any barf bags, but I held my tongue.

"Well then." Mrs. James pulled out a clipboard and clicked her pen. "Let's begin."

As she called each name, talented candidates—or at least mostly talented minus a few sour notes—got up and sang their lungs out. Almost literally, organs on the stage.

I slouched lower and lower in my seat. It was like being on a U10 soccer league and facing a college team. You know it's going to be humiliating, but you stay rooted on the field because you don't want to trip over your shoelaces as you flee screaming.

She could call my name any minute now. I'd already settled on the song "Ninety-Nine Bottles of Beer on the Wall" because, though lacking any ethical value, it came from a time-honored family vacation tradition meant to boost our immunity to torture should we be forced to visit such hot spots as Geraldine's House of Wax Teeth or Ancient Aliens' Toilet Bowls.

Just kidding. I picked "Let It Go" from *Frozen.* Sol and I had crooned that song so many times, I could sing it backwards.

But what would my monologue be? Perhaps the wedding scene from the classic comedy *Princess Bride?* Wuv. Twue wuv. Yeah, I could swing that. If I could remember what came after *wuv.* Or how about the scene from *The Wizard of Oz,* where Dorothy confronts the phony man hiding behind the curtain? Like *Frozen,* Sol had recited the confrontation enough to tattoo it on my brain. Of course, I hadn't practiced either one. Which could set me up for a colossal failure that rivaled my unsuccessful Cruyff Turn.

Sudden panic sent my pulse racing. I traced the contours of the room. Were the brick walls and musty black curtains closing in on me? I'm used to open space. Clean air. Real birdsongs. Dirt and grass and balls and sun and—

The room spun. Sweat drizzled down my neck. I plucked the collar of my t-shirt. "Is it hot in here?" I whispered.

"Dani." Worry creased Sol's forehead. "Are you okay?"

I shook my head.

"This is overwhelming you." She put a hand on my shoulder. "Take deep breaths."

Eyes wide, I sucked in air.

Sol swallowed hard. "I'm sorry, Dani. I didn't realize it would be this hard for you. You don't have to do this. We don't have to. We can leave right now. Together. Besties. No one will judge us."

"Sol Garcia," Mrs. James announced.

Sol winced, and my heart broke. Leaving this dream

behind was her testimony to our friendship. But I couldn't let her do that.

I squeezed her hand. "You got this. I'm rooting for you."

Sunshine had nothing on the happiness that poured over Sol's face. "You sure?"

"Break a leg," I said.

Sol rose and sauntered to the stage with the grace of a tiger. Those killing machines were quite elegant when they weren't trying to eat you.

She gave me a quick wink, then handed her sheet music to the pianist. The room quieted. Stage lights glittered off her dangling earrings. "Hello, I'm Sol Garcia, and I will be singing 'You'll Be Back,' from *Hamilton.*"

She nodded at the pianist, who played a single note that hung in the air with expectation.

Lifting her head toward the heavens, Sol seemed to draw in the air surrounding her and wrap its magic around her like a cloak. When the words "You say" blossomed from her mouth, the room hooted their approval.

The spirited melody swelled and swirled around the room. A choir of angels might have joined in had they dared compete with Sol. I sat up in my seat, swaying to the verses. When she hit the final chorus with its playful scatting, Michael stood and joined in. *Da-da-dat-dat-duh. Da-da-datta die-ya duh. Da-da-dat-dat-die-ya duh.*

Next thing I know, everyone else is on their feet to conclude the song. *Da-da-dat-dat-duh. Da-da-datta die-ya duh. Da-da-dat-dat-die-ya duh-uh.*

"Well," Mrs. James said when the twittering of laughter stopped. "That was highly unexpected. And I loved it."

The crowd clapped and Sol flushed, and I simply stared at my friend.

Growing up with Sol, I was aware of her many talents. Soccer, of course. Writing. A strong vocabulary. A magnetic personality. But this singing?

It blew me away.

Sol had never sung like this before. Instead, she sprinkled little tunes in the middle of conversations so often, they'd get stuck in my head all day. I didn't know how many times I'd found myself humming the tune to "If I Were a Rich Man" whenever I borrowed money from Dad.

But this? This was enchantment, pure and simple.

Then she launched into her monologue, and I got goose bumps. No denying it. Sol was to theater what Reb was to our soccer team. Mrs. James inclined her head toward Sol when she stepped off the stage. A show of respect maybe? She jotted something on her clipboard and underlined it three times. Either that or she was crossing several items off her to-do list. With a sniff, she called the next person. Me.

How do you follow an act like that?

Legs shaking as if I'd just finished running wind sprints, I stumbled up the stairs and onto the stage. The spotlight blinded me like the midday sun, and I blinked to adjust my vision. The glare made it difficult to see the audience, a small comfort at least. I squinted at the ghostly bodies anyway, until I spotted Sol.

She flashed me a thumbs-up, syphoning some of my tension. Or maybe she was jerking her thumb toward the exit, telling me to get out while I still could. I chose to generously interpret her gesticulation as encouragement.

"Whenever you're ready," Mrs. James said. She clicked her pen out and in.

Taking a big breath, I opened my mouth. "I'm Danielle, and I'll be singing—" My throat froze.

After several seconds (or years, maybe centuries), Mrs. James cleared her throat. "I understand you have no sheet music, so you're singing a cappella. But what's your song, dear?"

Was the woman prompting me? I struggled to focus.

That's when Sol's voice sang from the audience. "Look for the silver lining whenever a cloud appears in the blue ..."

She stood, facing me. That wasn't the song I picked. But I knew it. The words hung there between us, tugging at my memory.

Yes, an old song from a failed musical, *Zip Goes a Million*. Sol used to sing it on rainy days. And we had a lot of rain last April.

I found my voice, much like a mewling cat. "Remember, somewhere the sun is shining. And so the right thing to do is make it shine for you."

"A heart full of joy and gladness will always banish sadness and strife," Sol continued, locking eyes with me.

"So always look for the silver lining," we sang together, "and try to find the sunny side of life."

An odd stillness filled the auditorium when the song ended, punctuated by the clicking of Mrs. James's pen.

"Well, it seems today is full of irregularities," she finally said. "But since we can all draw inspiration from that touching moment, I'll let it pass. Now, Ms. Dani, before you do your monologue, I'm wondering if you've considered being on the stage crew?"

"She can't," Sol said. "She's on the soccer team. No offense, Mrs. James, but she belongs on the field. Our team needs her more than you need a prop manager. In fact"—she lowered her eyes and her voice—"we're both on the soccer team."

"But Sol was born to sing," I said, stepping forward. "This

stage is where she belongs. So I hope you'll still let her stay despite breaking the rules. And if you do, I'd like to watch."

Mrs. James dabbed her eyes with a tissue. "Yes, I think I can allow that. They're really more expectations than rules." Clearing her throat, she checked her clipboard. "Jesse Moreno. You're next. Please tell me you're singing something lively."

"Will 'I Just Can't Wait to Be King' from *The Lion King* work?"

Mrs. James chuckled. "Bring it on."

As I sat through the rest of the morning, my stomach and nerves settled. I had done the right thing coming to support my friend. And I had done the right thing bowing out. I might have made a few friends. I mean, I made eye contact with Michael. Yay me.

Only one little worry kept worming into my heart.

If Sol landed a lead in the production, how could she keep up with her *Heart and Soul* blog? Would she have to give up soccer? And if she didn't blog or play soccer, would we still be best friends? Or would Harper take my place?

CHAPTER TWENTY-NINE

THE CAST

Sol stepped close to the paper taped on the auditorium door and skimmed her finger down the list. "You'd think with today's technology, Mrs. James could send a text announcement, right? Or post it on the school website under the theater tab like she did for the callbacks. But no. She's old school. Although, in a way, this makes it kind of exciting too."

"At least you got a callback," I said. "That's a victory right there."

"Yeah, but I don't want sit on the bench for this one." Her finger stopped and her eyes widened. "No way! No. Way."

Yanking her hands back to her face, she squealed. "Dani, I'm Cinderella. That's one of the leads. I'm in the play! I'm an actress!"

I let my jaw drop. "Way to go!"

We both screamed, "Yaaaasss!" and danced around.

Two students passing in the hallway exchanged glances and snickered. I ignored them, letting my friend get all the giggles and spins out of her system. Why not? The first period bell hadn't rung yet, and we had an adrenaline rush to burn.

When Sol finally calmed down enough to breathe again, I gave her a push on the shoulder. "I'm proud of you. Your first audition, and you nailed it. Are you excited?"

"Well, yes, I'm excited and scared." She sang those last words, and I recognized them from a snippet of one of Little Red Riding Hood's songs from auditions.

The song made my heart twinge as the reality sunk in that Sol would be fully immersed in an activity that didn't include me. "Look at you." I pulled away and hugged myself. "You're ready to steal the show."

"As Cinderella, I'm going to have a ball."

Just not a soccer ball. Sadness bled into my happiness and twinged my heart.

"Dani, are you okay?" Sol put a hand on my shoulder.

Swallowing, I nodded. "I just realized you're going to be busier than ever. And that means we'll probably have to double up on our coffee runs."

She laughed. "We'll make time to hang out, I promise. Even if only to suck down more liquid heaven while we mourn our loss of sleep. Which, right now, doesn't sound like a bad thing."

"I'm going to invent new fairy-tale jokes to keep you on your toes. Like what do you call your character when she goes on a shopping spree? Spenderella. Or what kind of shoes does a Cinderella soccer player wear? Grass slippers." I paused for breath. "Oh, one more. What do you call a princess who goes viral? Trenderella."

"Ha-ha." Beaming, Sol pulled out her phone. "What a great way to start a Monday morning. I'm making a social media post, texting Harper, and texting my mom, in that order." She leaned toward the list, pointed at her name, and snapped a photo.

Before she checked the picture, Harper rushed over.

"Is that the list?" Her breath came in gulps. Had she sprinted down the hall?

Sol dropped her arm. "Yes. And Harper! Guess what? I'm Cinderella." She cupped her chin. "Call me Cindy."

Harper squealed, her smile nearly bigger than her face. "Is my name on there?" She pushed past me to examine the post. Seconds later, she let loose another squeal. "I'm Red Riding Hood! I have a lead role too!"

And then we went through the whole squealing, dancing, fist-pumping sequence again. Our trio could not contain our happiness. It was like the bubbly joy you experience from squeezing a tubful of rubber duckies.

"Here," Harper said, shoving her phone in my hands. "Take a picture of us."

As I gawked at the device shoved into my hands, my euphoria drained. A chasm in my heart had opened with the passing of the phone. A "we're in this circle" and a "you're outside it" type of division.

Sol shoulder-hugged Harper, and the forced smile on my face stiffened. Harper would be front and center in Sol's media post today. And I would not.

I shook my head, clearing those negative thoughts. Better

for me to be on this side of the camera. Unlike these two actresses, I wasn't a fan of the spotlight.

Ignoring the uneasiness growing in my stomach, I snapped away. The two stars struck a variety of happy poses.

After a dozen shots, Harper reclaimed her phone. She and Sol bent their heads over it as she flipped through the images, murmuring things like "That's a good one," and "No, my eyes are closed."

"Do you know the rehearsal schedule yet?" I asked, interrupting their media mining.

Harper cocked her head and squinted at me, as if wondering why I still stood there. "I've got it." She swept her hair behind her ear and typed on her phone. "Sorry, Dani, I don't have your number, but I'll send it to Sol. Hang on."

A moment later, Sol's phone pinged.

"Thanks." Sol opened the file and pinched the screen to enlarge it. "Oh, this is detailed. Listen to this, Dani. 'In addition to immediately working on learning their lines, actors can expect the following schedule. Week one, learn the musical pieces and blocking.'" She glanced at Harper. "At least I already know the songs."

"Blocking? I don't get it." I scrunched my nose. "A block in soccer prevents the ball from reaching the intended target. But don't you want to move forward with the production?"

"What?" Harper said.

Sol put a hand on my shoulder. "Outside of my soundtracks, this is new to Dani. The girl's world revolves around soccer. And I only know about blocking because I've seen the director's cuts to tons of musicals."

"Gotcha," Harper said. "Well, okay, blocking in theater is different than soccer. It's when you walk through the script and everyone learns what part they're in, when they're needed, where to stand, where the action takes place, when to walk forward or fall back, and when to exit the stage."

As if that definition of blocking made any sense. Why not just call it *Acting in Slow Motion?* Or *Show Motion* for short.

Or maybe *blockheads.* I liked that one better.

Still, the first week of rehearsals didn't sound difficult. "Okay. Sounds like you could still make it to soccer practice."

"Oh, no, no, no." Harper shook her head. "Dani, it's not just a one-and-done kind of thing. Everything we do on stage has to flow, just like your offense on the field. And that takes time. Lots of it."

Had I heard her correctly? I cleared my throat. "What about soccer?"

Sol's broad smile softened into a grimace. "I'm sorry, Dani. When I went into this, I had hopes for a big part, but I figured I'd end up in the chorus." She wrung her hands. "Now that I landed a lead role, I think I'll have to quit the team."

"Wait—what?" My chest tightened. "Why?"

"She won't have time." Harper gave me a sympathetic look. "When you're not blocking, you're running your lines. Actors go over and over the play, sequentially and methodically. Did you notice the six-hour weekend rehearsals too? On the accelerated timeline we have, everything will be doubled up."

"Like summer sessions, where we work out in the mornings and the evenings," Sol said.

"I even expect the stagehands to start setting up props and backdrops right away. We don't have much time until—" Harper showed Sol something on her phone.

"No more scripts after week two." Sol gulped and slapped a hand against her forehead. "In a short time, I've got to have an almost two-hour play memorized."

"And keep reading." Harper nudged Sol. "This is the best part."

"On Wednesday, we get fitted for costumes." Sol gasped. "So soon? This is awesome. Do I put on my own makeup, or do they recruit people for that too?"

"We get a hair and makeup crew," Harper said.

Sol caught my eye. "Speaking of costumes, Dani, do you remember when I wore that Princess Leia costume for May the Fourth last year? I had the hair all loopy and the belt. You should have seen us, Harper. And Dani was—what were you again? Yoda?"

I nodded.

"Wait, wait, wait. I've got pictures of us." She whipped out her phone again, and Harper leaned in. Once again, the two scrolled through the images together.

Harper laughed. "Girl, you rocked the princess look."

Nothing about my Yoda attire?

My mood tanked. I was beginning to see a pattern here. Sol had introduced a new factor into our friendship, and just like Little Red Riding Hood, we now traveled an unfamiliar path. Soccer was the one thing connecting me to my best friend. And now, that line was threatened by the musical. She'd go one way, and I'd go the other.

Except Sol would be fine. She'd thrive in this new environment, just like she always did. She took to making new friends like a fish to water.

But me?

I would flounder on the shore.

A compulsion to grab Betty and hit the field overwhelmed me. I needed to sweat, to run, to numb my heart. I staggered, trying to keep my balance.

Sol steadied me. "Whoa, Dani. I feel a little dizzy too. It's a lot of changes to take in all at once. Maybe we should start planning our coffee sessions now."

I smiled. "I'm thinking we might need that intravenous option."

"But you're okay with this play?" Her forehead wrinkled.

"Yes." I gulped air. I would be okay. This move would force me to stand on my own more instead of relying on Sol so much. It could turn out for the best. "It's a new adventure. Anything else I need to know about?"

"Toward the end of the soccer season, there are three days of dress rehearsals with lighting and a pit orchestra." Sol planted a fist on her hip. "I love how the school involves as many students as possible. Technical crew and band members work together as a team with the actors."

Harper laced her fingers together. "It's a thing of beauty, like a well-oiled machine."

Coach Hering called us a well-oiled machine sometimes when we passed the ball well. Would Sol remember that? Miss it?

The first period bell rang, flooding the halls with students scurrying to class. I hefted my backpack. "I gotta go. Math is on the other side of the building."

"And we're this way," Sol said, hooking arms with Harper. "See you at lunch, Dani."

With a spring in their steps, the two walked off, chattering without a backward glance.

I told my feet to move, but they didn't listen. I stood as isolated and unsteady as a newborn calf finding its legs. Only when the tardy bell sounded did I dab my tears and drag myself in the right direction.

By then, my heart was as empty as the hallway.

What would our soccer team be like without Sol?

CHAPTER THIRTY

LUNCH

Sol texted at lunch. Her third period teacher had released their class early, so she and Harper ran to get a celebration meal at Taco, Taco, Taco. Did I want anything?

I did. But nothing she could buy at the restaurant. *No thanks,* I said.

Instead of hiding in the bathroom for lunch, I sat in my car and listened to music. The vehicle was just as lonely, but it smelled better.

I scrunched down so no one would see me. I mean, how embarrassing would that be?

I couldn't bring a tray out of the lunchroom, so I ate the entire box of granola bars I'd packed to share with the team after practice.

Except I saved one for Sol. I knew she'd be hungry later.

CHAPTER THIRTY-ONE

PRACTICE

I forgot Sol quit the team.

She texted before practice to remind me she'd turned in her jersey and let me know Harper would give her a ride home.

Before warmups started, I had to make three trips to the bathroom to clear my system.

Too many granola bars.

CHAPTER THIRTY-TWO

JAY

"Defenders must be tireless." Coach Hering scooped up the ball, stalked over to Reb, and pointed to a spot on the right. Spinning on her heel, she motioned for Erika to move backward. "But they gotta be smart too."

Bending to put my hands on my knees, I used Coach's interruption to suck in air. Pushing myself hard had its drawbacks. Like lack of oxygen to the brain.

Or maybe it was a blessing because I didn't have enough energy to think about Sol. I'd made it all the way to the scrimmage part of practice with that tactic.

"Always watch the play and move accordingly." Coach side-shuffled toward Reb. "The closer you get to the attacker"—she beckoned Erika forward, then held a hand up to stop her—"the more cautious you must be. If the attacker approaches quickly, leave a cushion so you have time to react if they change direction. Move in and put pressure on the attacker if they're stopped or edging forward slowly. You'll be better able to anticipate their next move. Got it?"

Erika dabbed her face with the bottom of her shirt. "I move in when Reb's guard is down, and I fall back a little when she's on the fly. Got it." She allowed a hint of sarcasm into her voice, as if reminding Coach Hering she already knew that tip. Not enough cynicism to raise any eyebrows, but enough to show her competitive attitude.

"Great." Lips pressed together, Coach Hering turned her focus on me. "Dani, you hold your dribble too long when the defenders are on you. Pass more. Look for chances to give-and-go with Reb."

"Especially when I'm open." Reb lifted her chin. "Which, let's face it, is most of the time since I'm fast."

Grinding my teeth, I turned away. Yeah, I remembered almost blowing it last game.

"You're on the same team. Play that way." Coach tossed the ball to Wren. "Let's set this up again." She pointed to the sideline. "Throw-in from midfield, and we'll go from there."

The ball arched through the air. I dutifully headed it toward Reb, who took off down the field with Erika on her heels. I trailed after our striker, steadfast as always, cleaning up any crumbs our alpha leader left behind like a common goldfish, both eager and fearful to surge ahead.

For the team's sake, I kept my body and emotions in check. When practice ended, I moved with all the speed of a drunken snail, collecting balls and cleaning up any plastic one-use water bottles forgotten on the field. I studied my teammates as I loaded the equipment and trash on Coach's cart. Reb's confident banter, Wren's nervous nail chewing, Erika's quick smile, Sandy's bulldog stride. My other teammates, yanking on hoodies, pushing and laughing and scrolling through their phones.

For the past four years, I'd spent the best part of my day with this family of athletes. I knew their strengths and weaknesses, their motivations and dreams. Yet without Sol and her ability to help me connect with other people, I felt awkward.

Reb wiped her face on her sleeve. "You're dragging, Dani. C'mon. I know Sol's not here, but ya still got us. And lucky for you, I don't sing all the time. My body is the only orchestration needed on the field."

I lifted my chin, acknowledging her. But didn't she get it? I missed Sol's singing and the easy companionship. "Thanks. I'll try to get in tune with you."

"Now you're talking." Reb laughed and headed toward the school.

Lagging behind, I dug through my duffle for gum. I found stinky socks, a receipt, and my taser, but no gum. At least my unnecessary treasure hunt had allowed the field to clear so I could walk alone to my car. I needed the space and hated it at the same time.

The lure of distraction led me to Hayden's practice field. Easing into the bleachers, I sought his familiar mop of hair. Anything to lift me out of my funk.

Jay sat in the first row, scrolling through his phone. Not wanting another lengthy, mostly small-talk encounter, I pretended not to notice him. Instead, I picked a spot several paces to the left and turned my head to scan the far corner of the field. I spotted Elijah first, the muscles in his legs bulging as he sprinted after a ball. I smiled. Cute but hopeless. He'd need a burst of speed faster than his wit to outmaneuver two defenders.

When he switched to defense, Elijah looked my way and lifted a hand.

After flashing Elijah a thumbs-up, I checked the sidelines for Hayden. My pulse raced when I spotted him waiting for his turn to come in for the drill. I laced my fingers together, fighting the urge to wave.

Would Hayden think I was needy if I hung around?

I threw a sidelong glance at Jay. He lounged, tracking the plays, toying with his candy, seemingly unaffected by the fact I hadn't acknowledged him. Maybe he figured I didn't see him. At the time, that was my goal. Now, I wouldn't mind moving closer so Hayden wouldn't think I was too desperate.

But then I'd have to initiate conversation.

Well, I had made a pact with Sol to try new things. Like engaging in social interactions. Besides, any friend of Coach Campbell couldn't be so bad.

From across the field, Hayden shot a look my way and worked his jaw.

What did that mean? Irritation? Condemnation? Constipation?

I balled my hands. *Look like you have a purpose to be here.* Now or never.

"How's the scouting report?" I turned so Jay would know I was addressing him.

He startled. "Say what?"

"The scouting reports." I raised my voice. "Which player on the team stands out to you?"

"All of them." He chuckled. "They got skills. By the way,

you were right about that Elijah kid. I checked out his stats. Solid player."

"Yeah." I shifted, daring a peek across the field. Hayden was back in business and struggling to protect a ball.

And since I was with someone, I didn't stand out as much.

I relaxed. Crisis averted.

On the downside, I'd unleashed the talker.

"It's interesting to note that your other boy, Hayden, leads in fouls and goals. Aggressive players like that often dominate on the scoreboard. Is he aggressive in school too?"

I shrugged. "I don't have any classes with him."

"But you like him, I can tell." Jay clicked his tongue. "Back in the day, Coach Campbell and I both had our eye on the same girl. Claire. Tall, blonde, with legs that just wouldn't quit. Campbell made a bet he could score a date with her before I did. So what does he do?"

He paused as if waiting for an answer.

I shrugged. "Ask her out?"

"Nah." Jay waved a hand in the air. "That'd be too easy. He found out she'd joined a tennis class, so we both scrambled to sign up. Get close to her, right? Only Campbell, he's fast and feisty and decides to show off how athletic he is. Thinks all he's got to do is swing the racket with her and she'd swoon for him."

I glanced at Coach standing on the sidelines with his arms crossed over his middle-aged belly and tried to imagine him fast and feisty. "Did it work?"

"It might have," Jay said. "Except he either sent the ball soaring off court or slammed it into the net. Not impressive. He came off like a braggart, and I ended up taking Claire to Homecoming."

Curiosity got the best of me. "How?"

"I played the helpless fool who didn't even know how to hold a racket correctly." He grinned. "And since Claire was such an expert, of course she didn't mind helping little old me."

Jay might have found the situation amusing, but I didn't. "Poor Claire," I said, "having her emotions played with like that."

Jay's jaw clenched for a moment, so fast I almost missed it. "It was a different time. Different era. We were just kids having fun."

"By treating Claire like a target to be acquired?" For some reason, I couldn't let the injustice go. "By pretending you cared about her? I'm sure she had a blast."

His face paled. "I treated her well. Then. And after, I guess." Grimacing, he fished his pack of red licorice from a back pocket, peeled one loose, and tucked it into his mouth like a cigarette. "Look, I'm just a man reliving happy memories of my own high school days and helping a friend. At least, that's my script."

I narrowed my eyes. "We've all got a script to follow, don't we?"

"Humph." He snorted. "I need a sugar fix." He tore off the end with his teeth, glanced at me, and held out the bag like a peace offering. "Want a hit?"

Hayden breezed by on the field, close enough to see beads of sweat lining his face. He stopped when the whistle blew and glanced my way.

I needed to look like I belonged, so I grabbed the bag. "Sure."

Mimicking Jay's actions, I yanked away a crimson strip and passed back the rest. Like he had done, I bit off the tip of the stick. Though bitter on my tongue at first, the rubbery texture softened into something sweet and more palatable. Still, instead of swallowing it, I kept the chunk tucked in my cheek and sucked on it.

Jay turned back toward the field. "You criticize me, but you're like me, you know. Pretending."

"What?" Almost choking on the piece lodged in my mouth, I narrowed my eyes. "I'm not pretending anything."

"Oh?" He raised a brow. "You're pretending like you're not interested in that kid." He pointed at Hayden. "Pretending that other boy, Elijah, doesn't have a crush on you. Pretending like you enjoy licorice. Pretending you're fine sitting here alone. Where are your friends?"

Busted. I lowered my brows. "Busy."

"If you say so." Jay leaned back. "Let me tell you a story. It's about a boy who loved soccer. Let's call him Joe."

"This better not be another Claire story." I frowned.

"It's not," Jay said. "Joe is your typical kid. A dreamer. Wanted to succeed on and off the field. But Joe got into all kinds of trouble. He fell in with bad company. Made bad choices. Risky choices that left him compromised. Depression and paranoia set in. No one understood him. He would never measure up."

His words were a boa constrictor squeezing my heart tighter and tighter.

Nick had run with a rough crowd. Took dares. Tried alcohol, maybe drugs. All chasing the elusive promise of popularity. Of course, Jay couldn't know that. Could he?

I finished my candy and reached for more. He passed me the half-filled bag. Without hesitation, I sectioned off three pieces before handing it back.

"That boy, that talented but mentally unstable soccer player, longed for more. Needed more."

Nick wanted more. Was his own worst enemy. He turned from his faith and the church trying to find himself—and lost himself on the way. Nick tried to keep his struggles hidden, he tried to cover his insecurities with humor, but he'd gone too far down the path to self-destruction and got caught. Things weren't the same after he left for college. After the hazing incident. Now only his late-night or on-a-whim texts tethered him to me.

I swallowed the licorice past a lump in my throat and inhaled a second, then a third bite. The stuff was addicting.

Jay cleared his throat. "And then one day he took control of his life. He met a teacher who believed in him. A teacher who saw him." His voice lowered. "One who recognized his pain. His brilliance. One who also sympathized with his struggles."

My pounding heart threatened to overwhelm me. "How does the story end?"

"For Joe?" Jay lifted a brow.

Wait. Pressure built at the base of my skull. My vision spun. Was it possible to spike licorice? I pinched my eyes shut and shook my head. Not Nick. Joe.

"Yeah." I sighed and opened my eyes. "Joe."

Jay's gaze hardened. "You tell me."

What? There had to be a happy ending. That's how stories went.

"Heads up!" a player yelled.

Something slammed into the bleachers next to me, jolting me out of Jay's spell.

Jumping to my feet, I left the licorice on the bench and scrambled after the wayward ball. When I turned around with it, Hayden stood by the sidelines with his arm raised. A frown chased across his face, and his eyes darted over to Jay before returning to me. "Dani!" He waved his hand. "Here."

I tossed it to him.

He caught it. Before heading back, he hesitated and flashed a smile. As if acting casual. Chill. "Thanks."

All the emotions and memories of the fun we'd had dipping fries and battling one-on-one flooded my system at once. His musky smell. The precision of his soccer tricks. That sharp laugh. The way he charmed his way past my shyness. He was so nice.

Nice. I tightened my fists.

"Thanks for the licorice, Jay. But I gotta go."

"I'll catch you later," Jay said.

CHAPTER THIRTY-THREE

TIMELY TEXTS

My phone buzzed after dinner, and I snatched it up, thinking it might be Sol. But it was Hayden. Which shocked me like finding a three-toed sloth hanging on the shower curtains. Not that I minded. I just didn't expect it. I lowered myself on the couch and read his message.

I liked seeing you today. Did you try that Cruyff Turn in practice yet?

I grinned. He was thinking about me, obviously. *No. I spent my time passing the ball and trying not to trip on my laces.*

And eating licorice apparently. He attached an emoji face with a raised brow. *That's good for your game.*

Smiling, I settled into the oversized pillows. *The candy? Or not tripping?*

Laughing emoji. *The passing. But I guess the licorice and not tripping too. Who was that guy you were sitting by? I've seen him in the bleachers a lot.*

Coach Campbell's secret weapon. He evaluates your formations and gives tips and advice for improvement. Very talkative. I paused, considering if I was being too talkative myself, then shrugged and pressed send. I waited a full minute with no response, so I shot off another text. *At least he seems nice-ish.* Autocorrect changed it to "nice fish" three times before I got it right.

Or so I thought.

Hayden texted back right away. *Nice fish?*

Nice-ish. It should be a word. It's word-ish. You know what else should be a word? Parent-dippity. As in, it would be parent-dippity if my parents didn't work so hard all the time and could go to more of my soccer games.

Hayden sent a question mark.

Yeesh. I forgot I wasn't dealing with Sol, who would inhale my word choice, roll it around in her brain, and spit it back out as a masterpiece of wit.

My fingers flew. *It's a play on the word* serendipity, *which is when chance events work out to be beneficial.*

You're beneficial, he texted.

I beamed. *Thanks. Ish.*

I've got one. Contrapper.

It was my turn to send a question mark. It took another thirty seconds before my phone pinged. He must be doing something else at the same time. Eating maybe? Or wrestling with autocorrect like I had.

Trap and control. Like, contrapper the soccer ball.

I sent a winking face with a tongue out. *Shouldn't it be trapoller then?*

This time, I had enough time to chew off a fingernail before my phone lit up again.

Laughing face. *You're weird. Want to practice with me after school tomorrow?*

Pulse racing, I stared at my phone. Was he asking me to practice being weirder? Or because I was weird, I needed to practice more? Or was it a date?

Thank goodness I had an excuse so I wouldn't have to figure it out. *Sorry, I have a game.*

He sent a fast reply. A frowning face.

What exactly was going on between us? I bit my lip. I could read so much into that emoji if I wasn't careful. I stood looking over a cliff, fighting a light-headed heart urging me to leap over the edge while my dizzy mind screamed at me to shy away from the drop.

I followed my heart and texted back. *Would Wednesday work?*

No. My game day.

Of course. I knew that. My heart rivaled a koala for stupidity. Those critters often fail to recognize their own food and starve to death.

Swallowing hard, I tried to save face. *I'm free Saturday.*

Koala idiocy taking over again!

A thumbs-down emoji. *Not me. Club tournament.*

I almost typed that I could go to his game and watch, but I hesitated. He hadn't exactly invited me. And those things usually lasted all day. My stomach cramped. I'd be another tagalong if I showed uninvited.

Maybe some other time, he texted

I sent a thumbs-up and then waited ten minutes for another text from him, but it didn't come. What was I supposed to think now? I needed to bounce this developing situation off Sol. She'd know what was going on.

But a quick dial only landed her voicemail.

As the night stretched on, I tried to reach her six more times. I'd just have to wait until tomorrow morning when I picked her up for school. Because either she wasn't answering her phone, or this musical was sucking the life out of her already. She'd gone into the woods with Harper by her side, and who knew when she'd claw her way back out?

If ever.

Needing to work out my anxiety over two shifting relationships, I slunk downstairs to find Mom at the kitchen table. Head buried over her computer, she barely noticed me. I slipped my arms around her neck and leaned close. "Are you busy?"

Her eyes stayed on the screen, but she lifted a hand to press my cheek against hers. "I've got a little homework. What's up?"

I glanced at the patient history document open in front of her. She had paperwork to complete, and I didn't want to be a burden. My worries could wait. "Nothing. Want some help cleaning the kitchen?"

Her eyes widened. "Could you? You're an angel."

"I know." I forced a smile, which she didn't see, and went to the sink.

My phone buzzed in my pocket. Sol? Hayden? I glanced at it.

Elijah.

"But those who hope in the LORD will renew their strength. They will soar on wings like eagles; they will run and not grow weary, they will walk and not be faint." Isaiah 40:31, ESV

Another buzz. *Good luck at your game tomorrow.*

The kid might be invisible, but he kept his word. Timely words. And I knew just who needed to hear them.

Smiling, I tucked my phone away and picked up a rag. "Hey, Mom. I got a verse for you."

Chapter Thirty-Four

CAUTERIZATION

M acie was trudging down the sidewalk with her backpack slung over her shoulder when I drove past her house Tuesday morning. My heart sped, but my car slowed. Should I pull over and tell her I was sorry for what I said to her? Would she listen? Would she care?

I dropped my speed to a crawl, hoping she'd notice and I could wave. As if that universal sign could convey one idea. *We're cool now.* Then maybe my guilt would dissipate.

No such luck. Macie kept her eyes glued to a phone cupped in her hand. And talk about eyes! Since our last encounter, the girl had discovered makeup. Her eyelashes stood out like porcupine quills with matching black racoon-lined lids. Was that her attempt at looking more grown up? And was I partly responsible for the fiasco?

Poor thing. She probably thought she looked great. She was no better off than I was the first time I wore mascara to school. I had blinked and given myself a splatter of black, smudgy freckles. No one told me either. I discovered the disaster spots when I ran to the bathroom after lunch to check my teeth for broccoli.

I sat overlong at the stop sign, watching her progress. The middle school was several more blocks down the road. I still had time to catch her.

No, I didn't know how she might react to me, especially confronting her on the street. It might cause a scene, and if that happened, her mascara would run down her cheeks like melting wax. What ridicule would she face if she went to school looking like that? I couldn't take the risk.

I accelerated. Macie disappeared in my rearview mirror.

When I pulled into Sol's driveway, I sat for three minutes praying for Macie. For me. For Nick. For Mom. Mom said prayer changed things. Far as I could tell, only for the worse. Still, the act calmed me enough to text Sol. *Are you coming?*

After three more minutes, her front entrance opened. Bleary-eyed, she shuffled to the car and opened the passenger-side door. "Coffee. Please." She slid into the seat, leaned back, and yawned. "Two weeks into rehearsals, and I was up until two o'clock rehearsing my lines."

"That's late." I cocked my head.

Frowning, she held up a hand. "I know, I know. You don't have to say it, Squirrel. This hectic schedule is what I signed up for. But these thespians are hard-core. Even more committed than Reb on the field."

Competition ruled Reb. Bulldog tenacity drove her to the brink of exhaustion every game. I tried to visualize her type of intensity on stage. How did that translate? Reb, bellowing, "To shoot, or not to shoot. That is the question." And here, I imagine her kicking Hamlet's skull into a net.

"I feel guilty too," Sol said.

"Guilty?" I scrunched my face. "Why?"

She glanced out the window. "Most of the cast has performed theater forever, and they've worked hard to earn their spots. And here I come in out of nowhere and snag a lead role. It's like I stole it from them." Her head lolled my way. "So yeah, I stayed up late. I've got something to prove, you know."

I never considered the stress actors endured before. "Anything I can do to help?"

"Coffee. Intravenously if possible." She closed her eyes. "And let me rest."

"Besides that." I eased to a stop at a red light. "Do you want to run your lines with me? I am a good listener. One of my endearing qualities, remember?"

She dismissed me with a wave. "Thanks, but not needed. Mrs. James is opening her classroom during lunch so the cast can bond. She suggested it might help with our onstage chemistry, and we can practice our lines." She chuckled. "I guess that means I've got working lunch dates for the next month."

My stomach dropped, and I tightened my grip on the wheel. What about me? Who was I supposed to eat lunch with?

"I'm sorry. That puts you in an awkward spot, doesn't it?" A frown creased Sol's forehead. "It might not be exclusive. Maybe you can join us. I'm sure Mrs. James won't mind."

I gulped air, trying to negate the adrenaline spiking my system. Would Coach Hering allow an amateur to sit in on practice? I didn't think so. And imagine Coach Lofton's reaction. Eyes narrowed. Arms folded. Chewing gum like a cow's cud, each chomp emphasizing her displeasure.

Nope. Not gonna put myself in that position.

"It's okay. Gives me a chance to do my homework." I forced a smile as I turned into the Coffee, Tea, and Glee drive-thru.

"Good." Tension melted off Sol's face.

Holding up a finger to prevent further comment, I rolled down the window and ordered our usual fare. "My treat," I said, inching forward to the pickup window. "You've been working hard. You deserve it."

"Thanks." Sol rubbed the heels of her hands across her eyes. "How about you? How was practice yesterday? Or has it been another whole week already? Or two? I lost track." She blinked. "I gotta admit, I did not miss the conditioning."

"It was fine." I quieted, wondering if I should bring up Hayden, but one glance at Sol's sleep-deprived face told me she was not in a listening mood.

Silence reigned as I accepted our order and passed it to Sol.

She divided the drinks and took a sip from her steaming cup. "Too hot." She sputtered and thunked her drink in the cup holder. "Coffee can be so deceptive. It looks good and smells good, but it's bad news if your mouth jumps offsides."

A soccer joke. Gotta love that.

"There has to be a title for things that seem amazing but burn you," I said. *Theater rehearsals with Mrs. James* came to mind.

"There is." Sol blew on the top, a mischievous glint in her eyes. "It's called cauterizing coffee. Guaranteed to literally seal your lips with a scalding bliss."

I snorted, a noncommittal response on the humor scale. "You made that up."

"Guilty as charged. But you're in luck." Sol tugged on her seat belt. "I thought of a way you can help. How do you feel about being a guest blogger for *Heart and Soul* until I finish the play? I can show you how to sort through emails and create your posts."

Indecision immobilized me. With my parents working long hours, having to adjust my lunch period, my tenuous relationship with Hayden, the regular pressures of a competitive sport, and homework deadlines, I did not want the added responsibility of a blog. Especially a potentially time-consuming one. Besides, how was I supposed to advise other people when I hadn't dealt with my own issues?

But if it would help Sol ... give her more time to learn her part ... more opportunities to hang out with her new friends ... a better chance at succeeding ...

I sighed. "What do I have to do?"

"Nothing yet." Sol scrolled through her phone. "But I have an opening Thursday evening, and I can show you the ins and outs of advice columns. Then you can take over under the pen name Paige Turner, so no one knows it's you."

"You've thought this through, haven't you?"

"Yes." Sol tried her coffee again, this time managing a loud slurp. "Can I have Harper drop me off at your house after rehearsal? It will probably be eight o'clock."

"Okay. It's not like I have another commitment." Unless you wanted to count the therapy session I would no doubt require due to increased craziness in my life.

Chapter Thirty-Five

ANOTHER LUNCH

L unch was the worst today.

CHAPTER THIRTY-SIX

ANOTHER PRACTICE

S o was practice.

CHAPTER THIRTY-SEVEN

DEAR HEART

Dear Heart,

Three weeks ago, my best friend got cast in the school musical. Ever since, she's been too busy for me. When I pick her up in the morning, she talks about people and events I know nothing about. It's like she's sharing an inside joke I don't understand. Or she's too tired to say anything, which is weird because she usually talks nonstop. She hardly even texts me anymore. It worries me, the direction our friendship is going.

It's awkward at practice too. I never realized how much her presence made it easier for me to interact with my teammates.

She was my bridge. And now that's she's gone, I'm drowning. I struggle to connect with them, and I don't know how to fix it. I feel selfish for wanting her back on the team when I know how much fun she's having on stage.

I fear I'm mentally in a dark place, but I don't want to tell her how I feel. I'm afraid that might be hurtful to her. Or, worse, she might quit the musical, just for me, and then I'd feel horrible because I know how much she loves it. Besides, I want my friend to be successful and to support her the way she has always supported me. But other than answering letters for a blog, I don't know how. And I especially don't know how to do it without breaking my own heart.

You'll probably tell me to talk to my parents or a "trusted adult." Except my parents are busy too. I don't want to burden them. Coach Hering would tell me to toughen up. Coach Lofton—well, who knows with her? She'd probably grunt. Ms. Brown might overreact and baby me. And my other teachers seem distant. The only other adult I sort of trust shares licorice with me but talks too much. He might let something personal about me slip in a casual conversation with Coach Campbell. And that might somehow get back to Hayden.

I don't have a lot of options. Right now, I'm putting on a brave face, watching from the sidelines, and pretending everything is okay.

I think I do more acting in a single day than my friend will ever do in a lifetime.

Signed, What Do I Do?

Swallowing a lump in my throat, I read my letter on the school's blog submission page one more time before deleting it. A thumb flick sent the internet off the screen, leaving behind a black and white wallpaper shot of Sol and me on the soccer field, rows of apps, and the time. 1:56.

Pressing my lips together, I dropped my phone on the nightstand and pulled the covers over my head. Maybe my eyes would close before the alarm went off for school. Groaning, I wrestled into a new position.

Dolphins are insomniacs too. Only half of their brain rests at a time. The other half stays alert, enabling them to maintain awareness of any nearby predators.

Was loneliness a predator? Or did it simply make me more vulnerable?

CHAPTER THIRTY-EIGHT

CHANGE OF PLANS

A s usual, I picked Sol up twenty minutes early on Friday so we could go to our UCA meeting before first period. Except when we got to Ms. Brown's room, Sol kept walking.

"Wait." I stopped in the doorway. "Where are you going?"

Sol spun on her heel. "Oh no, is my brain so discombobulated that I forgot to tell you?"

I raised a brow. "Discombobulated? I hope that means your brain is telling you to take a restroom break before we walk in this classroom."

"No." Shaking her head, she stepped toward me. "Confused."

"Yes, very," I said.

"No, no!" She laughed. "The word means confused. Since most of the actors from the musical are in Thespian Club, I joined too. We meet in the auditorium on Friday mornings. I thought I told you about it yesterday, but apparently, I forgot. I'm too discombobulated these days."

"Oh." I kept my face neutral, unwilling to let my distress show. This musical continued to slice every thread holding us together.

"I'm sorry." Sol fidgeted with her jacket zipper. "It's only until after the performance. Then I'll come back to UCA, I promise."

I toed the floor. "Okay."

"So you're okay going to UCA without me today?" She caught my eye. "If not, I can go to Thespian Club next time instead."

"No, go ahead. We said we'd try new things." I drew in a breath and released it. "This qualifies as new."

"You're sure?"

"I'm fine," I said.

I wasn't. This new blow to our friendship was an armadillo in Texas. Roadkill.

I hefted my backpack and glanced through the classroom door. "I'll say hi to Barrett for you."

"Uh—" Sol squeezed both eyes shut, then skewed one open. "We broke up yesterday."

A coldness hit my stomach. "And you didn't tell me?"

"I was discombobulated?" She lifted a brow.

"Very." I scowled, but when her eyes welled, I relaxed my face. "We can talk about it later." *If you ever have time.*

"Thanks, Squirrel." She nodded. "I'd like that."

As she started on her way, voices filled the hall behind me, and then Harper rushed past. She gave me a wave, then caught up with Sol. They fell into immediate whisper-chatter sprinkled with laughter. Then, the two hooked arms and, singing snatches from some song, skipped-walked in synchronization to the end of the hallway and around the corner.

Great. Jazzy walks. I gawked after them. Was that a thing now? A new worry wriggled to the surface. With Sol gone, who would I sit with at UCA?

My pulse raced. I should skip it altogether. Clutching my backpack, I swung around to run back to my car and wait it out.

Instead, I bounced straight into Elijah.

The guy's pecs were well-muscled. Hard to miss it, even with that brief contact. He stood with a backpack slung over one shoulder. As I regained my balance, he pulled a Bluetooth headphone from his ear and smiled. "Did I miss the donuts?"

"I don't know." Frozen by his quiet charisma, my body trembled with indecision. Stay here or go? "I haven't checked yet."

"Well, c'mon. I'll race you to them."

He juked and rolled past me into the room, leaving me flat-footed and stunned. Snapping to my senses, I spun after him. My body-slamming threw him clattering into a chair. He scrambled around it and bumped me back, gaining an extra step toward Ms. Brown's desk, where the pack of pastries resided.

The chair toppled with a smack. Ignoring the chaos, we both lunged and slapped our hands on the box top.

"I call dibs on a chocolate frosted Boston cream pie," I yelled, ripping the lid open.

Wait! I gaped at him. Had he just inspired an action-oriented social interaction out of me?

"Relax, Dani." He straightened his back and grinned. "We both win. I wanted a glazed twist."

"If you aren't more careful, you'll both end up with what's better known as squash donuts." Ms. Brown folded her arms across her chest. "They're messy and flat, and they're not vegetables."

After apologizing, righting the chair, and grabbing a napkin and a carton of milk from the cooler to round out our meal, Elijah and I sat behind Barrett.

Elijah swatted Barrett's shoulder.

Barrett gave him a fist bump, but he avoided eye contact with me. I didn't blame him.

Leaning toward me, Elijah whispered, "Did you get my last text?"

Yikes! Since I immediately shared the verse he'd sent me with my mom, I'd forgotten to respond to him. Guess I was discombobulated. "Yes. Thanks. It was perfect."

He sat back, smiling. "Good. Glad you weren't ghosting me."

"No, I'm too nice for that," I said, a bitter taste in my mouth.

My tone must have sounded harsh because his forehead wrinkled.

I swallowed, uncertain about how to amend my tone. A tease seemed like a good alternative, so I threw one in. "Listen, if I ever forget to reply again, start praying, because something's wrong."

"Gotcha." He gave a crisp nod.

Hmm. He took me seriously. And I actually enjoyed his reaction.

He might not be my knight in shining armor like Hayden, but the guy was honest and eager, like a puppy. Nice, like me, I guess. He even gave me space to think by accepting my silence, which I tended to fall back on when things became uncomfortable.

A strange ease settled between us. With Elijah sitting quietly by my side, the tension in my chest since Sol ditched me in the hallway softened into something bearable.

Maybe I was alone. Maybe Elijah was alone too. But when we were alone together, the world didn't seem quite as bleak.

Chapter Thirty-Nine

UCA AGAIN

With the room nearly full, Ms. Brown checked the time, called our attention, and opened the meeting with prayer. After the amen, she turned on the screen display. "Friends, a few weeks ago, a news story captured my attention. Since then, it has not let me go.

"You probably remember it. A young girl—twelve years old—visits the restroom in a public place and disappears. After a desperate search, she is found. Alive. But beaten. Raped. Drugged. Prostituted into sex trafficking."

The air in the room grew oppressive. I held my breath.

With my own trivial worries, time and distance had faded the tragedy to a blur in my memory. Now Ms. Brown's description brought it flooding back.

Eyebrows drawn and lips pursed, Ms. Brown strolled across the front of the room. She paused by her desk, fists resting on the top, chest rising and falling. Her visible turmoil made my skin prickle.

When the quiet grew painful, she lifted her head. "When the story breaks, we are shocked." Her voice trembled. "Appalled. Outraged. How could this happen?"

She clicked a button, and the image on the board changed. "We tell ourselves this could never happen in our community." Ms. Brown resumed pacing. "We turn a blind eye to reality."

The camera captured a thin girl with sunken cheeks and haunted, hollow eyes. I doubted it was the actual victim from the news story, but the effect was the same. Horror.

Another slide appeared. "Here's the truth." Ms. Brown's gaze hardened. "The average age of the over forty million human trafficking victims is between eleven and fourteen years old."

She walked the length of the room, as if letting that fact sink in. Then, clearing her throat, she continued. "Runaways are picked up by traffickers within forty-eight hours. Some people go willingly into these situations, believing false promises of a better life. By the time they realize what's happening, it's too late."

A girl in the front raised her hand. Joy, a tennis player. "But how are they fooled? Can't they tell what's going on?"

Ms. Brown frowned. "But what if it's not a stranger? You'd be surprised what you can be manipulated into doing. For example, Elijah, what if I told you I'd give you a dozen glazed twists if you'd give me a hug? Would you do it?"

"Yeah." He bobbed his head.

"What if I gave you an unlimited supply? And after you enjoyed it for a while, I asked you to hug Dani for me?" She crossed her arms. "Would you do it?"

Heat rose in my face, but Elijah didn't blink an eye. "Yes."

"What about Meghan, in the back? Will you give her a kiss on the cheek for me?" Ms. Brown inclined her chin. "You don't know her as well, do you?"

"Not really." Elijah's ears pinked. "I'd feel uncomfortable doing that. But since you gave me so much, I'd feel obligated too. Like I owed you. So yeah, I'd do it."

"Ah." Ms. Brown lifted her hands, palms up. "And so, increment by increment, I have just proven how to lead someone down a path of danger." She turned back to Joy. "A trafficker is an expert at identifying moments of vulnerability. They scour places where people at risk can be found. Bus stations. Malls. Parks. Schools. Social media. Once they find their target, they form a bond. They commiserate. They compliment. They befriend them."

Ms. Brown advanced the slide to show a statistic, but I missed it because my brain exploded with thoughts.

Did we have traffickers in town? Macie was the right age. I saw her alone a lot. Conversation with her seemed to indicate she had trouble fitting in. Well, for that matter, I had issues too, so I shouldn't be too quick to jump to conclusions. But still. Something seemed off about Macie. And what had I done? Probably made things worse by pushing her away

The screen changed again. More faces. So young. So haunted. So anyone-you-might-pass-on-the-street. I saw Macie in every single one. My stomach churned.

"I read up on this. Talked to some local church ministries." Ms. Brown tapped her forehead. "And I learned how traffickers work. The criminals are good listeners who shower the victim with flattery and attention. Sometimes they even give gifts to make their target feel indebted. These manipulators leverage fears and insecurities and work all the angles. They offer what their victims need in a neat little package. Fulfilling the needs gives the trafficker power."

Macie fit the bill.

Unless I misread Macie's situation by projecting my own fears onto her.

My thoughts shifted inward. Did my parents' busyness, the break from Sol, and my own introversion make me appear vulnerable too? Had anyone spied me hiding in my car at lunch time? I curled my hands and lowered my face, thinking. I kept myself well hidden. Outside of school, the only person who might have witnessed my awkwardness was Jay. But Coach Campbell could vouch for him.

Ms. Brown lifted a palm-sized ball and squeezed it. "The traffickers make off-hand remarks criticizing the people in the child's support system, which plants seeds of doubt and undermines their confidence. They make their victim feel isolated. Alone. Bit by bit, they condition their thinking, making them totally dependent on them for the love they crave. And bit by bit, they gain control."

Ms. Brown's mouth twisted into a scowl. "Then, with their hooks in place, traffickers exploit the love and trust they so carefully cultivated." She strode over Joy and leaned toward her. "So now, is it hard to imagine how someone could be misled?"

Joy swallowed and shook her head.

"If you throw a frog into hot water, it jumps out," Ms. Brown said. "But if you put the frog in water and gradually heat it, it adjusts to the temperature increase. And then you can boil it."

Ms. Brown pushed away. "It's a trite visual, but it works. The process is called grooming. It's methodical. Intentional. Insidious. And it works. Because love—even false, manipulative love—is a powerful weapon."

She swept her gaze across the room as if judging our reactions. Finally, she sucked air in through her nose. "I'm still researching this plague on our society. And though it is a dark, evil blot on humanity, there is hope. Awareness of the problem is growing, and some churches and faith-based organizations are taking steps to combat the issue. They work with local police to track clues to where these pockets of crime occur."

Fear for Macie gripped me. I gasped for air and pulled in a strangled breath.

Embarrassed, I slunk in my seat, skin crawling as if I'd been violated. Was every eye in the room on me? Then someone else sniffled, and I realized I wasn't the only one grappling with this report.

Ms. Brown must have noticed. She held up both hands as if calming a storm. "I'm sorry if this information is upsetting. The Lord put it on my heart to share with you. I only wanted to raise your awareness of the situation since it's becoming a greater danger by the day."

Elijah shot me a look. His gaze softened, and he raised his hand. "What are we supposed to do?"

"Pray," Ms. Brown said. "Pray for God to work on the hearts of our nation. Our faith offers the hope our world so desperately needs. And pay attention to compromised people around you. Those who have a rough home life or who show signs of abuse. You might notice changes in someone's behavior or symptoms of anger, panic, or phobia." Ms. Brown's voice quieted. "And if you think someone might be a target, find a trusted adult and speak up. Before it's too late."

Tension lay thick in the room.

My mouth soured as my mind battled with this information. I didn't want to believe Macie was in danger. I needed more evidence. I needed to play detective.

On my own.

When the bell rang dismissing us to our classes, I staggered to my feet so fast, dizziness swept me. I stumbled sideways into Elijah.

"Whoa, Dani." He slipped his arm around my waist. "Are you okay?"

His strength steadied me. I regained my balance and squared my shoulders. "Yeah, I'm okay."

As okay as a baby harp seal on its forty-fourth day of abandonment.

CHAPTER FORTY

AFTER THE PRESENTATION

E lijah offered me a piece of gum as we left Ms. Brown's room.

"Thanks." I popped it into my mouth, hoping the minty freshness would overpower my sour breath, which was only slightly better than broccoli breath. I never talked much, but when I did, I didn't want people to turn green and pass out.

"Honestly, are you okay?" He stopped and circled his shoulders as if to shield me. His gesture reminded me of my brother being, well, all big-brother protective of me.

I nodded. "I'm better now. It's just—"

Sucking in air, I stalled for time to put my thoughts together. Should I tell him about Macie? About how the world felt less safe, and I viewed every stranger as a potential predator now? Or would that make me look like a paranoid wuss? Probably best to avoid it for now. "It's the statistics. And the pictures. You know. That's horrifying." I shuddered.

He tucked his hands in the pockets of his jeans while I adjusted my backpack. "I get what you're saying. But I don't think Ms. Brown wanted to scare you. She simply wanted everyone to be aware. We live in a safe community. What's the worst thing you've seen happen?"

"Other than school dances?" I raised an eyebrow. "Poor fashion choices and yesterday's lunch menu."

He didn't need to know I'd actually skipped lunch. That was a whole other issue unrelated to human trafficking.

Elijah mirrored my pose. "If that's all you worry about, I think you're safe."

"Well …" I dragged the word out. "I *am* worried about a fifth-grade girl who lives in my neighborhood. I see her alone a lot. And she's starting to act weird."

"Don't all girls start acting weird around fifth grade?" he asked.

"Very funny." I narrowed my eyes. "Girls aren't the problem. From my experience with my brother Nick, it's the boys who go off the deep end. Their raging testosterone pushes them to butt heads like rams working out their dominance."

"We're all just trying to get attention," he said, straight-faced.

"By acting like idiots?"

"It works." He jerked his head toward an intertwined couple in the hallway. "We might be bullheaded, but aren't girls known for being overly sensitive?"

"That's a stereotype." I smacked him—lightly—in the stomach, just enough to double him over.

He lifted his hands as if offering peace. "Easy! I was joking."

"Me too," I said. I could have stayed sheltered next to Elijah and his laid-back way for the rest of the day, but I'd already wasted too much time. "I need to get to class. Maybe I'll see you later."

I started walking down the corridor, and he fell in step with me. "I gotta ask you something first. You know teenage boys. We eat everything that's not moving. And honestly, we'll even eat some things that are. What was wrong with the lunch menu?"

"They served raw broccoli." I kept my pace steady. "You have no idea how many birthday party photos that vegetable ruined for me as a child."

"You strike me as more of a meat and potatoes type anyway," Elijah said.

"Yeah, but veggies are supposed to help me grow. My main issue is that chocolate is my love language." Spotting my destination ahead, I slowed. "Thanks again for the gum. And the Bible verse." I threw in a sudden thought. "We have a home game tonight if you want to come." Hayden wouldn't mind, would he?

Elijah grimaced. "We have a tournament this weekend. And it's an important one. College scouts will be there. I need to be my best."

"Of course." I stopped in front of my doorway. "No big deal."

"I'll make it some other time," he said.

He was sweet. I shook my head. But what was I doing, inviting him? I didn't want sweet right now. I wanted Hayden with his spicy looks and his even spicier charm. I pushed

Elijah's shoulder before I made a fool of myself. "Get to class. You'll be late."

He shuffled sideways. Then, with a goofy smile, he turned and disappeared down the hallway.

Taking a huff of air, I slipped into my math class. Something about the black and white clarity of equations soothed the agitation still lurking under my skin like a shark's fin. I couldn't let my roller coaster of emotions rule me, not today. Our soccer team needed to win the game tonight, and they needed my focus and stability to do it.

But first, I had to make it through the school day.

Including lunch.

At least this time I packed a PBJ.

Sudden doubt made me whip open my backpack and fish around until my fingers landed on a crumpled brown bag. Only then did I relax.

Yeah, lunch. Then soccer. And all my questions about Macie could wait until I had a chance to talk to her again.

Then maybe I'd know a little more about what was going on.

Overly sensitive. Pfft!

CHAPTER FORTY-ONE

THE GAME

To advertise for the upcoming fall musical, the cast showed up to sing the National Anthem to start our match. The announcer put in a plug before handing over the microphone to Mrs. James.

I was one hundred percent convinced Sol had something to do with the arrangement. True, she had quit the team. But she would have been too excited to hold back, and Coach Hering wasn't one to hold grudges. Coach Lofton, yes, but Lofton wasn't in charge.

After the final note sounded and cheers raised, I lifted a thumbs-up.

When Sol's gaze fell on me, her face lit up—well, lit up even more, because she already wore a quokka-sized smile. Those Australian critters took the best photos on earth. And they were so friendly and fearless, they'd flag down a hunter and beg him for a hug. In other words, they were the Sols of the animal kingdom.

I don't know sign language, but I used gestures to try and communicate a question to my best friend. *Are you going to stay and watch the game?* Although, in all honesty, my movements might have conveyed *You are standing on binoculars.* Or worse, *you are a stiff-backed, beady-eyed, crazy quokka.*

It didn't matter. Sol shook her head and mouthed *sorry* before chasing after her fellow actors.

Still, maybe she'd be free after the game. I made a mental note to text her when we finished. Normally I'd shy away from a trip to Let's Shake on It with a horde of our classmates. But today, the idea appealed to me. Especially after the harsh reality Ms. Brown had painted this morning. Much as I disliked being surrounded by people, her presentation highlighted the importance of community.

While Coach Hering outlined the scouting reports, Coach Lofton folded her arms and glared at the opposing team with all the intensity of a scorpion. Any darker of a look, and no doubt she'd call down a plague from Heaven. Wish I could mimic that ferocity. Might save me from unwanted attention.

When Coach switched into her pregame pep talk and final tips and adjustments, I tuned her out. Stomach tightening, I scanned the crowd for my parents. They should be here by now.

But they weren't. At least, not yet.

My eye muscle spasmed, making it twitch. Maybe they got caught in traffic. Besides, their workloads had been heavy this week. So far, I'd eaten three microwave dinners on my own because of their long hours. And on Thursday morning, I caught them arm-in-arm, slouched over on the couch, asleep. Which was actually cute. I'd left them a note—*Didn't want to wake you. There are leftover egg burritos in the fridge. We didn't have bread for toast. Hope you aren't lack-toast intolerant. Ha-ha.*

I'm sure they appreciated my dad joke. But it would have been nice to see their reaction.

Pushing aside my disappointment, I refocused on Coach.

"Remember, practice patience." Coach swept an arm out. "Patience on offense. No offsides. And patience on defense. Stay in position and in a good stance. Let them make the mistakes—don't try to force it by yourself. That's when you end up overplaying the ball and getting burned."

She thrust her hand into the center, and we piled ours on top. "Team on three. One. Two. Three."

"Team!"

A lone cheerleader broke away from her squad and flipped several back handsprings while our teams took the field. Sparse cheering and loud chattering filled the empty spaces. And then, a solo voice. "Go Dani!"

Startled, I glanced at the sidelines. Jay sat in the front row, waving a stick of licorice at me. My heart quickened, and I waved back. My parents were still no-shows, but at least one person made it to the game on time.

Our teams battled it out the first half. Early on, I picked up a wayward pass in the middle. My quick footwork laid the ball on the line. Reb picked it up on the run and the keeper came out for the ball. Reb cut a side pass to the outside, and I made a break for the ball. From behind, a defender slid hard to the ground, tackling me. We went down, me on top, knocking the wind out of both of us. The ref blew the whistle, pointing to the spot of the foul.

"Good reactions!" Coach bellowed from the sidelines. "Settle down."

Chest heaving a lifeline of oxygen, I climbed to my feet and wiped the sweat off my forehead. I knew who to look for. Reb. We'd done this drill many times.

While the ref eased back, I lined up for the free kick. In the box, players pressed together, jockeying for position.

Concentrate.

Letting out a hiss of air, I took two quick steps and booted the ball.

Reb leaped into action, but her header went wide.

The pace of the game picked up after that as our team fell into a rhythm. Pass forward, back to the keeper, back to the wing, back to the keeper. Pass, press, pass, push, pass, press, pass, push. Our offense applied more pressure, and our back line pushed up.

One minute before halftime, Erika rifled the ball upfield after an inbound toss, and Reb closed in on it. On the give-and-go, she passed out to Wren, who shot it back out. Reb beat the midfielder on the dribble and cut back to open the field.

This time, Reb hit me. I took her pass and battled my defender one-on-one. From the corner of my eye, I saw Wren streak past, a decoy to draw attention. Reb slashed diagonal across the middle. Like we practiced, I clipped the ball, leading Reb toward their keeper, whose only option was to challenge the ball. A lunging block by the goalie deflected the shot, but Reb was too fast on the rebound. A slick twist of her head, and the ball whiskered past the post into the goal. Score!

Reb screamed, rushing up the field with her arms wide to collect high fives and hugs. I lifted fisted hands overhead, hooting my praise, and turned toward the bench.

And stopped dead cold in my tracks.

That was my habit. After a good play on the field, I looked to the bench. For Sol.

Except she wasn't there.

And she wouldn't be there for the rest of my senior season.

Reb's slap on the back snapped me out of my momentary melancholy. "Now that's what I'm talking about," she said. "Wooo!"

I joined her war cry, an outlet for the adrenaline flooding my veins.

We still had another forty-minute half to survive.

The rest of the game went by in a grueling, sweat-inducing, diving, falling, scratching, grabbing, shoving, kicking, grunting, slamming blur of action. My lungs worked harder than bagpipes, and I pushed myself until my muscles threatened to tear. For my team. To reach our goal.

To qualify for playoffs.

I played with a lot of heart, but absolutely no Sol. And the odd void only put me more on edge, making me fiercer and more reckless.

In the spirit of old routines, when the game ended with a 1–0 victory, I passed out granola bars and collected empty water bottles discarded on the ground. Players and parents and students gathered in clusters near the bleachers, too invested in their animated conversations to help.

When I finished, I searched the crowd for my parents again, spotting them on the far end of the announcer's table talking to Reb's parents.

Something stirred in my chest, both buoyant and wounded.

They'd made it after all, and that spot reserved for family filled with an aching comfort. Who cared if they'd missed the opening ceremony or maybe even the first half? They came.

Mom noticed me and waved. As I made my way over to her, she leaned over and said something to Reb's mom and then walked in my direction. She and dad met me halfway. "That was an impressive game." She had dark circles under her eyes, but they still managed to sparkle. "You really stepped up your efforts. Reb's mom said if you win two more games, you'll seal a playoff bid for your team."

"Probably." I side-hugged my dad. "We still have five games left in the season, but they're teams we've already beaten. Even if we lose one or two, we should make it, if only as an at-large invite. But we'll have a better ranking if we win."

Mom frowned. "Well, that takes all the tension out of it, doesn't it?" She glanced around. "Where's Sol?"

"I told you she quit, remember?" I pressed my lips together as we turned and walked toward the parking lot. "Weren't you listening?"

Mom tapped her palm on her forehead. "Right, sorry. I have so much on my mind lately." She chuckled and elbowed my dad. "Did I mention I need a vacation?"

He grinned, hefting his car keys. "Once or twice."

My ears pricked when we got closer to the dwindling groups of remaining students. Things like *party at Michael's house* or indiscernible snatches of conversation reached me. And I didn't have the nerve to ask for details. Cheeks burning, I ducked my head and slipped my hoodie on.

"Honey, are you going to Let's Shake on It with your friends?"

It took me a moment to realize Mom was talking to me.

"Um. No." I licked my lips. "I'm tired and sticky. Maybe you and Dad and I can watch a movie and eat popcorn instead."

"I have a report to file." Dad frowned. "But you girls can hang out and have fun."

I gaped at him. Who files a stupid report on a Friday night? And how could a report possibly compare to spending time with your family?

Nostrils flaring, I clicked my jaw shut. Tightened it. Why should I care? This introvert liked her alone time, after all.

Before I could turn away, Mom grabbed my hand and squeezed it. "I'd like that. And I'll try not to fall asleep. See you at home?"

Swallowing hard, my eyes tracked Reb and Erika as they piled into a Jeep with a couple of junior boys. "Yeah. Sure." I squeezed her hand back. "See you at home."

CHAPTER FORTY-TWO

DEAR SOUL

When the movie started, Dad buried himself in the office with the door closed.

Mom fell asleep on the couch halfway through the popcorn.

And I paused the movie, tucked a blanket around her shoulders, and cleaned up the mess. It was a chick flick anyway, a romantic comedy, not my favorite genre. But since Mom had picked it, I didn't want her to miss it. Her intentions were good, but her body couldn't physically keep her promise of "us" time. I scrawled a few words on a yellow sticky note and stuck it on the ottoman where she'd find it. *Sleep well. Love you!*

On my way upstairs to my room, I tucked my earbuds in and pulled up my music library. After selecting the soundtrack from *Inception,* I laid back on my bed and scrolled through my social media accounts. Hayden hadn't posted anything, but Sol had posted a video of her cast singing the National Anthem filmed by someone in the bleachers, and a behind-the-scenes look at her theater rehearsal. Should I shoot her a text? Shaking my head, I dismissed the idea. She'd reach out if she had time.

And Elijah—and therefore Hayden—had a tournament in the morning. No way I'd text either one or disturb their rest.

The easiest choice? Do nothing tonight. Recharge. Start tomorrow fresh and new. With the old tunes lulling my eyes closed, I let my mind wander.

Jay disappeared after the first half. Hayden had texted good wishes and Elijah had sent a Bible verse, but neither one came to the game. Sol only waved across the field. And my parents arrived late. What did a girl have to do around here to get some respect?

Remembering my commitment to Sol, I rolled onto my stomach. I like to keep my promises. She'd sent me a link to access the *Heart and Soul* email submissions and instructed me to pick two each day to answer. One heart, one soul.

"Or do a bunch of them in a batch," she'd said. "That way, you can invest an hour creating several days' worth of material and then schedule them to post during the week."

"Is that what you do?" I had asked.

She'd laughed. "You know me. I'm too spontaneous for that. Now, remember, I'm an icon. Don't make me look bad."

I smirked at her lighthearted joke.

After clicking the file, I skimmed the entries. Most of the heart ones dealt with boyfriend or girlfriend relationships. I blew out a snort. *Yeah, like I'm an expert in that.* The soul ones dealt more with moral dilemmas. That was more my style. I opened one at random.

Dear Soul,

My older sister drives me to school, but she's a horrible driver. She tailgates slower cars. She screams at drivers, and when I remind her they can't hear her, she flips them off. She doesn't use her turn signal and rolls through stop signs. She even handles the steering wheel with her knees or asks me to steer so she can text or put on makeup or eat while she's driving. She's a disaster waiting to happen, and I don't have time to be killed in an accident or road rage incident. I've asked her to be more careful, but she says I should be thankful for a free ride. Help!

Signed, Horrified on the Highway

I cracked my knuckles and grinned. Now this I could handle. *Dear Horrified on the Highway, take the bus.*

After pressing the publish button, I leaned back. Hiding in my room, I welcomed this distraction.

The work preoccupied me, and I lost track of time finishing off a week's worth of entries. When I found myself yawning, I shut down my computer and turned off the light. Darkness, cool and comforting, blanketed the room. One by one, my muscles, still sore from the rigor of the game, relaxed. Outside, a cricket chirped its lonely tune.

Sighing, I rolled over and checked the clock. 12:47. Not bad. Like a rebel, I'd stayed up past curfew on a Friday night. Who needed to hang out at Let's Shake on It to have fun?

CHAPTER FORTY-THREE

SURPRISE

As soon as I woke up Saturday morning, I texted both Sol and Hayden. Something simple, wishing them good luck at their events and letting them know I'd prayed for them last night. After a moment's hesitation, I texted Elijah too. Sol texted back a heart emoji, Hayden sent a winking face, and Elijah sent a grin. Not much, but enough to get me going.

The smell of buttery pancakes lured me to the kitchen. I padded to the table and slipped into a chair. Mom swayed by the stove wearing her housecoat and slippers, evidence she'd moved from the couch to her bedroom at some point last night. Instrumental '80s music played on portable speakers, and she danced with all the awkward grace of a hip-hop artist with limited flexibility, no imagination, and a broken leg. She cocked the spatula in her hand like a microphone. "Yeah, yeah, yeah," she sang.

I coughed politely and she spun around. "Oh! Dani! You're up." Her cheeks flushed. "Did you sleep well?"

I lifted an eyebrow. "Apparently not as well as you did."

She laughed and flipped a cake. "Are you hungry?"

"Can an ostrich run faster than a horse?" I asked. "Yes!"

"One order coming up." Humming, Mom leveraged three pancakes on a plate and set them in front of me.

Chocolate chip. My favorite. So warm and melty, I could eat them without syrup.

I grabbed the syrup anyway and drizzled it on top. "You're awful perky."

"That's because I know something you don't." She set another plate beside me, stacked four high. "I'm dying to tell you, but I'll let your father do the honors."

Hmmm. A mystery. What could Dad have up his sleeve?

While Mom went to the fridge and grabbed the orange juice, I sectioned off a bite of pancake and shoved it in my mouth. "He's not working this morning?"

"He is not," my dad announced, entering the kitchen like a king. He lowered himself next to me at the table. "He is, in fact, eating a healthy breakfast with his lovely family and then packing his bags for a one-week vacation, which leaves bright and early Monday morning. We'll travel to a hotel tomorrow so we won't be late to the launch."

My jaw dropped. "What?"

With a wide smile, Mom handed me a glass. "We're going on a cruise."

Taking the drink from her, I frowned. "A cruise?"

"Of course," Dad said. "Your mother kept telling me she needed a vacation, and I finally found an opening in my schedule and snagged a bargain deal for the trip. I decided to treat her—to treat us—to celebrate our anniversary."

"Best gift ever." Beaming, Mom handed Dad a plate and joined us at the table.

Lowering my gaze, I pushed a chunk of cake around my plate, drowning it in maple syrup. "What about soccer?"

Mom set her hand on my arm. "I already checked with your coaches. They weren't thrilled, but they didn't say no either. Especially when I reminded them you'd be back in time for playoffs."

Letting my fork clatter to the plate, I drew a sharp breath. *"If* we qualify. Without a few more solid wins, there's no guarantee."

"Coach Hering said even if you missed one game and they lost, you could secure a berth by winning the next one," Dad said.

I scowled. "Coach Hering probably hated the idea but knew she couldn't stop you. And Coach Lofton will have me running wind sprints until I puke when I get back."

Mom's face dropped. Tiny wrinkles formed around her eyes. "I thought it would work out."

I threw my napkin on the table. "You should have asked me."

"We wanted to surprise you," Mom said, her voice rising an octave.

"Oh, I'm surprised all right." Heat rose in my cheeks. "Because of the timing. It may fit your schedule, but it doesn't fit mine. It's my senior year. Every season, my soccer team ends up third in our conference and doesn't qualify for playoffs. But not this year. This year we've got the skills and the experience to go far. Couldn't you wait for the season to end? Choose a different week to take off?"

"Your dad's schedule is packed, and he pays the bills," Mom said.

Dad tilted his head. "And did I mention *bargain deal?*"

"Did I mention *should have asked me?*" I shot back.

A million thoughts pillaged my head as my parents gaped at me. I knew what they were thinking. Nick was the loud, opinionated, difficult one. The badger with an attitude. I was the calm one. The easy one. The do-gooder. The compliant mouse who never spoke up. Where had this outburst come from?

I fisted my hands. *Figure it out. Please!*

Mom cleared her throat. "I'm sorry, dear. The tickets are nonrefundable."

"You don't get it!" I pushed away from the table and stood. "We can always go on a cruise. But if I fail to qualify for playoffs this time because I'm out sunbathing on the beaches of some seaport slurping down fruity drinks with umbrellas in them, I'll never have another chance." I folded my arms. "Ask Nick to go instead. I'm not abandoning my team."

My parents exchanged a glance.

Mom reached a hand toward me. "Honey, I'm not sure Nick—"

"He'd be fine with it. He'd love it." I gritted my teeth. "Might do him some good."

"I hate to pull him out of his classes," Dad said. "He needs that structure. Besides, you'd be stuck here by yourself for an extended time. We don't get back until a week from Monday." Dad frowned and glanced at Mom again. "I'm not sure I like that idea."

"I can take care of myself. And you can watch me." As if that was much different than what I was doing anyway. "Remember, you've got the phone tracker on me."

When Mom lowered her head and blinked, I realized I might have shouted that last part. Sweat broke on my upper lip. I hadn't meant to hurt her feelings or to sound ungrateful. But I already lost Sol. Hayden didn't want me for a girlfriend. Soccer was the one lifeline I had left. And now, they were asking me to miss one of the final games of my senior year because they couldn't wait a month to go on a cruise?

Taking a deep breath, I softened my tone. "I know it's been a crazy busy school year so far. Nick's trauma, your work, my classes and applying for colleges. And I love that you want to do something fun to balance it out." I paused, hesitant to go on. Frustration compelled me. "But did you consider my needs at all when you planned?"

The '80s music continued to jam in the background, its upbeat rhythm oddly out of place with the current mood. I walked to the counter and yanked the plug.

Mom's brows pinched and Dad's face lengthened. Their silence screamed in the void.

I leaned both arms on the table. "I like the idea of a vacation. Honestly. But I still don't want to miss a single minute of soccer. I would love to go on a cruise, but I'll blame myself if the team doesn't make playoffs, and I'll regret not being there to celebrate if they do. I can't go."

Dad rose, scraping his chair on the tiled floor. "This is not a negotiation."

Mom put a hand on his arm and locked her gaze with mine. "I think Dani's simply expressing how she feels right now. After all, we did spring it on her."

Her intervention robbed Dad of whatever else he might say. Instead, he worked his jaw and clenched his fists.

Watching him made my bravado wilt. Maybe I was acting selfishly. I studied the floor for a moment, then hardened my resolve. "I'm taking Betty to the empty lot. I still need to work on my Cruyff Turn."

"But your breakfast," Mom said.

"I'm not hungry."

Dad roughed a hand over his face. "Give me thirty, forty-five minutes tops and I'll go with you."

My heart twisted. When Nick and I were little, Dad kicked the ball around with us in the backyard all the time. He never asked us to wait for him. He just came. Still—

"I'll meet you there," I said, grabbing my housekeys. I stopped at the doorway. "Sorry for not helping you clean the dishes today, Mom."

I bolted before I could hear her answer.

CHAPTER FORTY-FOUR

THE EMPTY LOT

Physical exertion always allowed me to vent. Ball touches had the added bonus of developing my balance, agility, and speed. I chose a mindless, repetitious drill to channel my energy. Setting Betty on the ground, I used the outside of my right foot to push the ball a step to the side of me. Angling to use the inside of the same foot, I tapped Betty back the way she came.

It wasn't like I was mad at my parents. I loved them. But somehow, they had hyper-focused on their own challenges, forgetting we were a team.

In one fluid motion, I switched feet, doing the same move

in the opposite direction. I kept the ball close, bending my knees and leaning slightly over it to maintain control. *What would* Heart and Soul *say about the situation?*

As I searched my mind, letting my muscles shift to automatic, a memory surfaced. Mom, at the breakfast table, praying. As was her habit.

I had interrupted her routine that day, rushing through the kitchen trying to find my shin guards. She'd looked so sad, much older than I remembered her, and it made me pull up short. "Mom. Are you okay?"

"No." Her lip trembled. "It's hard when the first bird leaves the nest. I miss your brother."

Nick had only been at college for a full month. The house was definitely cleaner without him in it. And quieter. And duller. I could not rival the way he filled a room.

I had sat down next to her. Handed her a napkin to use as a tissue. "It'll be okay. You always tell me God holds the future. Listen to your own advice. Nick's in good hands."

"True." She wiped moisture from her face and sniffed loudly. "But I worry about him. He's always so reckless, barging ahead without thinking about the consequences." She smiled, despite her tears. "Offsides. Except in life instead of on the field. I have this awful feeling in my gut. Like something's wrong. I'm waiting for a phone call to tell me he's in trouble again."

"I don't think colleges call," I said. "He's nineteen now, remember? An adult."

Mom's face fell, and I put my arm around her. Her worry made it hard for *me* to admit I worried about him too. I had to be strong. For her. So I'd told her he'd be fine. I'd pretended I wasn't bothered by the empty bedroom, the lack of noise from his overly loud speakers playing rap music, or the hole left by his missing off-color jokes at the dinner table.

"He'll be back this summer, and everything will be fine," I'd told Mom.

Except Nick hadn't come home.

At least, not the strong, unstoppable, athletic superstar Nick I knew.

The college blamed the accident on a hazing incident gone wrong and suspended him from the soccer team indefinitely. Luckily, no permanent damage had been done to the other player, and the freshman had transferred to another school.

But not Nick. That ruling stripped him of his superpower—soccer. Reduced him to an ordinary, problematic student with too much energy to burn and nowhere to burn it.

That was two years ago. He still avoided coming home during breaks.

Nick's broken dreams went to show you never knew when the thing you loved most would be snatched away.

And now, pieces of my heart slipped through my fingers like sand. Sol, tied up in a fairy-tale musical. Hayden, a friend, maybe more. And me lost somewhere in between. And now I might miss out on soccer too. What else could I lose?

My feet moved faster and faster, and tears streamed down my face.

God, I don't understand my anxiety. Why is it so hard to accept this gift my parents are offering? In the grand scheme of life, this time loss seems a minor inconvenience. Help me sort out my emotions.

If I expected an instant answer, I didn't get it. Not even a sense of peace. My thoughts were a buzzing beehive angered to have their home of comfort uprooted.

CHAPTER FORTY-FIVE

MACIE RETURNS

Thirty-seven minutes had passed, and still no sign of Dad. Chest heaving, I settled on one of the broken steps that remained on the lot and cradled Betty between my knees.

He'd come. He had to. Like me, he kept his promises.

Not always on time, and not always the way you expected, but he kept them.

Squeezing my eyes shut, I pinched the bridge of my nose. What was wrong with me, lashing out like that this morning? Maybe I was more like my brother than I thought.

My shirt clung to me, sweat exorcising the toxins in my system. I wished, not for the first time, that I'd had the foresight to grab a bottle of water.

When the sound of footsteps on the sidewalk pricked my ears, I sucked in a deep breath. *Dad.*

I raised my head. But it wasn't Dad. It was Macie, her nose and racoon eyes buried in a cell phone, trouncing down the street with—

Wait—who?

I squinted. Macie told me she was a fifth grader. The boy with her looked to be around Nick's age. I studied the way she clutched the cell phone and how he stuck close to her side.

So maybe the guy was a cousin or an older brother—possibly a troublemaker—that just gave his favorite relative a new toy.

Or maybe he was a human trafficker who already had his hooks in her.

Yeah, right. Out in the open like that.

Even I wasn't dumb enough for that move.

No, I couldn't use the guy as an excuse to avoid what I needed to do. I hadn't treated Macie well. I had to make things right between us and then I had to warn her of the danger she might be in if she continued her isolation. Steeling myself, I strode forward and waved. "Macie!"

Macie lifted her head. Her eyes widened for a moment, then she looked away. "What do you want?"

"I want to apologize. For last week." I adjusted Betty on my hip. "I was having a bad day, and I took it out on you."

"I'm fine." Keeping her eyes on the ground, Macie bit her lip.

I tilted my head. "You didn't seem fine when you left. And that was my fault."

"I said I'm fine." Macie stiffened her back. "I know who my real friends are. I don't need your—"

Macie used language that quickly took our conversation downhill.

Stunned, I stepped back.

Macie turned and gazed at her companion. The adoration in her eyes made my skin crawl. As if in slow motion, I zeroed in on his face. Older than I thought. Early thirties? I glanced between them and then at Macie's phone. Brand new. Expensive. A necklace flashed on her skin, something I hadn't noticed last time. She wore makeup, more than a fifth grader needed, for sure. And the body language—it was clear who controlled the relationship.

Memories of our last UCA meeting came crashing back. My stomach churned. Suspicion seeped through my veins like the venom of a copperhead snake.

My first impression was right. Trey had to be a trafficker.

If only I could prove it.

Schooling my emotions, I turned to the man and took a risk. "You must be Trey. Macie mentioned you."

"Yeah?" His face clouded.

Confirmation number one. He was Trey. *Her only friend.*

I hugged Betty, thinking. How could I get Macie away from this guy? "Macie, do you want to stay with me and play soccer?"

Macie's eyes flashed. "I don't need your stupid game."

"Of course. I understand. Not after how I acted." I licked my lips, gaze darting between them. They oozed hostility. I'd seen the look on Nick before, one night when he didn't get to go to a party his junior year. Despite everything that could go wrong, he could not be reasoned with. Neither would Macie.

Numbness crept through me, and I took another step

back. What could I do? Call the police? With only suspicions and no proof? "Maybe I'll see you around sometime, Macie."

She sneered. "Don't hold your breath."

Helpless, I watched the two turn and waltz back toward Macie's house. Or maybe waltzing wasn't the right word. Swagger? Stride? Something that said, "I don't give a—"

Shut down. I pressed a hand to my forehead. *Shut down that line of thought.*

Maybe I was jumping to conclusions. Imagining things because of all the crazy human trafficking facts Ms. Brown had planted in my brain.

I lowered my hand, willing it to stop shaking. Stop overreacting. The guy must be younger than I thought. Kids always tried to look older. Besides, Macie didn't appear to be in any danger. Who was I to accuse, to point the finger? "Mind your own business. Leave me alone. I'm fine." That's what Nick would have told me. And I wasn't calling the police on him.

But Nick had needed someone watching out for him, hadn't he? Someone to save him from his own stupidity. So I could keep an eye on Macie. Watch. Observe. Dig around a little. I pulled a shaking breath and checked my watch again. Fifty-three minutes. And Dad had said—

Two hundred yards down the road, my father jogged into view.

He'd come.

A release of adrenaline sent a sweep of light-headedness through me. Fighting tears, I ran to him.

His forehead wrinkled. "Dani, what's wrong?"

I blubbered my whole story out. Ms. Brown's presentation at UCA. How I'd seen red flags with Macie. How I mistreated her. Her change in behavior. My suspicions about Trey.

Dad listened, his mouth in a straight line.

When I'd emptied all my fears, he sucked in a breath. "Well, this Macie girl sounds a lot like Nick. Impulsive. Moody. Kids go through emotional upheaval like this sometimes."

My stomach dropped. Dad planted doubt in my mind. Maybe because I didn't want to believe Macie was a victim. I wanted to be wrong. I wanted my dad's simple explanation to be right.

But I couldn't shake my gut feeling.

"What about this guy she's hanging out with? How do you explain that?"

Dad pinched his lips. "That is odd."

"Then what if it's not hormones? What if she's really in danger?"

He put a hand on my shoulder. "Would it make you feel better if I told you I know Macie's dad?"

My heart lifted. "You do?"

Dad nodded. "He works at a car dealership. I met him when I took the Mazda in for repairs last month. We got to talking when I found out he lived down the street. Single man with custody of Macie. He seemed nice. Doesn't take good care of his lawn, but that's not a sin. I'll stop by after work on Monday and let him know your concerns. Find out what he knows about this Trey guy."

A lump formed in my throat, and I lowered myself to the curb. "You mean, when you get back from the cruise."

Dad winced, squatting next to me. "Yes, as soon as possible. I promise. In the meantime, I brought you a water bottle. Mom said you left without one."

Accepting it, I sloshed water around in my mouth and then spat it out. The spit carried away a hint of the lingering foul taste. In the security of my dad's care, some of my misgivings bled away. We lived in a safe neighborhood where the worst things that happened involved ice cream, broccoli, or the degradation of well-trimmed lawns due to dandelion outbreaks.

"Thanks." I took another swallow. "I think I'm dehydrated."

"Then we should probably go home." Dad touched his palm to my forehead. "Can't have you overheating." He let his shoulders droop, as if disappointed he would not get to juggle with me, but he quickly hitched them back up again. "Need a piggyback ride?"

I took a long swig and then capped the lid. "Think you can lift me?"

"You're still my little girl." He stood and offered me a hand.

Grasping it, I let him pull me to my feet. My weight pulled him off balance, but he recovered. "Five-nine and 145 pounds of pure muscle isn't exactly little. Besides, what about Betty?"

He snagged Betty from my arms, then bent and signaled for me to hop on his back. I did, and he stumbled about five steps before dropping my ball and allowing me to slide off. "Okay! You're right. But I really wanted to pull that off," he said.

"I wanted you to pull it off too." Smiling, I picked up my soccer ball and fell in step with him. Our shoes scuffed the sidewalk, and an occasional dog barked in the distance. Sometimes, I think people shy away from silence because they fear what they might find in the void. But for me, words often got in the way. I let actions show how much I cared. For me, Dad showing up was enough. The fact he'd go to bat for Macie meant a lot too.

I reciprocated his peace offering by linking an arm through his.

As we rounded the corner toward home, Dad finally cleared his throat. "Look, I'm sorry I was late, but I want you to know, I heard you. At breakfast. And you're right. I had checked with your coaches, but I should have checked with you about missing soccer games before making plans."

For once, I missed the comfort of being invisible. Hearing Dad's apology almost overwhelmed me. As far as I knew, he'd never apologized to Nick. "It was a nice idea," I said, putting as much genuine gratitude into my voice as possible.

"Part of the reason it took me so long to get out here is I was on hold with a travel agent, trying to change the dates," he continued. "I wanted to show up at the lot with everything solved. I'd be the hero."

"You're still my hero. Even if it didn't work out." I quirked an eyebrow. He had to know that, right?

He shook his head. "Do you know how many fees are involved when you update an itinerary?"

I snorted. "Do I want to know?"

"No." He paused by our mailbox. "Let's just say it got so pricey and complicated, I started thinking about what you said. About inviting Nick instead of you."

My muscles stiffened. Hope, or a tiny seed mimicking it, sparked in me. "And?"

"We didn't part on the best terms, you know." Dad raised his chin, but not before I saw the pain in his eyes. "The boy needs to take more responsibility for his actions."

"But?"

Dad roughed a hand over his face. "I was hard on him. But this might be an opportunity to square things between us. He's my kid. And I love him." The last phrase came out with a hitch in his voice.

I slipped my fingers into his hand and searched his face. I'd never seen broken in my dad. I'd seen only his strength. "He loves you too, Dad." Couldn't he tell by the way Nick always sought his approval? And couldn't Nick tell by Dad's boundaries that he cared?

Men.

Dad squeezed my fingers and released them. "Yeah. Well. Anyway. I left him a message. But I wanted you to know, either way, you're off the hook. We'll save up and book another trip in the summer. One that won't interfere with soccer."

"And you're okay with that?" I asked.

He shrugged. "You'll be on your own, but we can still talk every day." He held up a hand before I could react. "You've got the tracking app on your phone. We'll be following you while we're gone. Just in case."

"Thanks." Like a humpback whale being lifted from the water, the weight of conflict lifted from my shoulders.

Now, if only Nick could find the same relief.

And Macie could stay out of trouble.

I pressed my lips together as I closed the front door behind me. How did Trey fit into the picture?

And Nick's voice echoed in my head. *None of your business.*

CHAPTER FORTY-SIX

DEPARTURE

On Sunday, we skipped church because my parents left early to pick up Nick from campus. After staying overnight, they would head to the port to load the ship.

Not that it had been an easy sell. On the initial call to Nick, Mom and Dad had the phone on speaker so they both could chime in. That also meant I could overhear the conversation. After three minutes—an eternity—of awkward small talk about the weather, Mom invited him.

Nick's voice had come clipped and tight. I imagined his face clouding over when he made his excuse, a good one, that he had classes and assignments due, so he couldn't make it. But I had come prepared and stepped forward. "Remember when you texted me this? 'I wish Dad would give me a second chance.' Nick … here's your chance."

The line had gone silent then. Mom tensed, her eyes welling. Dad worked his jaw, his gaze downcast. And I held my breath until my chest ached.

Finally, Nick had said, in a strangled voice, "If I agree to come, can we have some ground rules?"

The rest of the discussion was a blur for me. My heart swelled thinking about my role in a potential reconciliation. Maybe they'd talk, find common ground, work out their differences, and return home with smiles on their faces.

Although it was equally possible that unless he'd changed, the rebel son would ditch my parents at the first opportunity to go scuba diving with a group of bikini-clad girls. That, or he'd hang out with the crew and prank other passengers— possibly hiding broccoli under their pillows. Or he just might snag a costume and go high-kicking across the stage.

All I knew was that my parents were on their way to a cruise with Nick.

Now that the conversation was over, what could I do?

Pray. Even when I did not see the results I wanted, having a brother like Nick trained me well in that particular discipline. Other than that, I'd just have to wait and see what happened.

Besides, I had other things on my mind. Macie. Sol. And Hayden. Not necessarily in that order. You can guess who came first.

Exhausted and oddly content at the end of the day, I spent a quiet evening finishing my homework and binge-watching old *Star Trek* shows.

When I picked up Sol for school Monday morning, she was in a good mood.

"'Dear Horrified on the Highway, take the bus.'" Sol threw her hands in the air and laughed. "That's either the most brilliant advice on the planet or sadly lacking in any practical application. Order me a muffin this time, would ya?"

Sol's approval rang in my ears. Energized, I placed our Coffee, Tea, and Glee order and edged forward. "Glad you liked it. I went through the submissions folder and picked a few easy ones. Wanted to make sure I was doing it right before trying a harder one."

"Well, you're doing great. You have no idea what a relief it is to have that blog off my plate until after the musical." Sol released a yawn that set off a chain reaction in me.

"I have some idea," I said. "Now that I've added the blog to my to-do list, I spend all my waking hours thinking up witty comebacks to pet-peevy situations and passionate solutions to relationship woes." I paused and smirked. "Not. I'm kidding. I actually don't think about your blog much at all."

Sol grinned. "Love it. The sign of a true friend. Doing what they can to help so you can do what you must. Just stay out of the creepy file. Trust me." As her jaw stretched again, her words came out garbled. "How's the soccer season?"

"We're looking good. Reb earned herself another hat trick. Three goals in one game—she loves to shoot. Too bad you didn't see her victory dance." I fished around in my purse and pulled out my wallet. "Do you miss soccer?"

"Of course." She lowered her gaze and twisted her fingers together.

I handed my credit card to the woman at the window. "Maybe you can come back for playoffs. Which we are totally going to qualify for after this week."

Sol shook her head. "Coach Hering would never allow me to come back. And can you imagine what Coach Lofton would say?"

"She'd fold her arms and grunt." I took my receipt.

"Which would translate as 'oh no you don't, you little flat-footed prima donna Cinderella who runs away from the ball instead of using her head and sticking around.'" Sol quirked an eyebrow. "Or something like that."

Laughing, I handed her our food. "Sounds about right."

"What else have I missed since I disappeared into the woods?" She sniffed her coffee. "Give me the CliffNotes' version of your weekend."

So I told her about the cruise and having the house to myself for the week.

And since she'd brought it up, I told her about my touchy encounter with Macie, and how I worried about the guy she was with, and how my dad was going to take care of it when he got back from the cruise. "But am I imagining things? About Trey?"

"You've never seen the guy before?" Sol asked, nibbling on her muffin.

"No. I see an older man with an abnormal interest in Macie."

Sol frowned. "This could be serious. In our play, just like in the fairy tale, the wolf character is seductive and equivocal."

"Equivocal?" I clicked my tongue. "In normal English, please."

"Misleading." Sol rubbed her chin. "He beguiles Red Riding Hood into a trap."

"Sol!" I barked.

She waved vaguely. "Captivates. Entrances. Charms."

"In other words, the wolf is a friendly guy pretending to be something he's not to trick Red." As soon as the words left my mouth, my stomach clenched.

Jay. What if I was right about a predator operating in our community, but I pegged the wrong guy?

I gulped air, thoughts racing. No, Jay was a friend of Coach Campbell. That accounted for his presence on the field. I'm the one who planted myself in the bleachers. Besides, he had too many stories about their high school glory days to be—what was it? Equivocal? True, his conversation might be too open and not enough shut of the mouth, but excessive talking wasn't a crime. In fact, it made him more personable.

"Oh, Dani!" Sol shuddered. "I'm glad your dad is going to take care of Macie. I'd throw a relationship like that straight into my creepy file. Macie is lucky you noticed. Have you considered talking to Ms. Brown about it too? Or Coach?"

Frowning, I nodded. I had considered it. I ruled out my coaches. My experience showed them reluctant to act until faced with hard evidence. But I could reach out to Ms. Brown. She was the logical choice since she brought human trafficking up in the first place.

Still, the topic was uncomfortable. I sectioned the unease into a safe spot in my brain and changed the subject.

"Are you still practicing your lines during lunch?" I took a sip of tea to cover the conflict on my face.

"Yeah," Sol said. "But hang in there. Only a few more weeks, and things will get back to normal. I promise."

The hot liquid scalded my throat on the way down. I choked and covered my mouth. Another day facing the social scene alone.

I slogged through the rest of the day. Ms. Brown had a substitute in her room—another talker who informed me that Ms. Brown's mother had taken ill, so she'd be out the rest of the week tending to the elderly woman's needs.

Discouraged, I ate lunch in my car and listened to a melancholy Mozart playlist. I got a few flirty texts sent from Hayden, giving me a much-needed distraction, and Elijah texted me a soccer meme, good for a laugh.

Only at soccer practice did my tension leave and my thoughts become laser-focused. Toward the end, we divided into two teams lined up outside the eighteen-yard box on opposite sides of the goal. Both coaches served three balls in fast succession to the team diagonal from them. A long one for a player to take a power shot, a shorter one for a finesse shot, and one close to the goal in the air for a header. The only way to stay in the game was to get at least one of the shots in the goal. If you missed all three, you were out. If you made two, you could pull one of your eliminated teammates back into the game. Make all three, and everyone on your team who was out came back in. The last team standing won.

It was crazy. It was fun. It was exhausting. And by the end, even though worry over Macie still lingered, the hole in my heart from missing Sol didn't feel quite as big.

Still buzzing from the workout, I stopped by Hayden's practice when mine ended. I wasn't alone. Jay sat nearby, leaning on the bleachers. And since I'd already worked out that he was safe, I appreciated his company.

CHAPTER FORTY-SEVEN

CONSCIOUS DECISION

"Licorice?" Jay leaned over, offering his pack.

I accepted it. "Thanks."

"How was practice?" He bit off a chunk of his own piece and rolled it with his tongue. "Looked like you girls were working hard."

"Yeah. The season is almost over, and I think we'll make playoffs." I sucked on the tip, unwilling to eat too fast. "My parents will miss the last few games though. They went on a cruise for their anniversary."

"Good for them." He narrowed his eyes. "I hope you're taking extra precautions to stay safe while they're gone."

His question brought back some of my misgivings about Macie. Not trusting my voice, I held my stick in front of me, waiting to see if it would droop to one side or stay up straight. When it didn't move, I gave in and nipped the top off, holding the chunk in my mouth while it softened from bitter to sweet. "I'll be okay. I mean, I'm a little nervous being alone, but I keep the doors locked. And I've got a taser. And my parents keep tabs on me." I held up my phone.

"Smart." He grunted. "But if you're still worried about it, you can take my phone for backup. Just until your parents return. You can never be too cautious."

"I can't do that. How are you going to make calls?" I asked.

He shrugged. "It's okay. I have an extra phone at home I can activate. And if it makes you feel safer, I'd be proud to share."

I considered the offer. He had a point. I mean, what if I forgot to plug in my phone and the battery died and I needed to call 9-1-1 because a stranger was banging on my door in the middle of the night?

"Okay. Are you sure?"

Holding out his device, Jay inclined his head. "Of course. Just keep it charged and throw it in your bag or something. Give it back when your folks return." Licorice twitched from his lips when he spoke.

"Thanks." I tucked it into my backpack.

Jay refocused on the boys' practice. "You still hanging out with that Hayden guy?"

"We're friends." I sighed, thinking about how much more I wanted than that. "But yeah. I hope we can hang out soon."

He grunted again, strangely less talkative than usual. Not that I minded.

A whistle blew, and the coach signaled the end of practice. I checked my watch. Fifteen minutes early. Then again, the sky was darkening sooner these days. Fireflies already winked on and off, drifting like lazy Christmas lights.

"Time for me to be going." Jay stood and stretched. "You'll be careful with your parents gone?"

I nodded.

"And keep that backup phone with you."

"Of course," I said.

He scanned the field again. "Good."

My phone buzzed, and I fished it out.

A message from Hayden. *Want to review the science homework with me tonight? Remember, I got a seventy on the last test. I need help! Let's Shake on It is open until eleven.*

Eyes wide, I lifted my head to see Hayden looking my way with his duffle bag slung over one shoulder. He held up his phone and pointed.

My jaw dropped. Hayden wanted to go out again and since my parents were gone, I didn't need to worry about curfew.

Jay lifted his chin. Was he trying to peek?

I tucked my phone away. It buzzed in my pocket, as if eager for a response.

I wanted to go, but I probably shouldn't push my luck. With the phone tracker on, my parents would know if I went out after practice. But no way I would go out without a phone. What if I got in an accident?

I'd have to say no.

Unless I invited Hayden over. The tracker would say I was home but wouldn't reveal who else was with me. We'd have the whole place to ourselves.

That brought a different danger. If Nick's experience taught me anything, it was that it was easier to avoid temptation than resist it. Something else occurred to me. Jay's phone gave me another option.

I could drop my phone off at home so the tracker stayed there and take Jay's phone to Let's Shake on It. And why not? What harm would it do? I would be finishing homework, after all, not acting like some lawbreaking juvenile.

I glanced at Hayden again and flashed him a thumbs-up. He smiled and started walking my way.

My heart pounded, and my throat went dry. What was this new feeling? Fear? Or excitement? Maybe both? Is this how Nick felt when he took risks?

Jay interrupted my thoughts. "Take care of yourself, Dani."

"I will." I dismissed him with a wave. "I'll catch you later."

"Or maybe I'll catch you." Jay tipped his maroon cap, stuck his hands in his pockets, and strolled off.

Just in time too. Hayden closed the distance between us.

"I got your message," I said. "And I'd love to go. Is it all right if we drop my car off at home first? I'd like to ride with you if that's okay."

"Yeah." He smiled. "I'll follow you home."

I held up the keys. "See you in ten minutes?"

"I'll be right behind you," Hayden said. He walked me to my car.

With dusk falling rapidly now, I flicked on my lights and pulled out. In seconds, Hayden's headlights shone in my rear-view mirror.

When I got home, I parked the car in the garage. Hayden idled in the driveway while I dashed inside and set my phone on the kitchen table. I sent a quick text to my parents saying I was doing homework, I didn't want to be bothered, good-night, and I loved them. Then I grabbed my backpack with books and tucked my new phone in the front pouch. My parents could have peace of mind thinking me safe at home, and with Jay's phone, I could go out and still have a way of contacting help if I needed it.

At least, that's what I kept telling myself.

As I turned to leave, my phone lit up. I had to check it. *Love you too. Nick says hi.*

My stomach tightened. I pushed the device away and rushed to the door. With my hand on the doorknob, I paused, breathing heavily. I was about to do something just like Nick would do.

I lowered my head and squeezed my eyes shut. As an introvert, I asked questions and listened. That was my survival mode. Now seemed like a good time to try it. *God, should I go through the door?*

An unmistakable feeling of wrongness permeated my gut. There were two ways out. Ignore the unseen warning and proceed. Or disappoint Hayden by ditching him.

An idea flashed in my mind. Once again, an unexpected option.

Scraping my fingers through my hair, I went back to the kitchen table and picked up my phone. I pulled a full breath, let it out, and selected the microphone. "Hey," I dictated, "I know it's a school night, but would it be okay for me to go out to dinner with a friend? We can go over our science homework too."

I reread the message, bit my lip, and pressed send.

Mom replied five seconds later. *Sure. But don't stay out too late.*

Conscience cleansed, I sagged with relief, tucked my real phone in my pocket, and bolted out the door.

CHAPTER FORTY-EIGHT

QUALIFIED

Even though I knew my parents wouldn't be at my Tuesday game, I kept glancing at the bleachers. Old habit, I guess.

I read Elijah's text one more time before tucking my phone away. *"My flesh and my heart may fail, but God is the strength of my heart and my portion forever." Psalm 73:26, ESV*

Words to inspire.

Coach Hering huddled us up before we took the field. "For the past two weeks, we've been coasting. A few close wins against mediocre teams. Not today. This team boasts a strong front line and relentless defenders."

"We got this," Reb said.

"I like your confidence." Coach Hering pointed to me. "Remember to follow through when you pass and shoot. Improves your accuracy. Push wide and look for Reb on the diagonal."

"Got it." I nodded, mind already imagining the play.

"Coach Lofton gave me a scouting report on the Raiders, and here's the key." Coach leaned forward. "We gotta run on full cylinders and we gotta work as a team. Trust each other. Know your position and what you bring to the table. Work hard off the ball. We do that, and we're one step closer to playoffs."

"Woo-hoo!" Erika yelled, her cry echoed by the team.

As we took our spots, I scanned the crowd again. No Hayden yet. But Jay sat there, twirling a red stick. I smiled. Nice of him to show up.

The whistle blew, and the ball bounced into play. The possession went back and forth like tug-of-war. Midway through the first half, the black shirts pressed past our back line. One player, number eleven, cut back, juked Erika, and broke free. Forced into a compromised position, Erika tackled her from behind.

The ref whistled. "Foul."

A free kick on goal.

Sucking air, Erika stood and planted her palms on her knees. The pinched expression on her face screamed frustration.

"Shake it off, Erika." I jogged over and patted her back. "You didn't have a choice."

Jaw set, she shrugged me off. "I know."

Reb came and fist-bumped her. "Trust us."

Erika's look softened. "Gotcha."

Eleven lined up for the strike. Two steps and a boot. Sandy lunged right, but the ball went low and to the left. Score.

At halftime, Coach Lofton was red-faced.

But Coach Hering was red-faced and *hoarse.* "Girls, we cannot take those risks in the backfield. Offense, press as a team. And find your positions. When you take up the wrong one, you limit our options and effectiveness. Keep your defense-to-offense transitions strong. When they drive to score, implement counter measures."

This was not new information. We'd focused on these skills all week.

"How bad do you guys want this?" Reb yelled.

"Ha!" we shouted.

"How bad?" Reb lowered her voice.

"Ha! Ha!"

"How bad?!"

"Ha! Ha! Ha!"

We exploded like thoroughbreds out of the starting blocks in the second half. After intercepting the ball in the center circle, I beat the initial defender and pushed ahead. Controlling the pace, I shot a pass to Reb, who battled one-on-one and then knocked it back to me. I dragged the ball wide, surging past my defender, watching for Reb to cross over in the frame. Anticipating her move, I chipped the ball waist high. Reb bulldozed in for the strike. The ball hit the crossbar and ricocheted, but Wren was positioned perfectly and headed it in on the rebound to finish it. Score! An equalizer.

Turquoise jerseys swarmed Wren, hooting. Less than one minute into the half, we'd tied the game.

"Nice play." Reb drew us all into a circle. "Do I get the assist for my remarkably well-placed ricochet off the frame?"

Erika pushed her, but in a playful way. "Show off."

"Talk to Wren about that," Reb said, winking at our forward.

I gave a feral growl. "I'll pass it your way, Reb. Next time, the score is yours."

Reb gave a toothy grin like a crocodile anticipating an easy dinner.

But keeping that promise proved difficult. The game's intensity rose three notches. More aggressive challenges. More corner kicks. More quick pounces on loose balls. More headers.

More sweat, grit, and hustle.

As time ticked down, their backfield pressed. Reb and I toyed with them, passing to see if they would bite so we could kick the ball over the press. They took the bait, and we flooded their box. A defender cleared the back, and the ball came to me in the corner. Voices screamed from the sidelines, from teams, cheer squads, fans, the noise building to a frenzy.

I took a calming breath. Spotted my target. Reb.

Time shifted into slow motion. I took a strong step and pounded the ball. It sailed high toward the center. Three defenders jumped. Reb held back for a split second, then launched herself upward. Connected. Headed the ball past the goalie, into the net.

"Yessssss!" Screaming, Reb sprinted toward our teammates, pulling the number on her jersey forward as if to say *notice me, world!*

And they did. After the 2–1 game, a cluster of spectators surrounded her.

Coach pulled the rest of us together. "Girls, Coach Lofton has some news."

She held out her arm, and Coach Lofton stepped into our impromptu circle. A distinct spark marked her steely eyes and the edges of her lips curled. "Qualified," she said.

We exploded. Erika danced—if that's what you want to call her awkward moves. Wren and Sandy jumped up and down screaming. My pulse raced so fast my knees went weak. And while I'd never call myself bubbly—I reserved that term for giggling, outgoing, over-the-top optimists—today, the word fit. My feet barely stayed on the ground.

I turned, ready to sweep Sol in a hug, and stopped short.

She wasn't there to share the joy.

Neither were my parents.

Well, I could still text the news.

Digging my phone out of my duffle took less time than a chameleon's tongue to snag its food.

For Sol, I sent, *We just qualified for playoffs!*

For my parents, I added, *Thank you for letting me be here to celebrate with my team.*

I even shot Nick a text. He was the only one who responded right away with the words *Show off,* and ten seconds later, a laughing emoji and *JK, way to go.*

"Nice game," a voice called.

Licorice man. Grinning, I lifted my head and waved. "Thank you. We're going to post-season play." Was it possible for a smile to literally split your face?

He flashed a thumbs-up.

Before I could respond, Erika body-slammed me. "Righteous!" She held up her phone with one hand and flashed a number one sign with her other. "C'mon, get in this. Smile!"

More players pushed around from behind as Erika snapped a dozen shots. Reb even rushed over from the bleachers and photobombed us.

"We've got to celebrate. Let's head for Let's Shake on It." Reb crooked an arm around my neck. "Dani, the assist queen. Are you in?"

"I—" I glanced toward the bleachers. Jay was gone. "Yes. Absolutely."

While fun, the festivities at Let's Shake on It overwhelmed me. I left early. Still, hanging with my teammates left a warmth in my heart. It still hadn't reached the same level of comfort I had with Sol's support, but I viewed tonight as a baby step in the right direction. I fell into my bed and drank in its softness.

Later that night, something buzzed. I woke with a start, mind full of cobwebs, and squinted at my clock. Eleven forty-five. The abrasive sound didn't come from there.

Wanting to mute the offending ring, I stumbled out from my sheets and tracked the noise to my backpack.

Blinking, I knelt beside it and fumbled with the zipper. I thought I'd left my phone by my bed. But my hand fell on it, lit and vibrating.

I answered. "Hello?" My voice had the rough texture of leather.

"Hey, Champ. I was thinking about you and thought I'd call."

"Who is this?" I asked.

"You didn't think I'd forget my old phone number, did you?"

I lowered the device and looked at it more carefully. Oh. Not my phone. The phone Jay lent me.

He was still talking, so I quickly tucked the phone to my ear. "… and I didn't get a chance after your game."

Jay knew my parents were gone. He had to know a phone call this late was unusual. But he made it anyway.

Why? "It's almost midnight." Cradling the phone, I crawled back into bed. "On a school night."

"I'm sorry, guess I lost track of time. But did you remember to lock your doors? Turn on the house alarm?"

"Yes." I yawned, comforted by his almost fatherly concern. "I think so."

"Well, good. I needed confirmation you were safe tonight."

I sighed. Did every adult in my life think me incapable of taking care of myself? Still, I'm sure he meant well. "Uh—thanks. But I'm fine."

"Okay. Sleep well, Dani."

The line went dead.

After rolling over, my senses suddenly spiked into overdrive. Outside of general concern, did Jay have another reason for calling so late? Had there been a break-in downtown? Police sirens on the roads? Reports of a missing person? Another abduction?

The conversation, probably meant to calm me, had the opposite effect. The quiet in my house roared, and the streetlight cast dark shadows across the floor. Shivering, I pulled the covers up to my chin.

Sol would have crawled under the covers with me.

Nick would have teased me for being chicken.

My parents, both busy, might have overlooked my sudden discomfort.

Coach Hering might have called me offsides for letting my mind jump to a dark place.

And I would have argued that even animals use their God-given senses to detect danger.

I laid in bed for an hour, listening to the clock tick in the hall. The last thoughts I had before sleep pulled me under were about harp seals and Macie.

CHAPTER FORTY-NINE

REVELATIONS

"Hey, Squirrel," Sol said when she climbed into my car Wednesday morning. "You look tired. Dreaming about a certain someone? Or dreaming about playoffs?"

"Playoff hype." I turned on my signal and eased out of her driveway. Should I tell her about my flirtatious outing with Hayden, which involved less physics notes and more chemistry? No, I needed more time to unpack what he meant to me.

"Good." Sol slapped her hands against her thighs. "Good, good, good. Well. I read the blog last night. Your answer to Hamburger Hog—hilarious and helpful. 'Don't worry about the beef. You've got bigger fish to fry.' Classic Dani."

I smiled. "Thanks. I should probably work on another set tonight. I let it slide after that first round. How is the musical coming along?"

"Amazing. It's what I want. And—" she sang her next words to a tune from the musical, "that's how I know who I am, 'cuz I know what I want." She broke off and raised a brow. "I took liberties with the lyrics."

I laughed, treasuring my limited time with her. I missed having her around more often. Missed her on the soccer field with me. Missed our inside jokes—like the way Coach Lofton sometimes tooted and walked away, leaving a cloud of stench for someone else to claim. We called it The Fog. Missed our lunch time, my midday oasis in a sea of noise, which was now reduced to brown bag leftovers in my car. And I missed our phone calls and texts. Sol turned her phone off while at rehearsals, and with the rapidly approaching opening date, that happened more and more frequently.

"Want to run your lines on the way to school?" I asked.

She pounced like a fox on a mouse. "Can we? Although it's really more singing than memorizing lines."

Ever get a song stuck in your head? After Sol and I parted ways at school, one stanza kept cycling through my mind. During math class, numbers swayed in rhythm to it. It hummed through my mind when I tackled science lab. Almost drove me nuts. How did Sol put up with it? Clearly, music was her superpower.

By lunchtime, rain had arrived. I stood by the exit closest to the parking lot, looking through the windows. Should I make the mad dash to the car and then sit in stinky, wet clothes for thirty minutes? Or should I brave the cafeteria instead? A trip to a musty bathroom didn't appeal to me.

"Dani, wait up. Are you leaving?"

I recognized Hayden's voice and turned around. What would he think of me standing here gawking? I played it cool. "Maybe. I'm undecided."

"Well, I'm headed to the counselor's room." He held up a brown bag. "She keeps it open during lunch for anyone who wants a break from the cafeteria, no questions asked. Want to come?"

It made sense that a school counselor might care enough to give up her lunch period to help a few kids. I shrugged. "Why not?"

When we walked in, Hayden swept his arm wide. "Welcome to the lunch bunch."

Our counselor, Mrs. Cook, worked at the computer on her desk. She acknowledged us with a lift of her chin and went back to whatever held her attention. Probably emails. Unless teachers surfed social media during their breaks, in which case she'd be pulling up memes like, "My face when the loudest noise in the room is the kid reminding everyone to be quiet" or "My face when I ask if there are any questions and a student raises their hand and proceeds to tell a ten-minute story about their grandma visiting the doctor to have a wart on her left toe examined."

Okay, that last one might have been too long for a meme.

Four boys lounged in the back playing cards. One groaned before throwing his hand into the middle. Laughing, another boy collected his cards and began to shuffle.

Near the front, three girls bent their heads together as they talked quietly and nibbled on their food. Sandwiches, crackers, yogurt cups, and—what was that? I wrinkled my nose. Better not be broccoli.

One of the boys from my math class sat alone in the middle with an electronic gaming device, and Hayden guided us to two desks next to him. "What's up, Ben?"

Ben kept his eyes glued to the screen. "Level fifty-six, baby! Die, zombies, die!"

Uncertain about the social rules in this room, I lowered myself behind a desk and set my lunch on top. "Guess this explains why I never see you at lunch."

"Right." He pulled a sports drink from his sack and twisted the lid off. "I'm familiar with broken places. Last year, before I moved here, I went through a—" He paused and cleared his throat. "A rough patch. Mrs. Cook read my file and offered her room as a midday sanctuary if I recruited other kids that were"—he licked his lips—"struggling like me. You get good at recognizing them after a while."

I snorted. "I guess I looked desperate enough to invite today."

"No offense, but when you spend your lunch hour hiding in the car, you kind of fit the profile."

He knew?

How embarrassing! As we say in soccer, time to deflect the ball.

"Or maybe I dislike crowds." I flattened my lips. "Ever consider that?"

He shrugged, nonchalant. "Either way, here you are. Here with me."

How curious. Narrowing my eyes, I studied his face. I had suspected Hayden had authority issues like my brother. Sometimes he seemed on the edge, fidgety, like he was threatened by someone else's success, or jealous, like when I talked with Elijah. Whatever challenges he had faced, it was hard to tell from his actions or read from any facial clues if he bore any scars.

What trauma had he suffered? Divorce? Or a death in the family? He'd referred to beer before. Maybe he'd overcome an addiction. I resisted the impulse to press him for details. If he felt comfortable enough, he'd tell me someday. Even so, his momentary vulnerability made him even more attractive. He rubbed his eyes.

"Allergies again?" I asked, resisting the urge to lean into him. Comfort him.

He sniffed. "You been around Sol?"

"Yeah." I plucked my shirt, looking for hairs. "And her cat. Sorry."

"It's okay." He slurred the words, so they came out *S'okay*.

"Anyway—" he drew the word out like a sloth blinking.

His hesitation made me reconsider. Maybe he'd invited me not because I looked desperate but because he was. Desperate for what though? What did he hope to gain? Did he find me too adorable to resist?

I clung to the idea. "I'm glad you asked me to come." Unwrapping my sandwich, I inclined my head toward Mrs. Cook's desk. She looked intent on whatever task she had. "Wish I'd known about this arrangement a month ago." I took a bite. "How'd you do on the science quiz?"

"An eighty." He smiled. "I had a good study partner."

We spent the rest of the period laughing. I got on a weird animal kick and entertained him with pictures of the emperor tamarin, a small monkey with a white moustache that inspired the Lorax from Dr. Seuss, and the markhor goat, whose long, spiraling horns reminded me of curling ribbon, only hard enough to skewer you. Hayden brought up the Komondor again—like we had our own inside joke.

When the bell rang, we scooped up our trash and headed for the halls.

"Thanks for this." I lingered by the doorway, unwilling to part so soon. "It was a nice change in my routine."

"I'll be here tomorrow too." The skin around Hayden's eyes tightened. "If you decide to come back."

I nodded. "I might."

I waltzed off without looking back. *Waltzed* because a warm, almost syrupy feeling lifted my heart. Is this what drove Sol to dancing and singing? And *without looking back* because I didn't want to appear overeager, like one of those socially struggling students Hayden said was easy to recognize.

By three o'clock, the rain hadn't let up, and now lightning came in bright flashes. Coach Hering cancelled practice.

Normally, disappointment would have crushed me at the announcement. But tonight, with a spring still lingering in my step from lunch and a blog assignment for my best friend, I welcomed the break. Wednesday evening was all mine.

When I got home, I threw my backpack in the corner, balanced Betty on the table, and raided the fridge. Like a true soccer parent, Mom fed us a healthy diet, which, unfortunately, often included broccoli. But since she wasn't there, I nabbed the milk and poured myself a bowl of cereal instead.

"Snack of the gods," I told Betty.

She didn't answer. Not surprising. As a soccer ball, she's usually grounded.

Once I finished, I turned on my computer and accessed *Heart and Soul's* email submissions. If I did batch work, I wouldn't have to look at this for another week. Or two, if I threw myself into it.

After cracking my knuckles, I scanned the entries. Which one should I answer this time? A pet peeve? An annoying sibling?

I got on a roll, answering five Dear Souls in a row before opening the Heart tab. The first one I picked was easy—a freshman girl who feared she'd fall head over heels in love with a senior she just met. "Slow down," I typed. "Try wearing sneakers instead."

The next one caught my eye.

Dear Heart,

Let's fight sexism together. I'll get all dressed up. You can take me on a date, buy me dinner, and beg me to—

No. I stopped right there. Some words you can't unread. I debated sticking this in Sol's creepy file, but I deleted the obscenity instead. Who needed that kind of garbage? Sol would never know.

I finished answering the rest of the cache, scheduling each to cover the next two weeks. Sol would be happy.

"Betty," I said, leaning back in my seat. "This has been a productive day."

She smiled in a ballsy way. Which is to say, not at all.

My gaze fell to Sol's creepy file. *I wonder what she's got in there.*

Curiosity gnawed at me. I clicked open the file.

CHAPTER FIFTY

THE CREEPY FILE

The file held more entries than I expected. I didn't need to read them all—only a glance at the first line suggested where the email was headed. How many ways could you interpret "Hey, gorgeous"? What creep would address a teen like that? Even if it came from another teen, it reminded me of what Ms. Brown had brought up last week in UCA. Human trafficking. She'd claimed people from any race, religion, gender, age, education level, or nationality could fall victim.

The emails gutted me. So graphic. So sleezy. How could the school tolerate them? *Because Sol hadn't told them.* She loved her blog enough to slide these into a closet of sorts. Which begged the question—was someone targeting my best friend? Because for sure, whoever sent those submissions exhibited aggressive behavior. Was it someone at our school or an outsider who'd gained access through the website? The drop-down menu listed Academics, Advice, and then Athletics. Anyone looking up department staff or sports stats would spot it. Was Sol even aware of the potential danger?

Stomach churning, I dug online for a list of characteristics a predator might look for in a victim. I found several lists, quickly read them, and pinpointed common features. Red flags included family problems, signs of abuse, and avoiding social interactions.

Releasing pent-up breath, I leaned back. None of those described Sol. The description was closer to me than her.

I patted the top of Betty. "Don't look so smug. I got myself bent out of shape for nothing."

Another link caught my eye. "Romeo pimp." I clicked on it.

The article said some predators sweep young girls off their feet. They gain their trust by filling a need. They might shower them with gifts or affection. Anything to hook them. To isolate them. To control them. Ms. Brown had called it grooming.

I knew love was powerful, but this scenario painted love as a manipulative tool. No one became a victim on purpose. They were deceived.

Heart pounding, I closed my computer. That scenario sounded more plausible for the area we lived in.

And then I knew exactly where I'd experienced this behavior. Macie.

Nausea gripped me.

I'd suspected it but passed the problem off to my dad. He convinced me she was safe, but if not, he'd contact the father. But what if it was too late? Was she in immediate danger?

I could talk to my dad again. But would he take action, especially from so far away? No, he already believed he'd dealt with my issue.

A dark misgiving clung to my heart, something vile and sinister. The whole idea I might be right about my suspicions paralyzed me like the fast-moving poison of a black widow's bite. I bowed my head and prayed. *God, give me wisdom, and grant Macie protection.*

I opened my eyes with new resolve. I'd call 9-1-1 right now.

As I reached for my phone, I hesitated.

And say what?

That I thought my neighbor was in danger based on her clothing and makeup choices? That her attitude changed? That I didn't trust—or actually know—the guy she was hanging out with?

The police would no doubt ask me a bunch of questions I couldn't answer. If I wanted anyone who could do something to take the threat seriously, I'd need more proof of illegal activity. Which meant I had one option. I'd watch Macie and take good notes.

That night, as the rain continued to drizzle, I slept fitfully. A sense of urgency pushed me to act—like when you have an open shot in front of the goal. But reality kept me in check. I did not control the ball, and I wasn't even certain who my opponent was. When the morning sun broke the horizon, the hurry-up-and-wait combination left my bedsheets in tangles and lingering nightmares.

CHAPTER FIFTY-ONE

DEBATE

"Can you believe my opening night is a week from tomorrow? This accelerated production schedule has been crazy intense." Eyes dancing, Sol blew the steam off her coffee. "We have tech dress rehearsals all week, and then the curtains open."

I wanted to bring up the creepy files with Sol and talk about my suspicions, but she jumped into my car with guns blazing, so to speak. She had theater on the mind, and I hated to dampen her excitement. Besides, I'd driven by Macie's house that morning and spotted her waiting for the bus like a normal kid. She'd even dropped the mascara. Perhaps my late-night worries were ungrounded. My concerns appeared less urgent with the new day.

I held up a hand. "Tech dress rehearsal? What's that?"

"That's when we have the people who run the lights and sound in place and the backstage crew are there to switch the set and we wear our costumes and go over the script to work out any glitches. It's one step away from a full production." She slapped a hand on my knee. "I checked your soccer schedule. You have a game opening night. But you better have tickets to one of the other performances."

"Of course." I nodded. "I'll nab front row seats."

Sol leaned forward. "The view is better back a few rows."

"Hmm. Thanks." I sipped my tea, my face much calmer than my heart, which threatened to choke me. Would now be a good time to bring up the creepy file? Macie?

"How's my blog holding up?" Sol asked. "I don't even have time to read it anymore."

The tension eased from my chest. Sol had provided me with the perfect bridge to start a conversation I dreaded.

"I uploaded two weeks' worth. That means when your cast party ends, my job is over." I took a quick breath and kept going. "Speaking of *Heart and Soul,* I opened your creepy file."

"What? Why?" Sol couldn't disguise the surprise in her voice.

I steeled myself. It was time for Sol to be the listener and me to be the speaker. I stepped into the role as best I could. Starting with a review of Ms. Brown's presentation on human trafficking, I spent the rest of our drive to school explaining what I had learned and what I feared after reading those files.

We sat in the parking lot then. Me, having emptied my guts, and Sol, biting her lip as she processed it. After an eternity—which was probably less than a minute—I couldn't wait any longer.

"What do you think?" I shut the car off. "Am I crazy?"

Sol drew her eyebrows down. "I don't think I'm in danger. Those email submissions are just spam. Someone fishing. If I don't bite, they don't act. And I ain't biting. But Macie." She frowned. "Maybe. It's the second time you've brought her up. Are you certain?"

"Honestly, no, not a hundred percent." I pressed my lips in a line. "And my dad did say he would contact the family when he got back."

"But you don't think you should wait that long?"

I shrugged. "That's why I'm asking you. If I'm wrong, I undermine my dad. If I'm right—"

"If you're right, are you in any danger?" Sol's forehead creased. "Like, if you call and the police check it out but don't arrest anyone, will someone know it was you and go after you?"

"Macie might suspect I'm the one who blew the whistle." Sol's back stiffened. *Might* is too big of a chance for me. I don't know what to do. It sounds so risky. I could talk to Mrs. James. I mean, that situation comes up in the play more or less. But I still think your safest bet is to wait for your dad to come back."

Safest bet for who?

Swallowing hard, I nodded. I told myself Sol was the advice columnist. She knew best.

She patted my knee. "I know it's hard. But there's nothing else you can do right now."

Hands trembling, I pulled my keys from the ignition. "Yeah, you're right."

Except I couldn't shake the feeling she wasn't.

CHAPTER FIFTY-TWO

SUSPICIONS AND STAKEOUTS

S till preoccupied, I met Hayden on my way to the counselor's room for lunch.

"You're walking fast." He fell into step with me. "What's the hurry?"

"Something that's been eating at me all morning." I explained to him what I had learned at UCA and my suspicions about Macie and her older friend. "Sol encouraged me to wait—safety issues, you know? Mostly mine. But I have this itch to do something."

He listened without interrupting, even when I stopped in the hallway short of the classroom to finish unloading. The longer I spoke, the longer his face grew. Part of me felt bad about that. If he had suffered some trauma like he claimed, talking about a compromising situation like this might be a trigger for him. At the very least, it was bound to make him uncomfortable.

The other part of me needed his insight because of that same traumatic experience. He'd know if I was going … well … offsides.

When I finally finished, he wrapped an arm around my shoulder. "I understand how you feel about the Macie kid. Sol said you might put yourself in danger if you go ahead with the accusation. Do you feel like you're in danger?"

His protective squeeze encouraged me. I pulled in a breath and released it, letting my pulse calm. "Not with you around," I said. "That and I have a taser in my purse."

Nodding, he smiled. "What's the one thing holding you back?"

I didn't hesitate. "Actual proof."

"Do you think you'll ever get that?"

"No." I hung my head.

"Okay." He squared his shoulders. "That settles it then. You wait."

"Unless …" I said.

He frowned. "Unless what?"

"Unless I stake out Macie's house. If I spot anything out of the ordinary, I can report the activity with confidence."

He grabbed my hand.

Despite my state of mind, my skin warmed at his touch.

"Spying on people? That doesn't sound safe. What happened to my shy little Dani?"

"She's scared." I lifted my chin. "For Macie. I don't want to be right. But what if I am?"

He narrowed his eyes.

My bravado wilted a little. "Am I being paranoid?"

"A little." He pinched the air to show how much. "Look, even if you're right, I'm with Sol on this. It's not safe for you. Wait for your dad."

Tears burned my eyes. I almost backed down then. Doing nothing was the easy choice. The safe one.

But something inside me rebelled, and I surprised myself. "I can't wait."

"Hey, it's okay." He reached up and gently wiped my cheek. "Tell you what. Why don't I take you out for lunch today? It will give us more privacy, and we can figure out what to do. Are you okay with that?"

Relief washed through me, and I nodded. I needed clear thinking on this with someone I trusted.

Burger Barn proved to be as busy and crowded as the cafeteria, so we took our order outside. Hayden's calmness to my storm made me aware of my hunger, and I snarfed down my food.

"Training for the zombie apocalypse?" Hayden asked.

With a painful swallow, I shook my head and set down my burger. Ketchup leaked from under the smooshed bun, dripping onto the wrapper. Better there than on my shirt. How embarrassing would that be?

After another ten minutes of talking in circles, Hayden crushed his drink cup.

"You're determined to do this then?" He leaned forward and brushed a crumb off my shirt, then ran his finger down the length of my arm. "To stake out Macie's house tonight after soccer practice?"

Fighting goose bumps, I dotted my lips with a napkin. "Yes."

"I can't believe I'm saying this," he said, shaking his head, "but if you're that determined, I'll come with you. I'll bet Macie has seen your car on the street, but she won't recognize mine. We can hide in the open."

"I didn't think of that." I gulped. "What if some creep spots us outside the house?"

"I'll kiss you." Mischief danced in his eyes. "People tend to look away from public displays of affection."

My face heated. As much as I might enjoy that, I didn't want some phony first kiss like a stage performer. "I got a better idea. I'll bring my backpack. If anyone asks, we can say we're on the way to the library for a different kind of one-on-one session." I hoped my light humor would make his last idea less awkward.

"Or that." His eyes narrowed ever so slightly. Was he disappointed? "What about Sol?"

Like visualizing a play in soccer, my mind raced through possible outcomes. "I'm not going to say anything. She might try to talk me out of it. This is something I've got to do on my own. With you, of course."

"I understand." He checked the time on his phone and sighed. "Lunch is over. I'll see you tonight."

School couldn't end fast enough after that. When the final bell rang, I threw everything I had into soccer practice, even pulling off a Cruyff Turn that left Erika in the dust. It wasn't until after I rushed home and changed into dark clothes that my nerves set in.

Seconds crawled like a tortoise while I sat at the kitchen

table and waited for Hayden to pick me up. I passed the time by sending a text to my parents and offering a few short prayers for wisdom. My stomach was a roller coaster, so I avoided any food.

Dusk arrived. Hayden knocked on my door twenty minutes later. I slung my backpack on my shoulder and let him in.

"Are you ready?" he asked.

"Yep." Showing more confidence than I felt, I lifted my taser and my phone. "I got these all charged up, just in case."

"Your phone?" He shook his head. "Didn't you say you had a tracker on it?"

Lowering my arm, I nodded. "Yeah. So my parents know where I'm at. Macie is down the street, close enough they won't think twice about it."

"What if we have to follow her somewhere? Like she walks down the street, and we don't know if she's on her way to the store or to the park to meet some guy." He raised a brow. "Do you want your parents to worry and call you? Let's leave your phone here. I've got mine, and it's fully charged. But bring the taser."

"It's shockingly handy," I joked.

"Can I carry it?" Hayden asked. "If we ever need it, I always wanted to be the hero."

"Sure." I slapped it into his outstretched hand. Then, fighting equal parts of excitement and terror, I set my phone on the table. "Let's go."

Hayden drove his car down the block and parked across the street behind a truck. Then he shut off the motor, cracked the windows, and sat. After a few minutes, Hayden produced a set of binoculars—his dad's, he claimed, for football games—and we took turns scanning the back and side of the house for movement.

My whole body tingled. "I feel like an international spy."

"Yeah?" Hayden checked the time on his phone. "If we sit here long enough, those feelings will change into boredom. And I'm okay with that because it means there's nothing going on."

"But it also means we'd need to come back another night." I wasn't naïve enough to think this stakeout worked like the movies, where actions and resolutions happened on an accelerated timeline. "I'm not letting this go because of one failed attempt."

"I wish you would." Frowning, Hayden pressed a few buttons on his phone before lifting the binoculars to his eyes. "I set a timer. We should probably move to a new spot in an hour."

The sky faded to an inky darkness. Chilled air snaked in through the window, and the faint chirping of crickets came with it. Hayden and I communicated in low tones, and for once, I didn't mind the small talk.

After a while, my stomach growled. I'd skipped dinner and was paying the price. "How much time is left on the timer?"

He glanced at his phone. "Seventeen minutes."

"Then we've been here for almost forty-five minutes. And other than some lady walking her dog, the night is dead." I leaned my head against the console. "This was a bad idea. I should just call 9-1-1 and get it over with, even without evidence." I put air quotes around the last two words. "I'm done holding back. We could blow this whole thing up."

"If we had anything." Hayden pressed a button on his phone screen. "Give it ten more minutes," he said.

He was right. A few minutes later, the garage door opened, and a gray Ford Focus pulled out from Macie's driveway. After centering itself, it accelerated down the road.

Mind racing, I held my breath. Who just left? Her dad? Or maybe Macie herself with someone?

"Should we follow the car?" I asked, nerves like needles.

"No." Keeping his gaze fixed on the house, Hayden passed me the binoculars. "Wait. She'll sneak out. I have an instinct about things like this."

Apparently, he did, for not a minute later, Macie slipped out the side door with a backpack. She hung back in the shadows, face lit by her phone as thumbs flashed over the screen. Three seconds later, a black BMW with tinted windows pulled to the curb. With a furtive glance, Macie hustled to the passenger side and climbed in. Her door clicked shut, and the car reversed and sped off the way it came.

Hayden pressed the button to turn on his ignition, and his muscle car hummed to life. "This one, we follow."

I lowered my spy gear. "Why? We got our proof."

"Of what?" Hayden shook his head. "We need more."

"How?" I lifted my hands, palms up. "She's not being kidnapped."

"But she is being sneaky." Hayden jerked the wheel. "And that's something else I have an instinct about."

CHAPTER FIFTY-THREE

THE HOTEL

ike glowing cobra eyes, taillights led the way in the growing darkness. I lost track of how many turns we took, fearing to even blink, lest I lose sight of them in the gathering gloom.

"Where do you think they're headed? What if they drive out of state?" Queasiness seized my stomach. "Do you even know where we're at now?"

"From the number of homeless people I see, we're not in the safest part of town." Hayden checked his rearview mirror. "Don't worry though. Some girl gave me her taser for protection."

If his words were meant to reassure me, they failed. "Should we call the police?"

"And send them where? And tell them what?" Hayden scowled, slowing for a stoplight. "You wanted evidence, but what do we have?"

"I'm sorry, it's not like I'm familiar with these types of situations," I snapped. "Put me on a soccer field, and yeah, I know what moves to make. But how do you anticipate a faceless opponent who might not even be playing by the same rules?"

"Calm down." He punched the car forward and switched lanes to keep pace. "We have a face for this opponent. This Trey guy, right? We'll catch up to him."

I ground my teeth. "You don't understand what can happen to a girl out here." Panic made my voice harsher than I intended.

"Men are victims too." Anger colored his tone. He rubbed at his eyes. "Look, I'm trying to be cautious for both our sakes. So stop talking so I can concentrate."

His order hit me like a slap in the face. Even if he was right, they stung. But maybe his gruffness was what it took to help me focus.

And what about Macie? If she was deceived, would she see us as saviors or not?

I held my tongue.

As we zipped past streetlights, the buildings thinned and the traffic lights came farther apart. An overpowering sense of dread, of wrongness, weighed my heart down. What was I thinking, doing a stakeout? We were way out of our league.

Hayden finally broke the knife-like silence. "Look, Dani. I'm sorry for the way tonight is going. I'm doing the best I can in a bad situation. Just like you. I don't have a lot of options."

Macie's car pulled into a hotel. If you could call it that. More like a seedy halfway house. Weeds lined the parking lot and the peeling paint screamed of neglect.

My apprehension spiked. "This can't be good."

"I'll park a few spots over. Maybe you can look around and figure out what's going on."

Heart pounding, I nodded. Trey had seen me before. I couldn't let him spot me, so I slouched.

Peeking over the dashboard, I saw Macie get out. Someone climbed out of the driver's side too. A man. Trey? Yes, Trey. He pulled her into a lusty kiss that made my stomach sour. How many years older than her was he? What kind of promises had he given that made her willingly follow?

"That's him," I whispered. "That's the guy I saw with Macie." I clenched my fists. "This is against the law. She's underage. We're witnesses. *Now* we've got proof. Make the call."

Macie looked around and hugged her backpack closer as Trey pulled a key out of his pocket and opened the door of a first-floor room. They hadn't checked in. This must be a regular haunt for him.

Without hesitation, Macie walked right in. The door shut behind her.

I slouched even lower in the seat and glanced at Hayden. He sat, phone in hand, slack jawed.

I pushed him again. "Make the call!"

"You asked for it." He lifted his phone and pressed a button. "Hello?"

Muscles wound tighter than a rope, I held my breath. I knew the script. *9-1-1, what is the nature of your call?*

"Got her," he said, and hung up.

I blinked at him.

He smirked. "Guess you *didn't* figure out what was going on."

He clicked the button that unlocked my car door. It flew open, and hands latched onto my arms. Jerked me out the door. Twisted me around. A bulky man pressed his body against me, pinning me to the side of the car. My face pressed against the window. I kicked. Bucked. He slammed me back again.

"Hayden!" I screamed. "Use the taser."

"I will if you don't stop screaming," he said.

From behind, the man clamped a hand across my mouth.

Hayden sighed and waved a dismissive hand. "It's too bad, really. I liked you. Didn't want to use you. But you have yourself to blame. You wouldn't let things go. Insisted on bringing in the police. You forced me to do this."

Realization slammed into me. My heart raced, then pounded in my skull.

He'd charmed me like Romeo.

I thought we were working together. Flirting with love.

Instead, he'd executed the ultimate Cruyff Turn.

I bit the man's hand. He yelled, and I lunged to escape.

Cursing, he tripped me. I fell, knee connecting with hard concrete and hands scraping on the rough surface. Pain lanced up my leg as I tried to scramble away, stumbled, and fell again. Meaty arms locked around my middle, crushing my lungs. I yanked a hand free and clawed at his face. My nails raked across skin. The man spat and tightened his grip, cutting off air. I choked and gasped, panic cutting raw and deep.

A wet cloth with a pungent odor smothered my mouth. Burned my eyes. Overwhelmed my senses. I tried to scream, but my tongue didn't respond.

My lids fluttered. The struggle fled my body. I sagged, and the world fell in and out of focus. Someone put their hands under my armpits and lifted me. Dragged me. My head lolled to the side, but not before I saw Trey saunter over to Hayden and hand him a package of white powder.

Drugs? Was my life being traded for drugs?

"My man," Trey said. "Everything clear?"

"No phone on her. Left it at home. Her parents will think she's in bed." Hayden pocketed the drugs. "But you'd better take her backpack." He fished it out of the back of the car and handed it to Trey. "I don't want to have to dump any evidence. You're better at that."

"Yeah. You're too sloppy," Trey said. "You almost let this one get away."

Hayden stepped over to me and touched my hair.

I blinked, clinging to awareness. And hope. Did his eyes hold regret?

No, they were cold as a dead fish.

He leaned over and kissed my cheek. Lingered there for a moment, breath hot on my skin. "Bye, Dani," he whispered. "I really did enjoy getting to know you. So far, you're my favorite."

You wolf.

I lost consciousness.

CHAPTER FIFTY-FOUR

KEEP FIGHTING

Dizziness and nausea swept through me. Head splitting with pain, I squinted against darkness. *Where am I?* My face smelled like disinfectant. My science-class knowledge kicked in. *Chloroform?*

Memory of my struggle and Hayden's betrayal slammed into me, and I gasped.

Or tried too. Duct tape covered my mouth.

I lay curled on my side with my feet and hands bound.

I sucked short, desperate breaths through my nose. Like a fish tossed into the bottom of a boat, I couldn't get enough air to calm my pounding heart. *Lord, be with me. Lord, be with me. Lord, be with me.*

Keep fighting. My mind clung to a memory from the field. *Win your position.*

A pale strip of light lined the lower edge of the door. As my eyes adjusted to the darkness, I heard voices.

"I thought you were going to teach me how to model before we went to California." Macie's voice slurred on the other side of the door. Sluggish. Was she high? "Why are we leaving tomorrow?"

Tomorrow? Would I be with them? Or dead?

"Change of plans." Trey's voice was oil. "We have a package to deliver first."

"Why can't you mail it?" She giggled as if being tickled.

Didn't Macie understand what was going on? Bile soured my throat and a tornado of light-headedness swept me. I'd done my research. Read the statistics. I knew where this was headed. Either she was the package, or I was the package. Or we both were.

A low laugh. "Don't worry, Sweetheart. You'll still get your photoshoot."

The voice was a different pitch than Trey's. Sharper. Rougher. Maybe the man who took me down? Was he the supposed photographer?

I shuddered. This was bad. *Lord, send me your angels to protect us!*

Something Coach Hering said came to mind. *They have strengths. Doesn't matter. They have weaknesses too. We have to expose them and then capitalize on them.*

I stamped down a growing panic. Elijah had told me about mental toughness. I had to find my strength. Or their weakness.

Disoriented, I tried to make sense of the lumps on the floor around me. Maybe I could find a weapon of some sort.

A notebook. A pencil. My backpack must have dumped out when they threw it in the closet with me. Nothing useful there. Unless—

Jay's phone. A corner of it peeked from under a notebook. Hayden saw me leave my device at home. He had told Trey I had no phone. But he didn't know about the extra Jay gave me—the one I had kept in my bag for backup.

Which meant neither did the kidnappers.

Was it still charged? If I could grab it, maybe I could make a call.

Right. With my hands taped behind my back. How could I dial 9-1-1 if I couldn't see the numbers?

Helplessness tore at my heels like a dog. Would I ever see my parents again?

Memories of Ms. Brown's voice filled my head, sending a sharp stab of pain through my skull. *Don't just believe in yourself. Believe in something beyond yourself.*

I had to try. *I can do all things through him who strengthens me.*

Wincing, I wriggled closer to the phone. Inched my way onto my knees. Tape dug into my flesh. My eyes watered as I fought the urge to scream. I couldn't make any noise. It would draw attention.

And this pain was nothing compared to what might happen if I failed.

I heard odd sounds on the other side of the door. Groans. Macie? Was she okay? What were they doing? I blocked the sounds from my mind. My skull throbbed. This wasn't real. Nothing was real. Only the phone, inches from my face. Only the prayers on my lips. Nothing else. Nothing else. Nothing else. I had to reach it. *Lord, be with me.*

The phone lit up. In the dark recesses of the closet, it seemed a beacon of light. Panic struck. Would they see the glow? I had to answer. But what if I couldn't? It was too tight in here. Too tight. Too tight. The only thing I could move was my face. My nose. If I could just touch my nose to the green receiver button on the screen like I had on the bus ride home from our game.

I pushed. Missed. Repositioned myself.

The screen went black, and I choked back a sob. Whoever tried to call gave up. Exhausted by my efforts and the continuous overdose of adrenaline, I closed my eyes. *I give up too, God. I am in the belly of the wolf, swallowed whole, and there is no woodsman around to save me.*

The terror in that realization sent a new round of shakes through my body.

And then, the phone lit up again.

Like a shot of lightning, I renewed my efforts. Bending. Straining. Straining.

Touch.

"Dani?" Thankfully the voice came out in a whisper.

Jay's voice.

Licorice man.

The person I suspected might be shady. The person I must trust. And the person I could not answer with my mouth taped shut.

Quietly, though it seemed loud as a gunshot, I whined in my throat. Just a split second. A cry saying, "I'm here."

"Dani." Did I hear relief or fear in that tone? "This is Jay. I'm an undercover policeman. And this phone has a tracker on it. I assume from your answer that you are in trouble. I know your location. Hang in there. I'm coming."

The line went dead.

Don't go, don't go, don't go, don't go. Don't leave me alone here.

The screen blacked again. I couldn't help myself. Tears welled in my eyes and streaked down my cheeks. Through my nose, my breaths were snotty. My throat hiccupped, making plaintive squeaking noises.

Stop. They'll hear you. I'd always been invisible. Shy. Introverted. People overlooked me. Why couldn't I be invisible now? *I'm not here.*

Someone yanked open the closet door. The light stabbed my eyes, and a face I didn't recognized filled my sight. A snap glance showed we were the only two people in the room. How long had I been silently struggling in the closet?

Whatever had happened with Macie, Trey must have taken her somewhere else.

I learned all that in the split second it took to hear the man's words when he opened the closet. *Lord, surround her with angels.*

"Well, look who's up. Hello, darling. Let's have some fun."

At least, I pretended the word he used was *darling* instead of what he actually said.

Digging his nails into me, he started dragging me out of the closet.

I thrashed, giving a muffled scream.

Chapter Fifty-Five

CHASE

Cursing, the man grabbed me by my hair. Wrenched my head back, exposing my throat. "You're feisty. But I like that."

Pain shot down my spine. There was no question of struggle. I was a butterfly caught in a web. I couldn't even stand without toppling since my legs were bound. Whimpering, I allowed him to pull me further from my cage.

The phone slid out with me and spilled on the dirty carpet.

The man's eyes widened, and he cursed again. Snatching the device, he pressed the screen. Zipped his tattooed fingers across it. Let loose another expletive. Kicked me in the gut, knocking the wind out of me. Then, yelling, he slammed the phone against the wall and crushed it. And with it, any hope of rescue.

Nostrils flaring, he stormed across the room and grabbed his own phone. Glaring at me, he made a call. "Hayden lied. The girl had a phone on her. The log showed someone made an eleven-second phone call. I don't know. Three minutes ago?"

He listened, threw some things from the couch into a bag and zipped it like a bullet. The muscles in his neck bulged. He paused and snarled. "No, we can't take that risk. Now move!"

Spittle flew from the man's mouth as he pinched my face in a vise grip and growled at me. "You'll pay for this!"

Then he shoved me away, the burn of his fingers scalding my skin.

Jaw clenched, the man strode to the dresser and grabbed a gun. His hands moved in a blur, the gun clicked, and he leveled it at me.

I squeezed my eyes shut, waiting for death.

Bang! The door burst open. I peeked to see Trey standing in the doorway. "Macie's loaded. And—whoa, whoa, whoa." He held out his hands and stepped in front of me. "Put the gun down. If we don't deliver her, we've got to find a replacement. And we don't have time for that."

The man ground his teeth, hatred burning in his eyes. "Can I take a finger?"

"You can do whatever you want once we're clear. Let's move."

After shoving the gun in the back of his pants, the man hefted me roughly over his shoulder. My mind screamed in protest, my stomach tightened to keep my body in balance, and the tape chaffed.

Sirens sounded in the distance. So faint. They'd never make it before we left.

The man threw me in the back of the car with Macie. The door slammed shut behind me and the engine roared to life. Tires squealing, the car shot backward, throwing me off balance. Macie's eyes fluttered open, then rolled back into her head, whites showing. Whatever happened to her, she was out cold.

The car accelerated at an alarming speed. Five ticks. Ten. Twenty. An eternity. Then another set of tires squealed. The roar of a motor sounded from outside, matching our pace. Our car jerked one way and then another, crunching against something metallic. We swerved, then bounced over something. The movement tossed me like a rag doll. With my hands and feet bound, my body was at the mercy of gravity. I plummeted onto the floor, a shot of pain lacing through my hips and shoulder, marking the damage done by the drop. Macie fell on top of me, her body a limp weight. An ear-piercing blam, blam sounded from the front seat. Was our guy shooting? I braced my legs against the floorboards to steady myself.

A sudden burst of noise speared the air, and the car spun. Air bags exploded. Broken glass sprinkled past flesh to land on the floor. Both metal and men groaned. But the car didn't budge.

Heart pounding, I waited. Had we hit a wall? Another car? The sirens grew louder. Louder. Beyond Macie's hair, which covered half my face, a flash of red and blue cut the night. Voices. Men yelling. Jostling. What was going on? I held my breath, not daring to move. As if silence might make me unnoticeable.

Something creaked and scraped, metal on metal, like a door opening. My captors? Or something worse? I couldn't look. I squeezed my eyes shut and focused on controlling my thundering heart. Macie was lifted from me and then a hand clamped on my shoulder. Shook me. "Dani? It's over. You're safe now."

I wept, for I recognized that voice, and the bittersweet smell of licorice that went with it

Chapter Fifty-Six

CLOCKWORK

Macie and I had separate rooms at the hospital. Patient confidentiality kept me from knowing the extent of her wounds, but I'd watched enough cop shows to surmise they'd keep her for observation.

My injuries, while extensive, were not life-threatening. A bruised rib. Several cuts on my ankles and wrists and an angry red stripe on my face from the tape. Bruises over a good portion of my body.

A police officer stopped by and asked questions. His voice echoed hollow and distant as if passing through water. I answered as best I could. It's hard to think clearly when you're numb. Ashamed. Frightened. Betrayed.

My parents had been informed of the event. I talked with them on the phone, briefly, with a doctor's supervision. They rebooked their flight to leave as soon as they docked. Not soon enough for me.

I shivered, pulling my blanket tighter around myself. I'd been lucky. I'd been saved. How many thousands of girls were not so fortunate?

A knock sounded on the door, startling me. Funny how such a simple thing could make me jump.

Jay stuck his head into the room. "Hey, Dani. Mind if I come in?"

I nodded, not trusting my voice to speak.

He sat next to me on the bed, his weight making the thin mattress squeak and sag. "Doing okay?"

My eyes teared and I shook my head. I was not okay. Maybe not okay for a while.

"Hey, hey." He reached out as if to touch my knee, then pulled his hand back. "You're safe now. I thought you might like to hear the timeline of what happened. Sometimes that helps. But if you're not ready, I can leave."

"No," I croaked, finding my voice. "No, don't leave." I sucked in a breath and released it. "I would like to know how you got to me so fast. The police didn't tell me much. Just asked a lot of questions."

"Yeah." He sat for a moment, as if absorbing my fear. Then he reached into his pocket and pulled out a bag of licorice. "I brought this special for you. But I'm hoping you'll share it with me."

I snorted, taking this gift. I tried peeling the corner of the wrapper, but my fingers shook too hard.

"Here." He cupped gentle hands around mine and reclaimed the bag. "Let me."

He tore the plastic apart and pulled off a stick. "Thanks for this," he said, tucking it into his mouth. "The rest is yours."

Lowering my gaze, I peeled off a strip. The act gave my mind something to focus on, my hands something to do. I took a big bite and sucked on it, letting the bitterness bring life to my tongue. Another welcome distraction. "So what happened?"

He smiled. "Do you want the long version or short one?"

"Long," I whispered. "I need to know."

"Okay." He pulled my phone out of his pocket and handed it to me. "It goes back to your friend Elijah and your phone."

My jaw dropped. "What?"

"Apparently, Elijah sent you a Bible verse Thursday night around seven fifteen. According to him, you said that if you ever didn't respond right away, to start praying because you were in trouble. Or something like that."

"I was joking."

Jay cocked his head. "Good thing he took you seriously then."

"Wait, does that mean today is Friday?" I asked. "What time?"

"Two thirty a.m. But I don't think you'll be in any shape for school."

I smiled. "Probably not."

"Anyway, Elijah started praying. And then he started worrying. He said he couldn't shake the feeling something was wrong. So he texted your friend Sol, who had just gotten out of her tech rehearsal."

"She's Cinderella," I said, then winced. *The wolf.* "Hayden! Where is he?"

"You'll find out soon." Jay shook his head. "Are you going to let me tell my long story or not?"

Wrinkling my nose, I nabbed another piece of candy. "Keep going."

He raised a brow. "Your friend Sol texts you then and gets no response. She calls. No answer. She enlists her friend Harper to drive by your house just to check in on you."

"Harper?" I frowned. "We're not close."

"Apparently, Harper still counts you as a friend because she agrees to go the extra mile. The two arrive and see your car in the driveway. Sol thinks you've got to be home, but you still don't answer your phone or answer the door when she knocks. At first, she thinks maybe you fell in the shower or something, knocked yourself out. But the lights are out and it's dark, and she remembers what you talked about with Macie, and she gets worried. She calls Elijah and tells him the news. You're gone, and the girls don't know where. Then Sol calls your mom. And your mom calls the police. But they won't do anything until you're missing for twenty-four hours. You know they treat it as a runaway, especially when there were no signs of foul play."

I imagined my mom getting that answer. "Panic all around?"

"Your parents lit up our lines." Jay smiled. "As they should."

"How did you find me?" I asked.

"I'm getting there." Steepling his fingers, he studied me over them. "And I lied."

"About your job as a soccer scout?"

"About the licorice." Jay held out his palm. "Hand me another piece."

Choking back a laugh, I tossed him the bag.

"Now," he said, after freeing another stick, "this guy Elijah, he's not backing down. He contacts Ms. Brown from school, who shoots a text to the UCA members. They start praying. And one of the kids—can't remember her name—says her church has this ministry where people go out in teams and search seedy hotels for fancy cars."

"Fancy cars?" I puckered my lips and immediately regretted it. My face was still tender. "Why?"

Jay held up a finger and swallowed. "Because a fancy car is out of place at a cheap hotel. And that could lead—"

"—to people who get their money doing illegal things." I snapped my fingers.

"Exactly." Jay pointed at me. "When those teams got the call, they mobilized quickly. They took an assigned list of hotels, and they drove from place to place, looking for discrepancies. But when nothing unusual showed up, one of the men from the church called a pastor in the next town, and that church sent out their own teams. And all the while, your friend Elijah is praying. Sol is praying. And all your other friends at school are praying. For you."

My throat constricted. Mom always said prayer changed things. What power had my friends accessed?

"How many prayed?"

"I lost count," Jay said.

His words hit me. I always felt so alone. Was it possible I'd been surrounded by people who cared about me the whole time, and I just didn't know it? Or did it take a traumatic event like this to remind people what really mattered in life?

"Meanwhile, I'm checking my leads." Jay held up a hand. "I know what you're going to ask me, and I'll get to that in a minute."

I swallowed back my tears. "What am I going to ask you?"

"What I mean by *leads.*"

"Yes," I said. "I am. You're a brilliant detective."

"Undercover cop," he corrected. "And I'll tell you in a minute."

A burning question burst from my lips. "Did you really go to high school with Coach Campbell?"

He folded his arms across his chest. "No. But I did tell you that was my script."

He had used *script* in what I believed was a figure of speech. "Wow. You're good. I totally bought it."

"It's what I'm trained to do."

I took a thoughtful bite of candy. "Sounds like a tough job. What about the leads?"

"Yes." Jay roughed a hand across his face. "I checked my leads and noticed my phone, the one I planted on you, wasn't resting at your street address."

"Planted?"

"I told you I'd get to it." Jay frowned. "But not yet. So I'm tracking your movement, not certain if I should act or not, and I get overwhelmed with a craving for pizza in this little dive in the next town. Best thin-crust pineapple pizza you've ever had. The Maui Wowie. Trust me, it's worth the trip. And since it happened to be the direction my phone was headed anyway, I decided to go for a late-night snack.

"I'm five miles away when the tracker stops moving. About that time, I get a phone call. It's a tip from one of the out-of-town ministry teams reporting a car that appears out of place. And it's located at the exact same address as my phone."

My hands started shaking again. The timing. It was like divine clockwork. And it was too much. Too much to take in. But I needed to hear the rest. "Go on," I said.

CHAPTER FIFTY-SEVEN

THE REST

Jay stood, stretching his arms overhead. I forgot that he'd probably been up all night. "As soon as that piece of information fell into place, my instincts screamed you were in trouble, and I was the closest one to you. But I wanted to verify the situation first. I called. I mean—can you blame me? There was a hot pizza waiting for me."

My chest tightened. I lowered my piece of licorice. "I was in the closet then. On the floor. Confused. Scared. Trying to figure out if I could dial 9-1-1 with my nose."

"Yes. I read the report you gave the police." He paced, giving me time to slow my breathing, and then paused. "I can stop if you'd like," he said, his voice softening at the edges.

I shook my head. "No, keep going."

"Okay." He leaned against the doctor's computer desk. "I called again. And this time it went through. I heard a moan on the other end. I didn't know if the phone was in your possession or someone else's, but I took a risk and talked to whoever answered. I'm not sure why I did it. It was foolish of me. If the phone was in the wrong hands, I could have tipped my move. I should have just hung up."

But God was giving me hope.

"At any rate, I floored the gas pedal. And alerted local law enforcement. I was probably six minutes ahead of the nearest police officer, and good thing. Any later and your kidnappers would have been gone."

That fact slammed my composure. My hands started shaking. *Thank you, God!* "I'm pretty banged up." I held up a bandaged arm and swallowed. "How did you stop them?"

Jay raised his brows. "I thought you had figured that out."

Because figuring things out worked so well for me last time. "That's not my superpower."

"You're observant though. Guess."

"It felt like a car accident." I rubbed my neck, sore after the sudden, jarring stop.

"Close enough." Jay shrugged. "I corralled them back toward the cops headed our way. When they shot at me, I swerved. Accelerated. Ended up ramming them somehow. That forced them to hit a guardrail."

"You might have flipped our car."

"Or mine. But I didn't. And you know the rest."

An image of the flashing lights coloring the interior of the wreckage pulsed in my mind. And Macie's pale skin pressed against mine, blinking red and blue. Waiting, not knowing, not being able to see what was going on outside the car.

Closing my eyes. Holding my breath. Hands lifting, voices murmuring, bystanders watching.

What could have been. What might have been. If only.

"Did you catch everyone involved?" I asked.

"We believe there are more. Three people could hardly run an operation like this."

Fingers trembling, I hugged my blanket tightly around my body. "My friend Sol writes a blog for our school. She's got a file with creepy emails. Ask her for access. They might give you another lead."

"Yeah?" He pulled out a phone. "Can you give me her contact information?"

"Sure." I pulled up her number on my phone and handed it to him. "Her last name is Garcia if that helps."

"Thanks." He typed himself a note. "I'll look into it."

I shifted into a more comfortable position. "Will you tell me what you meant by leads now?"

"Sure." Jay cocked his head. "Do you remember when we first met?"

I nodded. "You were at Hayden's practice."

"And why would I be there?" His unblinking stare challenged me.

"You said you were undercover." I frowned, collecting my thoughts. "And Hayden traded me for drugs." My lips twisted, remembering his betrayal. "Were you there watching him?"

"Yes. And?"

"And when he started showing interest in me, so did you." I tilted my head. "Were you protecting me? Or using me?"

He frowned. "Is it bad if I say both?"

"Yes." I rubbed my neck.

He shrugged.

The pieces started falling in place. "You couldn't put a

tracker on Hayden or risk getting too close to him. But if he was hanging out with me, and *I* had a tracker, you could effectively follow his movements." I locked my gaze with his. "I was your lead."

He nodded. "You were."

Wow. And I had no idea I was playing with fire. "Do I get a medal or something?"

Grinning, he pointed to what remained of the licorice. "You get a bag of candy."

I ran my fingers over the smooth wrapper. "What about Hayden?"

"We tracked him down." Jay rubbed the palms of his hands on his pant legs. "He'll spend time in rehab and face felony charges. He's actually twenty years old—he was held back a grade—probably a direct result of family issues. Divorce. Neglect. I can't go into details."

"And Macie?"

"Confidential." He pressed his lips together. "But I can at least tell you she is surrounded by a network of caring adults. The church that helped locate you has some excellent programs for teens and tweens in distress, and I know they reached out to the family too."

He hesitated and gazed beyond me, as if reliving a memory. Some unspoken regret? Not my place to ask. I gave him silence to sort through whatever was on his mind.

Finally, he cleared his throat. "I suspect she'll need therapy to deal with the trauma. That might be an option for you too."

A knock sounded.

Jay stood, tipped an invisible hat, and strode across the room. He paused with one hand on the door. "Therapy is something you can discuss with your parents later. But you're tough. You will recover from this. It'll take time, but you've got a strong support system. Those friends of yours are sending lots of prayers your way. They're remarkable prayer warriors, you know? And prayer changes things."

"That's what my mom says too."

"A wise woman. Don't you agree?"

I couldn't argue with him. I'd finally seen the proof. "I do."

"Good." He nodded once and opened the door. As he walked out, Sol, Harper, and Elijah broke into the room.

"Dani!" Sol rushed to my bedside and threw her arms around me.

"Thank you," my throat was too thick to do more than whisper, "for always looking out for me."

"Right back at you." She hummed a little tune called "For Good" that I recognized from *Wicked,* one of her favorite Broadway musicals.

Some things never change. Thank goodness.

Finally, I pushed away so I could say hi to my other two visitors. "Thanks for driving Sol around for me, Harper."

She blushed and lowered her gaze. "Glad you're okay."

And then I turned to Elijah and held out my hand.

He took it and stepped closer, his ears pinking like they always did when he was put on the spot.

I didn't know what to say. Sol, Harper, and I—we knew what he'd done, the role he'd played. He was the first one who noticed something was off yesterday. He didn't brush off his misgivings. He pursued them. Pursued me. *Thanks* seemed an inadequate word to express my feelings.

So I didn't say anything.

Instead, I buried my face in his chest. Clinging to him, I sobbed wet, sloppy tears, the remaining ones I had been holding back.

He held me tight, stroking my hair and murmuring, "It's okay. Sh-sh. It's okay."

Then Sol sandwiched me on the other side and Harper from behind.

And then the door banged open again, and I felt the pressure of more people joining the hug. I peeked, shocked. Reb, Erika, Wren, Sandy, and …

Maybe the whole team?

And still they came. Kids from UCA. From church. From science class. Michael from the play. A murmured prayer here. A *thank you, God* there.

So many people.

So many hearts and souls.

An introvert's torment?

Or an introvert's comfort?

Maybe a little bit of both.

I sighed, drinking in their gentle, quiet warmth.

CHAPTER FIFTY-EIGHT

NICK

filled out more paperwork, answered more questions, and submitted to physical and psychological batteries before the doctors pronounced me well enough to leave. Since I was eighteen, I signed my own release from the hospital.

After sharing the information with police, I deleted most of the messages on my phone from that night. I couldn't bring myself to hear what my mom or dad or Sol had said to me. Didn't want to relive their panic. Their worry. I only saved one message, and that was the Bible verse Elijah had sent me. As if he somehow knew what I needed.

"I can do all things through him who strengthens me."
Philippians 4:13, ESV

It seemed a fitting reminder beyond soccer and gave me comfort.

Sol insisted I stay overnight at her house. We caught the news before crawling under the covers.

Because of the nature of the crime, the reporter didn't identify me or Macie. However, Sol's creepy file did bear fruit. The police traced several IP addresses and arrested five people in a human trafficking ring.

When the segment ended, Sol muted the TV. "We should publish a letter to our readers on the blog." Her eyebrows lowered. "Everyone knows we were involved. They're either going to be asking questions or gossiping behind our backs. Why not use this tragedy as an opportunity to educate people? As a character who witnessed Little Red go into the woods, I might have something to offer too."

She ended her last sentence with a dramatic pose. Probably she meant to lighten the mood. If I could syphon off some of her sunshine, I would.

"No." I picked at the edge of my shirt, trying to ignore the events replaying in my mind. I was too raw from the experience, like a mountain cat with a thorn in my flesh. Too horrified to put myself out there. In the spotlight. Vulnerable in front of the whole school. "No," I repeated.

"Okay." Sol reached out, but I shied from her touch. After a pause, she let her arm drop. "But people know bits and pieces about what happened, Dani. And they're going to ask you to fill in the blanks. Do you want to relive the trauma person by person?"

I cringed and shook my head.

Sol reached out again, and this time I let her rest a hand on my shoulder. "Then give them words. As soon as possible. Written words. Words crafted ahead of time to answer questions, ease anxiety, and bring healing. It might help you too. I mean, science is powerful. But words?" She squeezed me. "Words can change the world."

I can do all things through him who strengthens me.

The verse, the *words* Elijah sent me flooded my senses, and goose bumps rose on my arm. And I finally understood why Sol chose writing as her career path.

Sniffling, I rubbed my sleeve across my nose. "Okay."

"I know it's probably too soon but—" Sol's lip curled slightly. "There's no fight we can't win," she sang softly. "You and me. Defying *depravity.*"

"Nice." I snuffle-laughed. "A play on a song from *Wicked.* See, I pay attention."

Sol scoffed "You give yourself too much credit. I had to play that soundtrack nonstop for a month before you even remembered the title."

We did some research. Made some late-night calls. Brainstormed ideas. And it did help to talk about it. To sort through the emotions. To lose myself and find myself in the words.

Even though we stayed up well past one o'clock drafting the letter, it still wasn't late enough for me. It took forever to fall asleep. Too much think time remained, with my brain firing on overload. Every whistle of the wind and every shadow on the floor made my muscles tense. At one point I must have dozed off, but a nightmare shot me bolt upright with a start.

To nothing but the pounding of my own heart in my ears and my shallow gasps of breath. Lowering myself back into bed, I curled into a ball under the blankets. And prayed.

And prayed.

And prayed.

Exhaustion and Sol's soft snoring finally lulled me back to sleep.

The next day, I was in the kitchen eating pancakes for lunch and dressed in Sol's fuzzy, polka-dotted pajamas I'd borrowed, when the doorbell rang.

My eyes widened, and I dropped my fork. It clattered against my plate.

I looked at Sol and she looked at me, and then we both scrambled for the front door. I beat Sol there and slammed it open.

I pulled up short, ready to burst. "Mom! Dad!" I threw myself into their open arms. "You weren't due for another half hour!"

"I drive a little faster than they do."

The voice belonged to someone I'd longed to see for two years. I pulled back from my parents and smiled. "Nick!"

A familiar smirk on his face, he joined our makeshift huddle. "The prodigal son has returned. Hello, little sister."

After more hugs, kisses, reassurances, and tears, my parents followed Sol's mom into the living room, probably to talk about what she knew and to thank her for her help.

Nick followed Sol and me back to the kitchen and helped himself to three cold, unclaimed pancakes and a generous helping of syrup.

I needed time alone with Nick. I cleared my throat and gave Sol a pleading look, hoping she'd interpret it right.

She winked, then lifted her chin. "Uh—Dani? I just remembered I need to edit that letter we wrote this last night. Do you mind if I—?"

"Yes, go." I shooed her away. "Take care of your business."

She nabbed a banana and raced up the stairs.

Straddling the chair closest to me, Nick sectioned off a bite. "Glad you're okay."

"I'm glad you're okay too." I frowned. Small talk? We had

some deep issues to address. How could he act so nonchalant? As if we had spoken only yesterday? "Are you and Dad—"

"I apologized." He wiped his mouth with the back of his hand. "I was young. Impulsive. Strong-willed. Stubborn. And stupid. All of the above." He shrugged and shoveled another forkful into his mouth. "But Dad knows he didn't handle me well either. We're too much alike. Between the two of us, we sure made a mess of things."

I settled into my seat, more content to deal with his habitual problems than address my glaring lack of judgment. "I thought you'd never settle your differences. But I could tell it bothered Dad. He started working longer and longer hours."

"Avoidance tactic." Nick nodded. "Been there myself."

"But you agreed to go on the cruise."

Nick reached for my orange juice. I didn't object when he gulped it down. "After the hazing incident, I had a 'come to Jesus' moment. And ever since then, I've been praying for an opportunity to approach Dad, but I was afraid of—"

He paused, as if searching for the right word. Or maybe he needed to belch.

"Jumping offsides?" I suggested, quirking a brow.

He laughed. "Let's go with that. I didn't want to mess it up again." Then his face sobered. "Thank you for pushing them to invite me. For having a little bit of that stubbornness yourself. You saved me. That's your superpower. Relationships."

He leaned over and pulled me into a shoulder hug.

My face heated. How could relationships be my strength when I tried to avoid people most of the time? "When are you going back to campus?"

"Tomorrow." He released me and speared another bite of pancake. "I don't have class until Tuesday morning."

"Too bad. You'll miss my soccer game."

His jaw dropped. "You're going to play after all you just went through? You are one bad cookie, kid."

I wagged my fork at him. "That's the only kind of bad anyone should be."

CHAPTER FIFTY-NINE

DEAR HEART
AND SOUL

Dear Heart and Soul,

Human trafficking.

There, I said what we're all thinking about after what the news reported this past weekend. Human trafficking.

It's a story that has to be told, but no one wants to hear it. It's too awful. Too sickening. Too real.

Human trafficking is modern slavery. Often it involves sex. Sometimes it's labor. These are problems of epic proportions that we want to pretend don't exist.

And perhaps that's why the problem is growing. Every day, thousands of people are affected by it. Including our classmate.

She wasn't any different from you or me. She was someone you sat next to in class. Passed in the hallways. Maybe shared a granola bar with. Your average Joelle.

But she was often isolated. And lonely. And that made her a target.

Traffickers expertly find moments when people are vulnerable. As teens, we have an abundance of those. Social pressures. Academic pressures. A stressful home life. Divorce. Abuse. Take your pick. These issues plant seeds of longing in us. Longing for understanding. Stability. Love. Longings that can be leveraged by a trafficker. Perps use flattery, attention, and charm to manipulate and control their victims. Social media makes this whole process easier.

Hits close to home, doesn't it?

The problem is made a thousand times worse because it's an uncomfortable topic. We avoid it. We remain blissfully unaware.

Unaware. That's an odd choice we make. Because in almost every other area of our lives, we're constantly aware. Take soccer, for instance. Players are aware of their positions across the goal face. Aware of the player with the ball and her passing options. Aware of where the final defender stands. Aware of how much time remains in the game. How do you expect to win if you aren't aware?

But here is the truth, my Dear Hearts who yearn for relationships and acceptance. My Dear Souls who seek understanding and peace.

My Friends. My Classmates.

When it comes to human trafficking, we are unaware of

the dangers, we are ignorant of the red flags, and we are surrounded by potential victims.

What happened to our classmate is a wake-up call for
all of us.

Let's do better.

Love, Heart and Soul

VIRAL

On Monday at eight, Sol's letter posted on the blog and her social media outlets.

It went viral by noon that same day.

CHAPTER SIXTY-ONE

ALMOST NORMAL

"Girls, I know we've got playoffs locked in," Coach Hering yelled over the crowd, "but if we win tonight, we make a statement."

Coach Lofton grunted and crossed her arms.

"Oh yes." Coach Hering nodded at her. "Thanks for the reminder." She raised her voice. "We will also secure the third top seed in bracket play."

This statement earned a scream from all of us, but a chest-pumping, gorilla-level scream from Reb and Erika.

The week had passed in a blur, and, after missing a game, I got the go-ahead to return to action from the therapist. For the first time since the season's start, with my blessings counted, I knew I was fast enough. Strong enough. Smart enough. And good enough. On the soccer field. And maybe even in the social arena. I could carry this momentum into college. Play rec ball. Make new science-loving friends.

I would never wish what happened to me on anyone. But I learned God can take even the most horrible things in our lives and use them for good. Like raising awareness.

And I picked up a few other things.

Sol taught me everyone needs a friend. And anyone can be one.

By changing his choices, Nick modeled how anyone could change their life.

Jay proved there are still good people in the world.

And Elijah showed me God is never offsides. He's always right on time.

As our team took the field, the familiar tingle of adrenaline flooded me. I let my hand twitch at my side, a small release of energy. I needed to run. Sweat. Soar. Right after the National Anthem. I couldn't wait for that. It was opening night for Sol's play too, but she insisted on doing the honors.

During warmups, I scanned the bleachers and spotted my parents, several reporters, and Jay. Oh, and at the front of the horde of students stood Elijah.

My knight in shining armor.

I smiled and blew him a kiss. Admittedly, not an intimidating pregame move for a starting midfielder on a conference-winning team. But compared to what I went through, this game seemed like a party.

He'd sent me the perfect Bible verse last night. I'd read it a dozen times before tying my shoes on.

"Fear not, for I am with you; be not dismayed, for I am your God; I will strengthen you, I will help you, I will uphold you with my righteous right hand." Isaiah 41:10, ESV

The announcer cut the music, and I turned my attention to player introductions. When my name was announced, I got the biggest cheer I'd ever had in my life. We lined up, and Sol marched to the center of the field in full costume.

"Ladies and gentlemen. Singing our National Anthem, please welcome Cinderella, Sol Garcia."

The crowd, which had quadrupled in size since our last home game, roared as Sol waved. Just like before, her voice cast a spell. "And the rockets' great glare. The bombs bursting in air ..." The notes drew all attention to her.

When the final echoes of the song ended, the crowd roared again. That's when Sol held up a hand and spoke into the microphone. "Excuse me. Excuse me. While I was singing, did anyone notice the wolf?"

Murmurs swept through the crowd. And then Michael, who played the wolf, jumped from behind the speaker and yelled, "Boo! Remember people! Be aware of potential predators. And come see our musical after the game. Curtains open at seven thirty."

I broke ranks and ran to my friend to embrace her before she left. "Break a leg," I whispered in her ear. "And remember, you promised me excellent seats."

"Score a goal for me." Sol pulled away and looked me in the eyes. "And save me a granola bar."

I'm happy to say we dominated the game. I didn't score a goal, but I did pull off a decent Cruyff Turn, which set up Reb for her third goal. She loves hat tricks. Wren picked up a goal right at the end. Sandy shut out the other team. And Erika only got called for one foul—even though I'm convinced she got away with at least six more.

And as for Sol? She catered to a sold-out audience that included my parents, my entire soccer team, and one undercover cop.

With licorice.

SOCCER TERMINOLOGY

Assist: a pass to a player that scores a goal

Corner Kick: when the defense touches the ball over the out-of-bound end line, the offense places the ball in the corner of the field for a free inbounding kick

Defender: a position in front of the goalie that is the last line of defense

Dribble: when a player runs with the ball at their feet

Formation: the arrangement of all eleven soccer players on the field

Forward: offensive position on a soccer team that usually scores the most goals

Frame: the crossbars of a soccer goal

Give-and-go: a basic move where two players pass the ball back and forth between them

Goal: a point earned when the soccer ball is kicked into an opponent's net

Goalie: a player who can use any part of their body, including their hands, to guard the goal

Hat Trick: when one player scores three goals in a single game

Header: hitting the ball with your head

Keeper: see *Goalie*

Offsides: a foul called when an offensive player positioned behind the last defender receives a pass from a teammate

Midfielder: a position between the defenders and forwards that operates both offensively and defensively

Pass: when a ball is kicked from one teammate to another

Pitch: a soccer field

Shot: a kick aimed at the goal

Striker: an offensive player positioned to attack and score goals rather than defend

Tackle: a move, often sliding, meant to steal the ball from another player

Trap: stopping the ball with your body

Wall: a row of players ten yards away from the kick

RESOURCES

Ten Red Flags to Spot Human Trafficking

1. Neglect (hunger, malnourishment)
2. Abuse (bruises, promiscuous behavior or language, drug addiction)
3. Depression (loss of appetite, isolation from peers, inattention)
4. Poverty (homelessness, lacking necessary supplies)
5. Family dysfunction (divorce, instability)
6. Being controlled (older boyfriend, new friends, rehearsed responses)
7. Hyperarousal (anger, panic, irritability, crying)
8. New things (expensive gifts like purses, cell phones)
9. A disconnect (disengagement in hobbies and activities)
10. Personality change (change in behavior or attitude)

More details about some of these red flags can be found at https://humantraffickinghotline.org/en/human-trafficking/recognizing-signs

WHAT TO DO IF YOU SUSPECT HUMAN TRAFFICKING

1. Call the National Human Trafficking hotline https://humantraffickinghotline.org/en
2. Call 9-1-1.
3. Be aware. (See the Red Flag list above)
4. Join or support a local church with a ministry for recovering victims.
5. Donate to missions that provide a safe place for victims.
6. Pray for our nation and for our world.

SYMPTOMS OF DRUG ABUSE: CHECK THE FACE AND PERSONALITY

1. Red or agitated eyes
2. Dilated or constricted pupils
3. Rapid or random eye moments
4. Lip smacking
5. Frequent jaw clenching
6. Slow reactions
7. Mood swings
8. Personality change

If you suspect drug abuse, call this hotline: https://www.help.org/drug-abuse-hotline/

ABOUT THE AUTHOR

Former Wheaton College volleyball player Lori Z. Scott knows a thing or two about writing. Besides her **10-title bestselling chapter book series** (known by some as "the Christian version of Junie B. Jones" because of its heart and humor), she has contributed to 13 books and published over 175 short stories, devotions, articles, poems, and essays. Some of these won awards, including Pockets Magazine's fiction writing contest. She currently teaches second grade and writes articles for Story Embers, a growing website geared for Christian writers.